"Joe McKinney's first zombie novel, *Dead City,* is one of my all-time favorites of the genre. It hits the ground running and never lets up. *Apocalypse of the Dead* proves that Joe is far from being a one-hit wonder. This book is meatier, juicier, bloodier, and even more compelling . . . and it also NEVER LETS UP. From page one to the stunning climax this book is a rollercoaster ride of action, violence, and zombie horror. McKinney understands the genre and relies on its strongest conventions while at the same time adding new twists that make this book a thoroughly enjoyable read. That's a defining characteristic of Joe's work: the pace is so relentless that you feel like it's you, and not the character, who is running for his life from a horde of flesh-hungry monsters.

"And, even with that lightning-fast pace, McKinney manages to flesh the characters out so that they're real, and infuse the book with compassion and heartbreak over this vast, shared catastrophe.

"This book earns its place in any serious library of living-dead fiction."
—Jonathan Maberry, *New York Times* best-selling author of *The Wolfman*

"*Dead City* is much more than just another zombie novel. It's got heart and humanity—a merciless, fast-paced, and genuinely scary read that will leave you absolutely breathless. Highly recommended!"
—Brian Keene

THE
SAVAGE
DEAD

JOE
McKINNEY

PINNACLE BOOKS
Kensington Publishing Corp.
www.kensingtonbooks.com

PINNACLE BOOKS are published by

Kensington Publishing Corp.
119 West 40th Street
New York, NY 10018

All Kensington titles, imprints, and distributed lines are available at special quantity discounts for bulk purchases for sales promotions, premiums, fund-raising, educational, or institutional use. Special book excerpts or customized printings can also be created to fit specific needs. For details, write or phone the office of the Kensington special sales manager: Kensington Publishing Corp., 119 West 40th Street, New York, NY 10018, attn: Special Sales Department; phone 1-800-221-2647.

ISBN-13: 978-0-7860-2930-3
ISBN-10: 0-7860-2930-7

First printing: September 2013

10 9 8 7 6 5 4 3 2 1

Printed in the United States of America

First electronic edition: September 2013

ISBN-13: 978-0-7860-3312-6
ISBN-10: 0-7860-3312-6

ACKNOWLEDGMENTS

The book is done. Now comes the part where I get to sit back in my chair and stare at the completed manuscript and think about all the folks who helped me get here. This is where I get to say thank you to all those people who gave so freely of their time, knowledge and good counsel. Ultimately, they got this book into your hands. It had to pass through me first though, so the mistakes are mine. But what I got right, I got right because of them.

So, with that said, thank you David Liss, Gary Goldstein, Jim Donovan, Keith Milstead, Hank Schwaeble, Stephen Rieder, Rhodi Hawk, Robert Jackson Bennett, William E. Smith, Holly Zaldivar, Sanford Allen, Beckie Ugolini, Brian Allen, Thomas McAuley, Max Booth III, Lee Thomas, Kristina McKinney, Clay and Tiffany McKinney, and Joe and Jennifer McKinney. You guys are my inspiration and my bedrock. Thanks for everything!

CHAPTER 1

"Juan, you monitoring?"

It was Tess Compton, his second in command. Juan Perez touched the mic on his wrist. "Yeah, go ahead, Tess. Anything?"

"I've got nothing out here. A bunch of bankers and lawyers and soap opera stars, but nothing else."

Damn, he thought. "Okay, search it again," he said. "Top to bottom."

Juan had been checking the kitchen and the back hallways of the Washington Hilton for the last half hour, and so far he'd found nothing but a bunch of dishwater puddles that had soaked his best pair of shoes through to his socks. His feet were wet and he was pissed with himself. He had more than fifty agents working for him tonight, and another hundred uniformed cops working the perimeter outside. They had searched every bathroom, every closet, every inch of the Grand Ballroom where Senator Rachel Sutton was about to drive her latest nail into the coffin she'd made for the Mexican drug cartels. They had cameras everywhere, and the finest facial recognition software in the world scanning every person entering the building. There just weren't that many places an assassin could hide.

And yet they'd found absolutely nothing.

Juan took a deep breath and let it out to a slow ten count. There was some little thing he was missing. He was sure of that. He and his team were missing something. He glanced at his watch again. They were down to the wire on this one. The senator was set to give her speech in less than fifteen minutes. Once she took the podium and the cameras started rolling, they'd lose any hope of dealing with this quietly, behind the scenes.

There was a soft electronic chime in his earpiece and he switched over to the command frequency only he and Tess shared. "Yeah, Tess, what's up?"

"You ask me, I think we got bad intel on this. I'm looking around but there's nothing going on out here but a bunch of drinking and hand shaking. We've been through every inch of this place, ran everybody through the computers. I think this is a bust."

"The intel's good," he said. "We're just not looking in the right place."

"Then tell me where to look."

Juan nearly snapped back at her, but closed his eyes and forced down his temper instead. It wouldn't do to bark at her over the radio. She was just frustrated, like him. The Washington Hilton was a known quantity. He and his team had done at least fifty events here. They knew every inch of it. This shouldn't be that hard to figure out.

"Just get everybody to turn their areas over one

more time. Top to bottom. We've got a few minutes still till go time, so let's use it wisely."

"You got it, boss," Tess said. "You on the way out here? Piper is asking about you."

"Piper" was the Secret Service code name for Senator Rachel Sutton. The name held no special meaning. It was just easy to say and easy to understand when heard over the radio.

"What does she want?"

"She wants to know what the holdup is."

"Tell her I'm on my way. I want to make one more pass through here first."

They switched back over to the unit's main frequency, and while she relayed further instructions to the rest of the team, Juan continued searching the kitchen. This area was, really, the only weak spot in their plan. Outside the hotel, several hundred protestors had gathered. Already there had been clashes between Senator Rachel Sutton's supporters and those who wanted to see her impeached, but Washington, D.C.'s Metropolitan Police Department had those well in hand. And the protests were actually working in his favor. It gave him the convenient excuse—not that he needed one, but it was always nice to have—to lock down every exterior door the hotel had. Anybody wanting to get inside would not only have to get through the Metropolitan PD's barricades, but through armed teams of Secret Service and uniformed officers at each door.

Still, he wondered if it was enough. Senator Sutton had all but declared war on the Mexican drug cartels, and they on her. The International Asset Seizure Act, of which she was both architect and author, had given U.S. law enforcement agents the authority to seize, by computer hacking and piracy if necessary, the entire fortunes of confirmed cartel members, no matter where in the world they hid their money, and no matter what banking laws existed to protect those fortunes. It had been a risky political move, with both sides of the political aisle holding their collective breath to see how the world's banks would react. But in the year and a half since its implementation, the act had proven more effective than the rest of the forty years of the War on Drugs put together. This last was a fact not lost on Juan, who had been a member of the U.S. Army's 1st Special Forces Operational Detachment—Delta, the famed Delta Force, for five years before joining the U.S. Secret Service. He'd fought the cartels all over Mexico on countless undercover operations, and again in the United States as a federal agent. He'd fired a lot of bullets, shed a lot of blood, killed more than his fair share. But the senator's pen had, in the end, proved the mightier weapon.

He knew this for a fact from his contacts still working in Mexico. The cartels were hemorrhaging cash, and tearing themselves up internally through endless power struggles—and all of it because of the senator's law. They wanted her dead. And they'd already tried to kill her once, in San Antonio, about four months earlier. As the senator's motorcade had pulled away from the Mexican Embassy, it'd been attacked by twenty-three armed members of Los Zetas Cartel. The gunmen had descended on what they thought was the senator's limo. Instead, they found Juan and Tess Compton and the rest of his team. The resulting firefight raged down two blocks of downtown San Antonio, and by the end of it, sixteen cartel members were dead and the rest wounded and captured. It was a disaster for the cartels, but a huge shot in the arm for Senator Sutton, who used the failed assassination as a way to propose further measures against the cartels. She was scheduled to announce those measures tonight. He'd had good intelligence to warn him of that first attempt on the senator, and it was those same sources, sources that he himself had cultivated during his years in Latin America, in fact, that had alerted him to tonight's planned hit.

Busboys and dishwashers hustled all around him. The floor was a maze of dishwater puddles and scraps of food. Looking at bits of lettuce and half-eaten steaks, it never ceased to amaze Juan how much went to waste while putting on these events. As a boy growing up in the slums of Del Rio, Texas, he'd eaten dinners that weren't half as appetizing as the waterlogged trash on the floor here, and he'd been grateful for it. But he put that frustration aside, too, and refocused on the job at hand. Pots and pans clanged, instructions were yelled in a weird pidgin mixture of Spanish and English across the room, chefs and waiters barked at each other. None of them noticed him. Despite his tuxedo, and the radio earpiece, and the obvious gun bulging underneath his jacket, he was nothing new to them. They had all seen the Secret Service many times before.

He moved among them, watching them, studying their faces, comparing them to the background files his team had run on the entire staff prior to the senator's event. Everybody was accounted for. There had been no last-minute schedule changes, nobody had called in sick or switched shifts at the eleventh hour. Everything looked normal.

That is, until he saw a dishwasher carrying a large plastic bag of trash down to an open window along the back wall of the kitchen. It was the same wall that separated the kitchen from the loading dock.

A way in.

Juan froze, dread gathering in his gut.

"Oh, hell no," he said.

"Hey dude, come on," said a man's voice from behind him. "Trying to get through here."

Juan turned. One of the dishwashers, a slightly built white guy in a soaking wet T-shirt, black pants, and gray rubber Gators was standing there, holding a heavy tub of dirty dishes.

Juan said nothing, just gave the man a cold glare.

"Fine," the guy said, getting the hint. He backed up and walked around, muttering something that sounded like "Fucking asshole" under his breath as he went.

Juan ignored the insult. Instead, he grabbed the dishwasher who had just tossed the garbage out the window and demanded to know how long it had been open.

The guy shrugged.

"I don't know. All night, I guess. You guys won't let us use the door. All this stuff's gotta go somewhere."

He let the man go. There was no use jumping his case about it.

Halfway down the wall, on the other side of the sinks and drying racks, was a heavy, wire-mesh metal door. During his preliminary walk-through earlier that day, he'd ordered the restaurant manager to lock it for the duration of the event. The man had objected, quoting health code regulations about keeping standing garbage out of the kitchen, but Juan overruled him. "I want it closed," he'd said. And he'd hoped that the man understood the seriousness of why it had to be done. Juan thought he'd made that abundantly clear. But apparently not.

He went to the door and rattled it. At least it was still locked.

Two Metropolitan PD officers were standing watch outside, both of them smoking, neither of them paying the slightest attention to their post.

"Hey, officers," Juan said.

The two cops looked up, bored expressions showing in the glow of their cigarettes.

"Yeah?"

Yeah, Juan thought. *Yeah?* Those worthless mother . . .

"Can you come here, please?" he said.

One of the cops rolled his eyes. They both put out their cigarettes and walked over to the door. As they approached, Juan read their nametags. F. WALKER was a tall, lanky black man with corporal stripes on his sleeve. The other man, P. BOLAN, was a much older, and much fatter, white guy.

"You see that window down there?" Juan said, pointing to his right.

The white officer didn't even bother to glance that way. "Huh? What window?"

"That open window down there," Juan said. "With all the trash piled up below it?"

"Yeah, I see it," Bolan said. "What of it?"

Juan hated the sense of entitlement he sometimes got from uniformed cops assigned to his details. Cops like these two idiots, who were getting paid double time to watch an empty loading dock and a trash Dumpster, acted like national security was some sort of pain in the ass keeping them from their lunch breaks. And the fact that they couldn't see the problem disgusted him.

"I gave orders that all the windows and doors along this wall were to be locked up tight. Do you even know how long that window's been open? Have you been watching it?"

"I don't know," Bolan said. He was getting indignant now. "Go talk to the kitchen staff. They're the ones who opened it."

"Yeah, but—" Juan stopped himself from saying more. There wasn't any chance of impressing upon them the dangerous situation they'd allowed to happen, and besides, there wasn't time.

"All right," he said into the mic wired into his sleeve, "listen up, all of you. I've got an open window here in the kitchen off the loading dock. Frank, Soto, Sarantino—I need you three to break away and get down to the kitchen. I want this place searched. Somebody locate the PD supervisor, too. I want him down here right now. Tess, you monitoring?"

"Yeah, boss, I'm here."

"Get close to Piper, okay? I want you right on her shoulder. And make sure her husband and Mr. Godwin are accounted for as well."

"I'm on it," she said.

He was about to turn back to the two Metropolitan PD officers and chew their asses, but just then his earpiece chimed with a private message from Tess.

"Yeah, Tess, what is it?"

"Just wanted to let you know that the Good Doctor is already pretty deep in his cups. You want me to get Waller and Strahan on him?"

Damn, Juan thought. "The Good Doctor" was their unit's call sign for Dr. Wayne Sutton, Senator Sutton's infamously and perennially drunk husband. The man was still a practicing dentist, though how he managed to keep a handle on his practice Juan had no idea. He'd dealt with the man at least twenty times over the last six months, and each time Dr. Sutton had been resoundingly drunk. It was enough of a problem that every plan Juan and his unit came up with to get Piper out of danger now included a separate plan to deal with her husband.

"Yeah," Juan said. "Get Waller and Strahan to keep him close. Tell Piper to hold off on her speech. I'll be out on the floor in a just a moment."

"Boss, she's not gonna like that."

"I don't care, Tess. Just tell her to hold what she's got for a little bit."

The Metropolitan PD supervisor showed up a moment later. He was a young, clean-cut lieutenant named Brian Roth. He glanced from Juan to his two officers standing outside the metal door, and then back to Juan.

"Is there a problem?"

"I want you to get a squad down here to go through this area. I want every person checked and cleared against the staff roster, and I want it done right now."

The lieutenant's boyish smile evaporated. "I don't understand. Why the sudden change in plans?"

"You can thank your two all-stars out there," Juan said.

"Now hold on a second—"

Juan cut the man off. He didn't have time to be polite. "No, you hold on a second. Those two have been out there smoking and grab-assing all night while that window down there was standing wide open. Now you will get a squad down here, and you will account for every person who has been in and out of this kitchen since five o'clock this afternoon. Do you understand?"

"Now, listen," Roth said, "you can't talk to my men like that—"

"Save it for another time," Juan said. "Just get your people together and do as I tell you."

Roth looked like he wanted argue, but after meeting Juan's stare, he backed down. He finally nodded and said, "Yeah, all right."

"Good. I'll assign an agent to help you."

Juan walked off, toward the Embassy Ball Room. He passed Randy Soto, one of his agents, on the way out of the kitchen and explained what he wanted him to do with the cops back by the open window.

"You got it, boss," Soto said.

"Thanks, Randy."

He nodded to the man and stepped through the doors that led to the ballroom. It was crowded with movers and shakers from both sides of the border, most of them bankers and lawyers, a few Washington hardballers here and there. Juan scanned the room until he saw Tess chatting with a Mexican banker and his much younger soap opera star wife.

Tall and blond, able to move from English to Spanish with fluid ease, Tess Compton was in her element at parties like this. She wore a flowing red halter-top evening gown, a string of pearls at her throat, and was easily the match for any of the many beautiful women in attendance, even the soap opera stars. Despite his urgency, Juan managed a little smile. Very few people in this room had any idea Tess Compton was with the Secret Service, and none of them, save the other agents, had any idea how deadly she could be. Though she'd been raised in the finest country clubs in Atlanta, the daughter of a top executive for Kraft Foods and a Vassar graduate, there was nothing soft about her. He'd once watched her take down, and choke out a man twice her size when he tried to throw pig's blood on a federal judge they were escorting through the Senate lobby. She'd even made it look easy. Juan had seen a lot of agents come through the service. He'd even trained a good many of them. But none were as good as Tess. That was why he'd made her his second in command, and that was why they had become such good friends.

Tess spotted him as he approached, turned, and touched Senator Sutton on the shoulder, leaning in to whisper something in her ear. The Good Doctor stood a few feet off, a martini in his hand. He was swaying drunkenly, smiling at nothing in particular. Happy as a pig in slop, Juan thought. The senator's long-time aide, Paul Godwin, was standing just behind the senator, his fingers busily flying over his iPhone.

Both women turned to face him at the same time. The senator, dressed in one of her signature Hillary Clinton-style pantsuits, spoke first. "What's this all about, Agent Perez? You're cutting it kinda close, aren't you?"

"Yes, ma'am," he said. He explained about the open window he'd found. "I was hoping you could hold your speech off for a few minutes. Give us a chance to make a thorough search one more time."

"Ms. Compton already suggested that, Agent Perez. I told her no."

"Ma'am, please. After what happened in San Antonio, and given the intelligence we've had for tonight, I really think—"

"You've been conducting your searches all evening," she said.

"Yes, ma'am," he said.

"And you've found nothing so far."

"We've found an open window."

"An open window. Nothing else?"

"Ma'am, given the circumstances, I think—"

"I appreciate your professional concern, Agent Perez. Believe me, after San Antonio, I most certainly do. But I need to make this perfectly clear. I will not allow the cartels to dictate one minute of my schedule. Is that understood? Not one single second."

Juan's face flushed with heat. This woman was impossible. She had absolutely no concept of the danger she was in. Or was subjecting the rest of this room to, for that matter. It was arrogant and stupid of her.

Tess seemed to sense his frustration, for at that moment she put a hand over Paul Godwin's iPhone and leaned in to whisper into the aide's ear.

A moment later, he nodded.

"We could burn an easy ten minutes with you just

working the crowd on the way to the podium," he said to Sutton. "A few handshakes. A few quiet conversations. It'd be good for some camera time, and it wouldn't look like stalling."

The senator shifted her gaze from her aide to Juan. He was about to tell her she had no business wading into a crowd that he couldn't guarantee was safe, but Tess stepped in before he could speak.

"Ten minutes would be about perfect," she told the senator. "And Mr. Godwin's right, it'd be a good chance to work some handshakes on the way up to the podium."

Juan kept silent. His team was an elite wing of the service reserved for special operations. Every member of the team had proven themselves over and over again, and he encouraged his subordinates to think on their feet and take the initiative when it came to changing plans on the fly. It was hard to relinquish that kind of total control sometimes, but he trusted Tess. So he just stood there, waiting to see what Senator Sutton was going to do. And for a moment, Sutton looked like she was seriously considering Tess's suggestion.

But then she turned back to her husband. He was still smiling stupidly. He was a tall, thick man, with a ruddy glow and a smile full of perfect teeth. He tilted his drink to his wife and with a gesture that looked like he was stifling a hiccup said, "Absolutely! Do that."

Juan saw Senator Sutton's face harden, like she was gauging the size of the millstone hanging around her neck.

She wheeled around on Juan. "I'm going on right now," she said.

And with that she marched straight for the podium, leaving Juan and the others to sort it out.

"That's one determined lady," said Tess.

Juan nodded to her, and then turned to Paul Godwin. "Your boss is being foolish. People are going to get hurt."

Godwin shrugged and rolled his eyes. It was the oddly feminine sort of gesture Juan had grown accustomed to seeing from the man. "I have confidence in you, Agent Perez," Godwin said. "And Ms. Compton is right. The senator is one determined lady."

"Let's hope that doesn't get somebody killed."

But Godwin had already stopped listening. He was looking back toward his table, where a stunning, dark-haired Hispanic woman in a strapless black evening gown was holding a pair of martinis and smiling back at Godwin.

Godwin's iPhone chimed softly. He read the display quickly, then fired off what Juan realized must have been his millionth text of the night. The man never put that phone down. But then, much to Juan's surprise, he actually slid the phone back into its holster on his belt. He looked excited and nervous. He licked his lips and straightened his tie.

"Do you still need me for anything else, Agent Perez?" He motioned with a nod toward the woman. "I'd like to, uh, you know."

Juan shook his head. "No, we're good."

"Great," Godwin said. He started to leave.

"Good luck," Juan said.

Godwin looked back, confused for a moment, then smiled guiltily.

When he was gone, Tess said, " 'Good luck'?"

Juan stifled a smile of his own as he watched Godwin take one of the martinis from the woman. She giggled at something he said, and then the two of them walked off toward the back of the ballroom, her arm on his elbow.

"I have to admit, that's not what I expected to see," Juan said. "I kinda figured he was . . . well, you know."

Tess laughed. "You, too, huh? I actually figured he was kind of sweet on you."

Juan flashed a menacing look in her direction, but it only made her chuckle.

"Come on," he said. "We need to take our positions."

Without another word Tess moved to the middle of the room and took a seat next to a banker from Dallas. Juan withdrew to the corner of the stage on Sutton's right. From where he stood he had a view of the entire room. He watched the crowd as they took their seats and quieted down. He scanned the doors along the back wall and the railing of the balcony to Senator Sutton's left. Beneath the balcony was a staging area for the waiters, and beyond that, an entrance to the kitchen. He took all of this in with a practiced eye, his gaze constantly searching the faces in the crowd, looking for anything wrong.

Senator Sutton had barely finished her greeting when Juan spotted the waiter.

He was dressed in the hotel's signature white and crimson uniform, carrying a pitcher of water, but his gaze kept flicking back to the senator, like he was making sure she was still where she was supposed to be. A woman tried to flag him down for some more water, but the waiter moved by her as though he hadn't heard.

Juan stiffened, his gaze lasering in on the man.

His face was unfamiliar, but it wasn't until Juan saw the sweat beading on the man's forehead that he knew for sure.

"Rook and Carlton, heads up," Juan said into his mic. "I think we've got our man. The waiter with the water pitcher moving to the stage."

"We see him," Carlton said.

What happened next happened fast. Carlton and Rook rushed forward from beneath the balcony. Tess rose to her feet. The waiter put the water pitcher down on a table and kept walking toward the stage, his hand drifting to the brass buttons on his coat, pulling it open, and coming up with a black pistol that he leveled at Senator Sutton.

Juan got to the senator just as the first shot went off. He tackled Sutton to the ground and together they slid into the stage curtains behind the podium. He blocked her with his body, even as the room behind them erupted in gunfire and the sounds of people shouting, chairs being knocked over, women screaming.

"Stay down," Juan told Sutton. "I've got you."

He tried to push her under the curtains, but his left arm wouldn't move. Only then did he see the blood pooling on the stage between them. No, he thought, even as the pain blossomed in his mind. It felt like his shoulder was on fire.

Two agents came out of the wings, grabbed Sutton, and started pulling her back out of the way.

"You're hit, boss," one of them said.

"Get her out of here," he told the man. The agent tried to open Juan's coat, but Juan knocked his hands away. "Go!" he shouted. "Get her out of here!"

Juan rolled over toward the room, ignoring the pain in his shoulder. The room was in chaos. The shooter was backing away from the stage, moving toward the kitchen. The crowd was on its feet, falling over themselves as they rushed for the exits. Carlton and Rook were trying their best to swim through the panicked crowd, but they weren't going to get to the shooter in time to stop him. Tess, on the other hand, was standing in the middle of the crowd like a rock in a river. She already had her weapon in her hand, and as Juan watched, the pain threatening to pull him down into unconsciousness, the assassin aimed for Tess and fired.

The shot hit a woman next to Tess and knocked her down. Tess shot back, hitting the assassin in the shoulder and spinning him around. He slipped to one knee, but the next instant he was up and running for the kitchen door, holding his wounded shoulder as he went.

The room was spinning around Juan, and he knew the wound had to be bad. He wouldn't be losing consciousness like this from just a glancing blow. But he wasn't about to give up. Despite the pain, despite the waves of nausea that made it hard to focus, he got to his feet and ran after the shooter.

"Juan, no!" he heard Tess shout, but he pushed on.

The next instant, he was through the kitchen door, the shooter staggering on ahead of him, pushing his way through the confused staff. The shooter pushed a dishwasher with a plastic tub full of silverware in his hands over a prep table, forks and knives clanging loudly across the metal table and onto the floor. Juan forced the blurriness to the corners of his vision as he tunneled in on the assassin. Chefs and busboys were rushing between them, blocking his shot.

"Get out of the way!" Juan shouted as he leveled his pistol toward the fleeing man.

Another twenty feet and he'd be at the metal mesh door where the two uniformed cops were hopefully still on their post. Then a gap in the kitchen staff opened up and Juan took his shot, hitting the fleeing man in his leg and dropping him headfirst into an ice machine.

He ran forward just as the shooter was struggling back to his feet.

Juan planted his foot on the man's back and kicked him. The top of his head smacked into the wall and the man slid facedown into a puddle of filthy dishwater.

Tess appeared behind him while he was taking the gun from the man's limp hand.

She pushed her way around him, getting on her knees in the dishwater puddles and forcing the man's hands behind his back as she cuffed him.

She pulled the man to his feet. He was spluttering and coughing, his face ashen white from his injuries and dripping with dishwater. Other agents appeared behind them and took the man by the shoulder.

"Wait," she told them.

The agents held the man while Tess tore his shirt open, revealing a tapestry of tattoos.

"Juarez Cartel," Tess said, holding the man's shirt open so Juan could see.

Juan nodded. "Get him out of here."

When the man was gone, Tess said, "We need to get you a doctor."

Juan could feel his legs threatening to turn to water beneath him.

"How's Sutton? She okay?"

"She's fine, but you need a doctor."

He started to argue, but the pain was already turning his vision into a blurry mess. "Yeah," he said. "Yeah, I think that's a good idea."

CHAPTER 2

Finally, one of the Secret Service agents came over to get him. "Mr. Godwin, we're ready for you over here," the agent said.

Paul grunted impatiently. "It's about time," he said.

"This way, sir."

The agent led him to one of the tables in the Washington Hilton's lobby. Two agents were seated there, a man and a woman, both with laptops and a thick pile of adapters and cords spilling over the sides of the table. Paul didn't recognize either agent, and he thought he had at least seen most of the agents on Juan Perez's team. These two must have been from somewhere else.

"What's this all about?" he said. "I want to speak to Senator Sutton. Where is she?"

The agent who'd come to get him spoke up. "We need your cell phone, sir."

Paul felt a tinge of panic. His world was in that phone. "Why?"

"We're looking for pictures, videos, text messages. Anything that might have evidentiary value in our investigation."

"I didn't take any pictures during the shooting," he said. "I was too busy trying not to get shot."

"We still need to see your phone."

Paul glared at the agent. Right after the shooting, the Secret Service had locked the hotel down. Nobody went in, nobody went out. The wounded and their spouses were taken to the hospital, but everybody else was put in one of the hotel's meeting rooms and told to wait.

And for a while, Paul had done as he was told. He went where they told him to go and answered their questions in a numb haze. But now that the adrenaline had worn off, Paul was impatient to get back to work. He needed to check with Senator Sutton. They needed to script out their response to what had happened here tonight. There were press conferences to plan and meetings to set up, and all of it had to be done right now. The more time that went by, the more time Senator Sutton's enemies in Congress and the media had to spin this to their advantage. There was no way in hell he was going to let them take his phone from him at a time like this.

"Where are Agents Perez and Compton? I'm Senator Sutton's senior chief of staff and I've been dealing directly with them. I want to speak to them about this."

"Agent Perez is at the hospital being treated for his injuries," the agent said. "Agent Compton is with him. Now I need your phone please."

"This is crazy," Paul said. "What's your name again?"

"I'm Agent Frank Carlton. If you'd like you can lodge a complaint at a later time, but right now, I need your phone."

Behind him, another agent moved closer. Paul sensed the movement and glanced over his shoulder at the man, who stared back at him without expression.

Paul turned back to Carlton. "You should have a warrant for this."

"You're not a suspect, sir. We're just gathering information, such as pictures and videos of the crowd here tonight, that could be helpful in our investigation. We want to make sure your boss doesn't get shot at again. Nobody wants that, right?"

"Don't patronize me," Paul said. "And no, I won't let you have it. There's privileged information on there."

"Nobody here cares what your boss had for lunch last Tuesday," the agent said. "That's not what I'm after. Now please, sir, your phone."

Paul looked around, hoping to find somebody he knew, somebody who could intervene on his behalf, but there was nobody. He was pretty much stuck on his own. Realizing he was beat, he reached into his coat pocket and pulled out his iPhone. He punched in his security code and handed it over to Carlton. "I don't appreciate this kind of treatment, Agent Carlton."

"iPhone," Carlton said, as though he hadn't heard. He handed it to the female agent sitting at a MacBook. "This one's yours."

The female agent took the phone and plugged it into her computer. She made a few quick keystrokes and then wrinkled her brow. She glanced up at Paul.

"You have over four hundred photos in here from tonight alone."

"I told you," he said. "I'm Senator Sutton's chief of staff. It's my job to get pictures of her at events like this."

"Anything after the shooting?" Carlton asked.

"Doesn't look like it," the woman said.

"Okay, capture it all." He looked at Paul. "Did you take any videos?"

Paul lowered his eyes. "No," he said quietly.

"He has twenty-eight text messages from after the shooting," the woman at the computer said.

"To who?"

"Twenty-three of them to Senator Sutton. The others I don't recognize."

"All right," Carlton said. "We're gonna take it."

"What? No," Paul said. "No, you can't take my phone."

"You'll get it back as soon as we're done with it."

"How long will that take?"

Carlton shrugged. "I don't know. Three, four hours maybe. We've got to run every single one of those photos you took through our facial recognition software. That takes time."

Paul felt dizzy. "Please," he said. "Please don't do this. Capture whatever you need to. Download it or whatever you do. But please, I have to have that phone. Here in the next few hours I'm going to be scheduling press conferences and interviews and meetings. I have to have that phone. It's got everything in there. All my contacts, everything. Please, what happens in the next few hours could shape the rest of Senator Sutton's political career. Please."

Carlton glanced at the two agents seated behind

their computers. Neither returned the glance. Paul studied the man's face for some sign of mercy. Rachel Sutton's shift to the political middle had won her a lot of new friends in the Republican Party, and made a lot of enemies among the core faithful in the Democrats. If this agent was a dyed-in-the-wool Democrat, he might harbor some resentment, and he could sink Sutton, or at least help to sink her, by holding on to that phone.

"Capture a mirror of his device and return it to him," Carlton said.

Paul let out the breath he'd been holding.

"Thank you, Agent Carlton. Thank you."

Carlton nodded. "If we find anything, though, I'm gonna need the phone back. We have to have the source of the information to make a solid criminal case."

"Okay," Paul said.

Paul thought the agent was about to walk away when he suddenly stepped in close and whispered: "That boss of yours is doing a lot of damage to the cartels. I hope she keeps giving 'em hell. And you tell her, if she runs for president, it'll be the first time in my life I ever vote for a Democrat."

He turned and walked away without waiting for Paul's reply, leaving Paul standing there with a confused grin on his face.

The female agent kept his phone for another two minutes before finally handing it back to him.

"That's it?" he said.

"Yep," she answered.

"So, I can leave?"

"No," she said. "You can go back to that couch

over there and wait. Agent Carlton will tell everyone when they can leave."

"Oh. Any idea how long that'll be? I've got a ton of work I should be doing."

"I have no idea," she said. "But he's got Texas billionaires and Mexican movie queens waiting on the hook, too, and if he's not letting them go, I don't think your chances are too good for an early release." And then, with venom in her voice, she added: "And I don't care who your boss is."

He walked away, feeling equal parts relief and anger as the realization that the Secret Service now had records of every e-mail he'd ever sent, every photo he'd every taken, every appointment he'd ever made, and every website he'd ever visited. They quite literally had put his entire life under a microscope. The sense of violation was enough to make him physically ill.

He was walking across the lobby, sending another text to Sutton, when he bumped into a woman in a black dress. "Oh, sorry," he said, and then did a double take when he realized who it was. "Oh, my God. Monica, it's you!"

"Yes," she said.

"Wow. I didn't think I was going to see you again."

She smiled and lowered her eyes. "I was afraid of that, too. When the Secret Service men separated us, I was upset because I didn't have your number. I tried to get them to let me see you, but they wouldn't let me."

Paul shook his head. He couldn't believe his luck. Her name was Monica Rivas, and he'd met her earlier that evening, during the cattle call before Senator Sutton gave her speech. He'd sensed someone at his shoulder and turned, expecting to meet yet another Texas banker and his trophy wife. Instead, he came face to face with a stunning Mexican beauty. Never very good with women, he'd babbled some kind of lame greeting and gone on stammering, desperately trying to think of something cool to say, when Wayne Sutton had whisked him off on an errand "to find a decent martini in this goddamned place." He'd been almost grateful to be rescued from the botch he was making of it.

But later, Paul had caught her smiling at him from across the room, and he'd put down his iPhone and gone over to make a proper introduction.

Things had gone well from there. She was easy to talk to, with a bubbly laugh and eyes that seemed to make him the center of the room. She was a Mexican citizen, but had been educated at Harvard. She was a lawyer, a voracious reader, could speak four languages. Her insights into the potential legal barriers ahead for the senator's International Asset Seizure Law were nothing short of brilliant. He was having trouble deciding whether he wanted to debate her or make love to her.

Actually, it wasn't a very hard decision to make.

And then, when the bullets started flying, she'd thrown herself into his arms. He'd pulled her behind a table, and there, lying on top of her, the gunfire still crackling just a few feet away, he'd watched her eyes catch fire with fear and desire.

It was, for all the terror and screaming, one of the most erotic experiences of his life. But then the Secret Service had locked down the scene, and before he knew it, he was being pulled away. With everything that happened after that, and all that still needed to be done, he'd given up on seeing her again. Just another bad break in a string of bad breaks that defined his history with women.

But here she was.

And her brown eyes still held a touch of that desire he'd seen earlier.

"Listen," he said, "I'm gonna be crazy busy here for probably the rest of the day, but I would love to see you again. Would you give me your number? Maybe I could . . . call you?"

She shook her head, and her black hair moved like a wave over her bare shoulders.

"Oh," he said. "Oh, okay."

As many times as he'd been shut down like this, he thought he'd be used to rejection by now, but it was always awkward, and it always hurt.

Not knowing what else to say, he started to turn away. But then she put a hand on his wrist. He looked at her hand, at her slender fingers and perfectly manicured nails, then up to her face. She was smiling, and it was a wicked little grin.

"What is it?" he said. He wasn't sure why he was whispering, but he was.

"I was so upset when they pulled us apart, Paul. Please, let's not go away so quickly again."

"Well, okay. Sure. I have a lot of phone calls to make, though. You won't be too bored?"

Her smile turned demure. "Paul."

"What?"

"Don't you have a room here in the hotel?"

"A room?" For a moment he didn't understand. And then he did. "Oh," he said. "Oh, a room. Yeah, I sure do, but . . ."

"But what?"

"Well, Monica, I . . . God, I've got about a million things I have to do before I talk with the senator again. I have a press conference to put together and . . ." He trailed off there. She was frowning, the disappointment plain on her face. She looked embarrassed. He couldn't believe he was saying no to this woman, but what was he supposed to do?

And then, like she was reading his mind, she smiled and said, "I understand. You are a dedicated man. I like that. I respect that. A man should be a man when it comes to his job. Perhaps we will see one another again some time."

"I . . ."

But she had already turned away. He watched the way her dress moved as she walked, the liquefaction of her clothes, and he knew he'd never have a chance at something this good ever again.

Ah, hell, he thought.

"Monica, wait!"

Paul had his coat off and was struggling to get loose of his tie before they'd even closed the door. He had his hands all over her, and she on him, the two of them kissing, squeezing, exploring each other.

He groped for the light switch. Couldn't find it.

"Damn," he said.

"Leave it off," Monica said, breathing hard. Her

eyes were bright in the darkness, staring up at him. Paul had read in books of women whose faces were lit with passion like that, and he'd always thought such things to be the purple prose of hack writers. He certainly never thought he'd see it firsthand.

"Monica," he gasped.

Her long black hair had turned into a beautiful tangled mess after their ride up in the elevator. He loved the way it spilled over her shoulders. He loved the way her black dress clung to her breasts, to her hips. She was fantastic. She leaned in close to him, close enough he could smell the honeysuckle of her perfume and feel the heat of her breath on his neck. Her arms went around his waist, and the next instant, his cummerbund fell to the floor.

He didn't even feel the buckle come loose.

Staring into her eyes, all he could manage was to shake his head in amazement.

"Paul," she whispered, "take me to your bed."

He nodded, his Adam's apple bobbing in his throat like a piston.

Still smiling, she led him into the room, where the couch was stacked with his work for Senator Sutton—journals and legal briefs and notepads.

He stopped in the middle of the room and waited, like a lamb on the altar.

Paul had left a reading light on over by the bed, and in its soft glow he watched her coming closer and closer.

"You are—"

"Shhh," she said, putting a finger over his lips. "You saved me tonight. You were so brave."

Even in his aroused, lust-blind state, he knew that

wasn't exactly true, but it didn't matter. When he looked into her eyes, nothing mattered. She made him feel like a hero, and when she turned those dark, doe eyes up at him, the rest of the world fell away.

She undid his cuff links and the studs on his shirt. Watching her loosening his clothes, he could barely believe the chain of events that had led them here, like it was meant to be.

"I can't believe you're here with me," he said.

"I am not in the habit of going home with strange American men," she said.

"Am I strange?"

He had meant it as a joke, but the smile slipped off her face. "I am sorry," she said. "I have been speaking English since I was twelve, but the idiom is still sometimes difficult for me. I did not mean that you were strange. I meant only that—"

"Oh, no," he said. "No, no, no. I know what you meant. I'm sorry, I . . . I was trying to be funny. I'm sorry."

"You do not think me easy that I am with you?"

He shook his head. "I think you're a goddess, Monica. I just can't believe it."

"You make me feel beautiful," she said. She turned in his arms and swept her hair away from her shoulders, exposing the back of her gown. "Will you . . . undo me?"

"Huh? Oh, yes."

With trembling fingers he unhooked her gown. It fell, puddling at her feet.

And just like that, she stood before him, wearing nothing but a lacy black thong and high heels.

"Wow," he said.

She led him to the bed and pulled him down beside her. He loved the way her hair spilled over the pillow, the way her lips glinted in the low light. Paul ran his fingertips lightly across her belly, over the tops of her slender thighs. Her skin was cool, smooth, a rich coffee–and-cream color that made his fingers seem unnaturally white.

She sucked in a breath, her back arching in pleasure, breasts straining toward him. She moaned softly. It was almost a purring sound.

Paul leaned in to kiss her, her mouth finding his hungrily, and soon they were tangled up together, arms and legs intertwined, flesh to flesh. A burning flush of excitement ran down his entire body as his lips grazed her neck, her shoulders, her breasts. He took one of her nipples between his teeth and another thrill shot through him to hear the gasp she made.

He found the edge of her thong, his fingertips dipping under the fabric. Her hips rose slightly, allowing him the room to pull them down. She found his boxer shorts next, and tugged them down. He was beside her now, naked, hard, and hungry.

His need for her overpowered him and he climbed between her legs. He grabbed her wrists and pushed them down into the pillow. He could feel great strength in her, and also that strength yielding to his pressure, accepting him, pulling him in.

She closed her eyes with a sigh.

He sank into her, closing his eyes as the warmth of her sex surrounded him. He began to move, her hips pressing against his, the two of them finding one another's rhythm, pushing toward a release that was, for him, like going over a cliff.

Paul drove into her, again and again, unable to stop. Being with her he'd found a need within himself that was almost feral. He'd been with maybe ten women in his life, probably fewer, but never had it been like this. Never had he felt himself so overwhelmed by a woman, so completely enthralled by her power.

And then he felt his coming orgasm coiling inside him, demanding release. He opened his eyes and saw her staring back at him, nodding hungrily for him, urging him to push deeper. Paul went faster, drove harder. He felt himself growing close, too close, too soon, and slowed down again, backing away from his pleasure so that he could feel her body shudder.

Then, her muscles tensed. She curled against him. Her gasps turned into little panting breaths, her lips forming a perfect O as her fingernails dug deep into his back.

That was too much for him. He sped up again, his breaths quickening, growing harsh, and he buried himself as deeply as he could go within her, his whole body stiffening as he exploded.

Afterwards, Paul held himself above her, like he was doing a push-up, smiling between breaths that felt like a hammer against his ribs. He kissed her, then sagged down beside her, sweaty and spent. She nuzzled against his chest, a fingernail running over his still-heaving chest like the tip of a switchblade.

He sank into his pillow, laughing and gasping for breath at the same time. The whole world, for a moment, was forgotten. All that mattered was this moment . . . and at the moment, life was pretty damned good.

Playfully, she bit at his nipple, giggling as he convulsed.

"Hey!" he said.

"That was very nice," she said.

He laughed again. He ran a hand through his hair, both surprised and proud of himself that he had worked up such a sweat.

"Very nice, indeed," he said.

"You liked being with me?" she said.

He turned toward her, brows furrowed. Those eyes that had thrilled him so were now looking at him for approbation, and not for the first time that evening he felt everything that made him a man melt into a puddle of goo. She was simply amazing. Absolutely and unequivocally divine.

"God, yes," he said, the hammering in his chest finally subsiding. "You were *so* nice. So very nice."

"You made me feel good," she said, and once again she cuddled against his chest, contented as a napping cat.

He didn't speak. This was a moment of victory. It didn't need any words, just his fingertips lightly dusting over her olive skin.

She smiled and closed her eyes with a sigh.

He was still running his fingertips over her hip when "Here Comes the Sun" started playing on his iPhone.

Monica looked up. "What is that?"

"That's the senator," he said.

"You have 'Here Comes the Sun' as her ring tone?"

"Long story," he said. Actually, it wasn't all that long of a story. She'd told him once that she'd been moved to tears watching the Clintons onstage as they'd learned he'd won the presidency, Fleetwood Mac's "Don't Stop" playing over the PA, and how she'd confided in him that she wanted "Here Comes the Sun," the Richie Havens version, for her magic moment. He'd changed his ring tone that very night.

"Here, let me up," he said, pulling his arm free from under her.

He went over to his pants and fished out his phone.

"Jesus, Paul," Sutton said, not even waiting for him to say hello. "What are you doing?"

Paul looked back at Monica. She had rolled over onto her stomach, slender legs in the air, crossing and recrossing as she watched him. She put her lower lip between her teeth. *A come on over here and fuck me* smile was on her face.

"I . . . uh, I . . . well . . ."

"Damn it, Paul. I need you here. I'm at the Colson. Finally got Wayne to bed, the drunken bastard. But now I've got CNN calling me. They want a press conference. Where are you?"

"Okay, okay," he said, trying to marshal his thoughts. "Hold on a sec."

He held the phone in front of him and scanned through the missed calls. Shit, he thought. A ton of them. He'd silenced everything but Senator Sutton's ring tone right before he got in the elevator with Monica, but he could see now that he'd missed calls from all the major news outlets. Christ, even Fox wanted to talk to him.

What in the hell was wrong with him? Any idiot should have seen this coming.

"Paul?" Sutton said.

"I'm here," he said, putting the phone back to his ear. He went into scramble mode, and suddenly, his mind cleared. This was where he lived, where he was in his element.

Okay, he thought, Sutton's at her apartment in the Colson. She wouldn't want to move. And besides, bringing the press to her would put things on her terms. She would be the one calling on them, not them ambushing her. And with a dozen or so of them together, none of them would be able to dig too deeply. It would be perfect for the kind of sound bites the press, and the American public for that matter, had come to love Senator Rachel Sutton for.

"You should stay there," he said. "Let's use your office for the press conference."

"Well, of course, we're going to use my office," she said. "I'm not going back to that hotel, not through those crowds."

"Of course not," he said. He was nodding to himself. This was already coming together. "Listen, just stay there. I'm going to get NBC, CNN, Fox—"

"Fox?" she said, sounding disgusted. "Those bastards will turn this into a right-wing feeding frenzy."

"You're a moderate now, remember?" he said. "And besides, with NBC and CNN there, they'll balance each other out. And, don't forget, this will give you a chance to reach out to the Hispanic vote."

"What? How? You heard, right? Evangeline Ramos died tonight."

The Mexican television star, he thought. He remembered her going down when the shooting started. A pity.

"We'll use that as our lead-in," he said. "Her husband is Juan Cavalos, president of Grupo Financiero Banamex. First thing out of your mouth, you express condolences for her many fans, then transition into her support for her husband. Put it in those terms and he can't help but come out on our side. Anything less would dishonor his wife, and he can't afford that."

"Yeah," Sutton said slowly, and he could picture her nodding into the phone, seeing the brutal logic of the move. "Yeah, okay."

A pause.

"Paul?"

"Yes, ma'am?"

"That was pretty scary tonight. A lot scarier than San Antonio."

He nodded to himself. She was right. In San Antonio, they'd been watching from the fourth floor of the Mexican Embassy as her motorcade drove into the ambush. They'd watched Agent Perez and his team engage the shooters from the Los Zetas Cartel, watched the gunfight rage down the street, watching the gutters fill up with blood. But tonight, they'd been right in the thick of things. The bullets had whizzed over his head while he cowered behind a table, a beautiful Mexican goddess trembling beneath him.

He glanced over at Monica. She was still smiling, but his own smile had vanished.

"I know," he said into the phone. "I was scared, too."

"How soon can you be here?"

Monica rocked her bottom back and forth for him. She licked her lips.

"Paul?"

"Yeah," he said, shaking himself. "Yeah, I'm here. Um, I'll be there soon, okay? Forty minutes maybe."

"Hurry, Paul. Please."

"I will," he said.

He hung up the phone, then looked over at Monica. "Listen," he said, "I hate to do this, but I have to go. Something's come up. I have to handle this." He knew he shouldn't say too much, but damn was she incredible. "It's about what happened tonight."

"Will I see you again?" she asked.

"Yes," he blurted out. "Yes. I'd like that. Can I call you?"

"May I call you?" she said.

She stood up, radiantly naked, and took her iPhone from her purse. She walked over to him and put her phone next to his.

He gave her his number and she dialed it.

"What ring tone will you give me, Paul Godwin?"

He thought for a minute. "Sam Cooke maybe. 'You Send Me.' "

"I do not know it. But I look forward to hearing it."

"And for me? What'll you use for mine?"

"For you, I think it shall be Vicente Fernandez. He is always the best. I think I shall choose '*Aca Entre Nos.*' "

He had to think a moment for the translation. *Just between us.* Hmmm, not bad, he thought. "I like it," he said. "Listen, I need to—" He pointed to the

shower. "I need to get cleaned up and changed before I talk to the press."

"Yes, certainly. Go ahead. May we leave together,
when you're done? I would like very much for you
to hold my hand to my car. The city can be very
scary at night."

"Yeah," he said. "Yeah, I'd like that."

"Me, too."

He went to the bathroom, and right before he
closed the door, he saw her standing there, still holding her phone, wearing nothing but a smile, giving
him a cute little wave.

He pulled the door closed, feeling like the king of
the world.

As the bathroom door closed, Pilar Soledad let
the playfulness and the encouraging smile that were
the hallmarks of her Monica Rivas disguise fall
away.

Her expression blank, she stared at the door,
waiting, listening.

The shower came on, but she didn't move until
she heard the shower door open and the pattering
rhythm of the water change. Then, sure that he was
in the shower, she went to her purse and removed the
adapter she had secreted away there. She plugged
one end into her iPhone and the other into his. His
phone was password protected, but that didn't matter. The software built into her phone broke the four
digit code easily enough. Having his phone number
already plugged in made the process so much easier.

Her jail-breaking software completed the rest.

She watched as the display on her screen recorded the software's progress. One by one, the Unix-based limitations Apple had built into the phone began to crumble until at last her phone had total access to his iPhone's operating system. E-mail, calendars, text messages, notepads: everything opened for her inspection.

These Americans and their toys, she thought. Everything was here. His entire life, everything that mattered to him—and more important, to Senator Rachel Sutton—was right here for her to examine.

It was almost too easy.

When the process was complete, the software initiated an untethered jailbreak, and set up a worm that would migrate to his other Apple devices next time he synched them. From here on out, every update, every e-mail, every text would send a ghost copy to her device, giving her what the Americans so primly referred to as "the fly on the wall," making his life, and hopefully that of Senator Rachel Sutton as well, an open book.

The program finished its run right as the shower stopped. Moving quickly, Pilar unplugged her adapter from his phone and put it back in his pocket.

She was a few feet from her purse, still wrapping the adapter around her finger when he stepped out of the shower, steam rising off his shoulders and a towel around his waist.

"Hey," he said. He glanced at the adapter in her hands and cocked his head to one side. "What's that?"

For a moment, she thought how easy it would be

to kill him. A single strike with the blade of her hand to his throat, just below his Adam's apple, and she could crush his windpipe. She could stand over him and watch as he choked and gasped away the last few seconds of his life. The whole pathetic display would be over in less than two minutes.

Unfortunately, as long as the senator was alive, and as long as he was her most trusted aide, Paul Godwin was worth more alive than dead. Far more, in fact.

Which meant this was a job for Monica Rivas.

"I was going to charge up my phone," she said and moved a little closer to him. "But I have brought the wrong charger."

"You can use mine if you want."

"But there is no time, is there? You must leave in just a few minutes."

"There's a little time," he said.

He wasn't a bad looking man, she thought. Just a hair shy of six feet, perhaps a hundred seventy pounds. When he hit his forties, perhaps his light brown hair would thin on top, perhaps his belly would lap over his belt, but for now, he had a good body and a dopey but still charming smile that made her assignment not altogether unpleasant.

She tossed the phone and adapter cable on top of her dress, then stepped a little closer to him, her fingers toying with the loose knot holding the towel to his hips.

"You have a few minutes still?" she asked.

Pilar Soledad, back in character as Monica Rivas, stared up at him with her best doe-eyed innocent gaze.

"I, uh—" he stammered.

But he said no more, for with that the towel fell to his feet, and the woman he knew as Monica Rivas knelt before him, commanding his complete attention.

CHAPTER 3

Outside her window, Dulles International Airport sank into the darkness. Pilar Soledad watched it fade to black, aware that something vital inside her was hardening. It was always the same on these return trips to San Antonio, as layer by layer she peeled away the fiction that was her life as Monica Rivas, Washington, D.C., lawyer, socialite and Mexican-American rights activist, leaving only a core of ice too numb to care for much of anything.

Her gaze shifted to her reflection in the window.

The woman looking back at her was gentle, kind, sweet. She wore silver hoop earrings and a light mineral makeup, a powder, with a cool, muted red lip gloss. Her black hair was pulled back in a loose ponytail that draped over the shoulder of her tweed suit jacket. It was a good look for her, professional and stylish, bespeaking of old money and cultured tastes.

But Monica Rivas was a lie.

Like everything else about her, Monica Rivas was a cold, cruel, carefully constructed lie. And in moments like this, as she faced the transition from Monica to Pilar, she felt so bitter. For all her struggles, all those years spent clawing her way out of the gutters of Ciudad Juarez, of fighting against the gangs that tried to turn her into a common whore, that for all that, she had achieved little more than a sort of pointless circularity, a racehorse going 'round in circles at full speed, never getting anywhere. There was so much hatred inside her, so much resentment at the world that had created her. Had she not learned to bury all that rage over the years she probably would have put a gun in her mouth and ended it all. Instead, she stared at her reflection and let the walls come up around her heart, one after another.

From beside her, she heard a sharp intake of breath, and turned from the window.

In the seat next to her was an old Hispanic woman, short and fat, her dark complexion indicating her Indio heritage. The woman was gripping the armrests of her seat, her teeth clenched, eyes shut hard.

Pilar reached over and took the woman's hand in hers. It was the kind of thing Monica would do.

Surprised, the woman looked at Pilar.

Then she smiled.

"Thank you," she said, breathing a little easier now that she had someone to lend her strength.

"Taking off is always the hardest part," Pilar said in Spanish.

The woman's smile brightened. "Oh, are you from San Antonio?"

"Yes. Well, years ago. I haven't been back in a long while." The lie was practiced. It came easily.

Speaking Spanish seemed to relax the older woman, for the tension was gone from her face now. She even turned toward Pilar, as though they were sitting on a porch swing together rather than roaring steadily up to altitude.

"Are you going home then?" the woman asked. "To your family?"

Automatically, at the mention of family, Pilar thought of Ramon Medina. It was hard to hold the smile on her face.

"Yes," she said. "I still have some connections there."

"How nice," the woman said.

She went on talking, that old woman, but Pilar, for the most part, tuned her out. She was nodding politely, offering vague noises of encouragement now and then, but in her mind she'd turned back to darker times. She was thinking uneasy, alone thoughts, the kind of thoughts that kept her awake at night, staring up into the darkness, even when she was playing at being Monica Rivas.

She remembered a time, twenty years ago now, when she was in the back of an eighteen-wheeler with a boy she knew only as Lupe and fifty-three other migrant workers trying to get across the border into Texas. She had to have been eight, or possibly ten, because she'd been small enough to cower behind a field box that had recently been used to transport onions. She could smell them even now.

And Lupe, he would have been younger than that, for she'd been able to shield him with her body when the old woman—an old woman much like the woman sitting next to her now—had gone into cardiac arrest from the heat and died.

She collapsed right next to them, and when Lupe saw the old woman was dead, her face slack and powdery white in the daylight that slipped through the cracks in the trailer's walls, he'd gone still. Even after all these years, she could still hear his silence next to her, how awestruck he had been at being closed in with the dead.

"Why won't they let us out?" Lupe asked. He huddled against her, trembling, even though it was hot like an oven in the trailer. They hadn't moved in a long while, and several of the men had kicked and scraped and pushed against the walls, one by one dropping from heatstroke and dehydration. Looking across the silhouetted forms crowded into the trailer, she could tell that most of them were dead already.

"They've probably left us here," she said. "Disconnected the truck and left us here by the side of the road."

"But why? We paid them, didn't we? We paid them what they wanted."

She thought about the frightened look on the truck driver's face when he opened the back and learned that four of the migrants riding in his trailer had died. She thought about the men surging against the doors when they closed, their screams of rage and horror as the padlock clamped shut.

"Yes, we paid them."

"Then why?" He was starting to whine.

She squeezed his hand until his whining turned to whimpers.

"Stop it," she said. "Be quiet. Somebody will come soon."

"My head hurts," he said.

"You'll be okay."

"I want to throw up."

"You'll be okay. Just stay calm. Don't move if you don't have to. Somebody will come."

To drive her memories of that time away she took the old woman's hand again.

"You're so very sweet," the woman said.

Pilar smiled, wishing that were really true.

It was nearly midnight when she disembarked at San Antonio International Airport. The airport was almost deserted, the shops along the concourse all closed up, nobody but a few bored custodians wandering around. Pilar never checked baggage on these flights back and forth between Washington, D.C., and San Antonio. Everything she needed, and that wasn't much, she kept in her carry-on.

She made her way with the other passengers down to the exits where she rented a car on her Monica Rivas credit card. Less than ten minutes later, she had the airport in her rearview mirror and was looking for a place to pull over.

She found it in an abandoned gas station parking lot.

She turned out the lights, rolled down the windows, and waited. Washington had been hot and sticky with humidity when she left. Here, in San Antonio, it was even hotter, but the night air was dry and still and scented by a nearby magnolia tree in bloom. It pleased her. Even if coming back here stirred up a lot of memories she'd rather forget, there was still something satisfying, even welcoming, like a narcotic sleep, about the South Texas nights.

And with the windows open and the night air moving across her skin, she could almost hear Lupe laughing at the sparks rising on the hot air above the open fire they'd lit the night before they were to board the eighteen-wheeler and make the trip across the border. They were out on the black hills above Ciudad Juarez, behind a cluster of tarpaper shacks sitting on car tires. They didn't have anything to eat but some gum she'd stolen from a shop down in the city, but that was okay. Lupe was happy just listening to her talk about the wheel of fortune and what was in store for them.

"If you start at the bottom of the wheel and rise to the top, that's a comedy," she said.

"And if you start at the top and you go to the bottom . . ."

"That's a tragedy," she answered. "But that's not us."

"We're like those sparks, right?" They both watched pinpoints of light rise into the air, winking out above their heads.

"That's right. Our life's a comedy."

Oh, how he'd laughed about that.

And oh, how it hurt now to think about him laughing.

At 12:30 A.M., she took out her iPhone and called up a Gmail account that she shared with Ramon Medina, head of the Porra Cartel. The inbox contained a few junk e-mails, but those were unimportant. It was the draft folder with which she was concerned. The cartels had learned early on that the NSA routinely monitored international e-mail accounts. Anything going in or out of the country was scanned for key words and hot button topics by some of the most sophisticated software analytics ever devised. And when items of interest were developed, they were copied and read and the senders placed on the watch lists for more intensive scrutiny.

The Porra Cartel had figured out ways to be careful. Anytime they needed to relay large amounts of computer files, as she'd done with all the information she'd lifted from Paul Godwin's phone, they simply typed up an e-mail on the dummy account they shared and saved that e-mail in the draft folder. A simple routine was devised. When a scheduled check of the account was due, as hers was now, she simply logged in using the password they shared and checked for drafts. Unless the NSA knew the account name and the password, they stood almost no chance of intercepting the message.

Waiting in the drafts folder was a single message, written in Ramon Medina's clipped, terse style:

M . . . esto es algo bueno que lo puedo usar . . . en el edificio gris en Potranco y Westover Hills . . . lo que necessita aqui y ahora . . . R

That was good, she thought. He'd liked what she'd sent him and felt like it was something they could use.

Great.

Now to see what he wanted her to do about it.

He'd given her directions to meet him, and she

had a vague idea of where he meant. Ramon Medina never used the same place twice, but he generally felt more comfortable on San Antonio's west side.

She got on Loop 410 and headed west. The roads were nearly empty, much as the airport had been. Pilar put the car on cruise control—even though her Monica Rivas identity was airtight and the cops would never find anything if they stopped her, there was no reason to leave a footprint if she could help it—and headed into the darkness at the edge of town.

Her thoughts kept turning back to Lupe. The Texas Highway Patrol had finally rescued her from the eighteen-wheeler, but not before Lupe and thirty-nine others died of heatstroke. After that, she went to sleep every night hating herself, blaming herself for his death. She'd wake up in the morning hoping it had all been a sick nightmare, but of course it wasn't. He was just a child. He had counted on her, believed in her, and she'd let him down. That was the part that really chewed her up inside. She'd been careless. And now he was dead.

The Border Patrol had taken her from the Highway Patrol, questioned her, assigned her an identity card, and put her on an old school bus with bad air conditioning. Then they'd driven her back to the border, back to Ciudad Juarez. There they'd turned her out, a ten-year-old orphan left to wander the streets of the murder capital of the world. Other girls her age were forced into prostitution, but not Pilar. She learned to avoid the gangs, and even managed to steal the food she ate from right under their noses.

Ramon Medina was a young man then, still in his early twenties. He'd made a name for himself with a string of eight-liner gambling houses that catered to the American tourists, dozens of whorehouses and, of course, a tight leash on the growing trans-border drug trade. His personal office was one of the places Pilar went to steal food, and, more and more, money.

For two years she stole from him, until one night when he and three of his men had surprised her rifling through his safe, which she had learned to crack on one of her first visits. One of the men tried to grab her, but she fought him. He was three times her size, and still she fought. She almost got away, too. She would have, if Ramon hadn't put a pistol to the back of her head.

"So young," he said. "And so ready to die."

She closed her eyes and waited for the shot.

But it didn't come.

For as different as the cartels were, they all shared a strong patriarchal structure. Women were good for decoration, and for recreation, but not for business. Still, something about her had impressed him. She was feisty. She was smart. At twelve, she had succeeded in robbing him blind, getting in and out of his compound with the ease of a professional burglar. She would have gone on stealing from him, too, if he hadn't been forced to come back here unexpectedly. Ramon knew talent when he saw it, and he saw it in her.

Over the next six years he made her into a real professional. By her late teens, she could slip in and out of any compound, government or otherwise, like a ghost. And she was a natural with computers, with financial networks, with business management. She became indispensable to him, helping in every part of his operation.

Even the killing.

As his operations in America grew, he created the Monica Rivas alter ego. He built a fictitious biography for her, making her the only daughter of one of Mexico's wealthiest coal barons. He got her into Harvard, paid her way. He paid her way through law school at the University of Virginia, too.

In return, she'd become his faithful spy in Washington.

Ramon Medina, she thought. There had been a time, years ago, when she actually believed she was in love with him.

But she was older now. She knew better.

She turned her car into a church parking lot that bordered the abandoned warehouse Ramon was using for this meeting and parked behind a large cluster of shrubs that had gone to riot. The church was small and poor looking, which probably meant it didn't have video cameras, but there was no point in being careless.

She went around to the side of the warehouse and saw three guys standing just inside an open doorway. She knew them at a glance. Knew their kind, anyway. They were like all the other common foot soldiers taken off the streets of Ciudad Juarez, tattooed, skinny, unkempt, with a perpetually feral look in their eyes, like dogs that were never fed enough. Men like these died by the dozens every day in Ciudad Juarez, their only claim to fame the horrors that were ravaged on their bodies.

They saw her coming and separated from the

shadows. One of the men—Jesus, she thought, he's
not even wearing a shirt—put out his cigarette and
walked right up to her. He looked her over, head to
toe, leering hungrily.

"I'm here to see Ramon," she said, not wanting to
waste time with these losers.

The man laughed. He glanced over his shoulder
at the two men behind him. *"Ramon se esta putas
caras en estos dias,"* he said.

This brought a laugh from all three men.

"I am no man's whore," Pilar said.

The man looked back at her, a stupid grin still on
his face. Perhaps, at that moment, he sensed the
change in her posture, or perhaps he saw the look in
her eye, but either way it didn't help him.

He was still grinning when she drove her fist into
his throat, crushing the hyoid bone. The man staggered backwards and fell over. He was choking,
holding his throat, rolling on the pavement like a
fish out of water.

The other two men were already pulling the pistols from the waistbands of their jeans, but they
weren't fast enough either. Pilar sidestepped the first
man, and when his right hand came up with the gun,
she caught his wrist, pushed it high to get the arm
and the gun out of play, and then brought the blade
of her foot down hard on the side of his knee. The
bone crunched beneath the kick and the man cried
out. He sagged into a crouch, his leg unable to support his weight. That gave her the height advantage
she needed. Using her weight as leverage, she
twisted the man's gun hand around, turning in a circle so that he was off balance. He tried to hold on to

the gun, and that was a mistake. She snapped the bones in his wrist and sent him tumbling away.

All of this happened in the time it took the third man to pull his weapon, and by the time he did, he found himself staring down the muzzle of the pistol in Pilar's hand.

"Enough!"

Pilar kept the weapon trained on the man's forehead.

He glanced back toward the warehouse door, where Ramon Medina was standing with several of his personal bodyguards. The man turned back to Pilar, and she could sense his uncertainty, his damaged machismo. What would Ramon Medina think of him now, beaten by a girl they'd had outnumbered and outgunned? That's what he's wondering, Pilar thought.

He looked at the two men behind her. Both were still writhing and coughing, unable to get up.

If he had any self-respect at all he'd try to slap me, Pilar thought.

She smiled at him, inviting him to make the next move.

He didn't take the bait. Instead, he muttered, "You fucking bitch."

Pilar had been dealing with jerks like this little man her entire life. As a child, she'd run from his sort, men who leered at her with dirty faces and bad teeth, their intentions and desires plain on their faces. For years, she'd lived in terror of what such men would do to her when they caught her. But that was a long time ago, and she wasn't a little girl anymore.

She wasn't running anymore.

And she didn't take insults from anyone anymore.

Pilar closed on him before he could react and slammed the butt of her gun down on the bridge of his nose, shattering it with a sickening crunch. The man wilted below her, but Pilar wasn't about to let him go. She was no whore. She was nobody's bitch. The nerve of the man. Who the hell did he think he was?

A red curtain of rage dropped over her.

The blood rushed in her ears. She let the rage fill her.

She knelt over the man and brought the gun down on his face, slinging blood everywhere, smashing teeth and sending them skittering across the pavement like spilled coins.

The man's eyes lost focus. His hands dropped to the pavement. But Pilar didn't stop hitting him. The rage was too strong in her, her need to crush this son of a bitch too powerful.

She slammed the gun down on his mouth. "Bastard!"

And again.

"How do you like that?"

Again.

"Tell me I'm a bitch now."

Again and again and again.

"I said, *enough!*"

Ramon's words cut through the rage that had momentarily blinded her. He was the only one that could do that to her, pull her back from the edge.

She looked down at the man she'd just attacked. He wasn't moving anymore.

Pilar's chest was heaving, the gun was still raised above her head, blood dripping down her arm. Every nerve felt raw from too much adrenaline.

"You're done there," Ramon said.

Pilar lowered the weapon, and was about to get up when the man groaned through his busted teeth.

She slammed the gun down one more time.

Then she looked up at Ramon Medina. "Now I'm done," she said.

Ramon sighed. He was wearing a dark blue tailored suit, a white silk shirt with a gray tie, and crocodile skin boots. When she'd first met him all those years ago he'd looked just like every other street thug trying to carve out a section of Ciudad Juarez for his own. But the years, and more lucky breaks than any ten men deserved had polished him. Just like they'd done her. These days, Ramon Medina looked more like the wealthy playboys of the Mexico City club scene than the leader of the largest cartel in Northern Mexico, and despite the rage still simmering within her, Pilar remembered again why this man had held her in such sway for so many years.

She stood up, blood dripping from her face, her clothes, her hands.

"I see you're trimming off some of the deadweight from my staff," he said.

She smiled. "Isn't that what you pay me for?"

"I pay you for all kinds of things, Pilar." He put his hands in his pants pockets and studied her. "How was your trip?"

She shrugged.

"Would you like to get cleaned up before we talk?"

"I thought you said it was urgent."

He nodded. "Always straight to the heart of the matter, eh?"

"You should know better than anyone."

His expression remained pleasant. If he had any idea of the heartache he'd caused her over the years, all the things she swore she'd never do but did anyway just because of what he meant to her, he made no sign of it.

Oh, he knew, she thought. He knows everything there is to know. He's the only man who knows everything there is to know about me.

He just doesn't care.

Ramon turned to his bodyguards and gave instructions for the injured men at Pilar's feet to be brought inside.

"That one there, the one that's all beat up, take him to Dr. Rosato. Tell him I want a demonstration on the floor in fifteen minutes."

The men were removed inside, and Pilar and Ramon were left alone. He stood to one side and ushered her inside.

"What, no hug?" she said.

His smile broadened. "It is good to see you, Pilar. I missed you."

"What exactly am I looking at?" she said.

She was standing in Ramon's office, staring through a pane of one-way glass. On the other side of the glass was a fairly large open room, a few boxes here and there, some rusting pieces of machinery, a few doors along the back wall.

Aside from the men she'd injured outside, now sprawled out on the floor, there was nothing much of interest.

Ramon flicked his wrist, checking the time on his slim gold watch.

"Any minute now. It takes about ten minutes for someone as badly injured as our friend out there to feel the effects."

"When did you get the watch? I don't remember you ever wearing jewelry."

He gave her his best smile, perfect white teeth gleaming in the lamplight from his desk. "Do you like it? It was a gift."

"From who?"

"Does it matter?"

She turned away. "You're a bastard."

"Come on, Pilar. Don't be like that."

She didn't take the bait. She wasn't going to get into this again. How many times could he play her like this, keep her coming back for more like she was on some kind of string?

How many times would she let him?

Nodding toward the window, she said, "Tell me what I'm supposed to be looking at."

He stood up from his desk and came over to the window to stand by her side.

"I've diversified quite a bit over the years. Drugs and weapons pay well, but the real money is in investing. American sports franchises, banks, software startups, you name it. And, among other things, I happen to own significant interests in six different biomedical research firms, which is why you're here."

She nodded toward the man she'd pistol-whipped. He was on his back, a puddle of blood forming around his head. "I don't think biomedical research is going to help that guy."

"No," he said. "You're right about that. He's definitely a dead man."

"So what am I supposed to be looking at?"

"Just wait." He looked at his gold watch, and then flashed that disarming smile of his again. "It should be any minute now."

She scowled, but said nothing.

Pilar turned her attention back to the three men out in the middle of the warehouse floor. Two of them were moving, rising shakily to their feet. The third wasn't going anywhere, though. She could see that from here.

Must have done more damage than I thought, she realized. *Of course, the bastard deserved—*

The thought broke off cleanly. The man she'd injured so badly was convulsing. He was coughing blood all over the floor. She'd seen men die from beatings before, and that wasn't what was happening here. It looked more like something was inside him, and trying to tear its way out.

"What's wrong with him?" she asked.

"Just watch."

The room wasn't lit very well, but as the man flopped around on the floor, Pilar got a pretty good look at his features. He was ghastly. Something was wrong with his face. She'd smashed him up pretty severely, but she hadn't caused that. Not those injuries. The cuts on his face looked black. That wasn't bruising. She could see that. That was disease. And the skin around the black, diseased wounds was mottled red and shot through with burst blood vessels, like fresh burn marks.

"I didn't do that to him," Pilar said. "What is that? What's going on?"

"I know you didn't. I did." Ramon pointed back to the floor. "Just watch."

The man stopped fighting. As Pilar watched, he sank to the floor and went still. Pilar's brow furrowed. Had he just died? It sure looked that way. But then, he climbed to his feet, stood there stupidly for a moment, and then started to look around the room.

"This is the tricky part," Ramon said. "Sometimes they don't attack. They just stand there."

Pilar looked at him. "What are you talking about? What is this? What did you do?"

"Always so many questions, Pilar. Even when you were a little girl, you always questioned me. What have I told you? Don't ask questions. It keeps you from hearing the answer." He pointed to the window. "Ah, good, he's one of the movers. See? Look."

Pilar turned back to the glass. Inside, the man with the ruined face was staggering forward, advancing on the man that Pilar had hit in the throat. Pilar didn't react when the first man attacked. She didn't react when he pushed the man's chin up and leaned into his neck, exposing the bruised throat. She thought maybe he was checking the damage she'd done to his friend. But when the man started to tear into that bruised throat with his teeth, pulling huge strips of flesh away with the broken stubs of the teeth he had left, Pilar gasped.

"My God," she said.

"Oh, no," Ramon said. "God has nothing to do with this, I assure you. That right there is good old-fashioned American biomedical research. Nearly a billion dollars of it, in fact. It took my labs almost two years to modify the *Clostridium* bacteria that's causing that reanimation."

Pilar's only response was a long, muted groan. The man was eating that guy. Actually *eating* him.

"Ramon, what have you done?"

"Incredible, isn't it?" Ramon said.

"It's ghastly."

He laughed. "Pilar, I'm surprised at you. Don't you see what's going on out there?"

A gunshot kept her from answering.

Inside the room, the third man was backing away from his two companions, a look of abject horror on his face. He held a pistol on the man with the ruined face, but Pilar was unable to tell where the shot he'd just fired had gone. The cannibal was climbing to his feet now, so he hadn't been hit.

Or had he? There was a blackish-looking hole in his right shoulder, and as he lurched forward, that arm didn't come up.

Four more shots rang out, all of them solid center mass hits to the chest.

Pilar nodded in approval as the man with the ruined face fell backwards onto his butt and sat there, staring up at the man who had just shot him. Strong will, Pilar thought. The human body, she knew from experience, could withstand a huge amount of violence and damage and still carry on. She'd once slashed an American soldier's belly wide open, and then been surprised when the man ran away from her. She'd chased him for four blocks through the slums of Ciudad Juarez, the man cradling his intestines as he ran, before finally putting him down. It all depended on the amount of fight an injured person had in them. This man, with four gunshots to the chest and one to the shoulder, might still hang on for a few hours, though he wasn't going to be getting back up.

But he did.

Pilar gaped at what she saw. The wounded man was actually getting back to his feet. His moans did not surprise her. The man must be in terrible pain. But the fact that he was on his feet, and stumbling toward the man with the gun again, shocked her. It wasn't possible.

"He only has one chance," Ramon said. "He needs to take out the medulla oblongata, here, at the base of the brain pan."

Pilar glanced at him.

Ramon pointed at the back of his own head, where his skull met the spine. "Right here," he said. "What snipers call the kill spot. Hit there and all autonomic functions cease."

Another shot.

Pilar turned back to the window. Out on the floor, the man with the gun had managed a head shot that blasted away most of the top of the other man's skull. A tattered flap of his scalp was hanging down the back of his head.

"Nope," said Ramon. "He missed it."

Pilar was speechless. It was impossible, completely and unbelievably impossible, but the man was still on his feet. She expected him to fall over any minute, but he didn't. He staggered forward.

The man with the gun started to plead with the man to stand back.

"That won't help," Ramon said. "Once somebody's infected, and the bacteria have had a chance to take over, the person can't be reasoned with. All they want to do is attack. Doesn't matter who, doesn't matter what. They'll even go after their own children. If our friend out there wants to get through this, he'll have to destroy the medulla oblongata."

None of what Ramon was saying made sense. He could be that way, cryptic, but she had never felt this over her head with confusion before.

"Hmm," he said. "Nope. He's done for. Look."

Pilar hadn't even realized she was staring at Ramon.

"Look," he said again, and pointed toward the floor.

She did as he commanded. The man with the ruined face had knocked the other man down. The room filled with screaming. Pilar watched it all with a blank expression on her face. What had Ramon done? That man should be dead, but he wasn't. He was missing the top of his head and his chest had a handful of metal in it, yet he was still making a meal of the man. Oh, God, he was eating him.

"He *is* dead, Pilar," Ramon said.

"What?" For a moment, she thought she'd said something out loud, but then she reminded herself that he had always been able to do that. No one else she'd ever known, except maybe Lupe, when she was younger, could read her face as well as Ramon Medina. Whether she liked it or not, she had no secrets from him.

"You're wondering why he isn't dead. That's because he already is dead. He died before he attacked that first man."

Pilar shook her head.

"It's true. Here, watch."

Ramon pounded on the glass. Out on the floor, the man looked up, trying to find the source of the sound.

"Though they're dead, they still respond to sight and sound. There's no other real brain function that we know of, though. Well, except that need to move around and grab stuff. In all other ways, they're dead though. No breathing, no thirst, no nothing."

He beat on the glass again, and this time, the man got up and crossed to them. He walked right into it. Then, to Pilar's horror, he started trying to chew his way through it, beating on it with his gore-stained palms, smearing blood all over the glass.

"He'll stay like that for hours," Ramon said. "Once they catch the trail of something, they just keep going until something else comes along."

Pilar stared at the man. He was ghastly. She'd seen people tortured before, dismembered, burned, scalded with acid . . . this was worse. Worse by far.

"It's the eyes, isn't it?" Ramon said.

She nodded, still staring at the man on the other side of the glass. Ramon was absolutely right. The look in this man's eyes was the same as what she'd seen staring back at her from severed heads on tables or looking up at her from inside duffel bags. Exactly the same. Distant, profoundly vacant.

"That's when you finally believe they're dead, when you look in the eyes."

"Are you saying that man's a zombie?"

He laughed. "Yes! That's it exactly."

"You made a zombie?" A thousand questions raced through her head. But there was only one that really mattered. "Why?"

"Pilar, you don't need me to tell you that. You've spent enough time in the United States to know them as a people. They consume. That's what they do. They always have to have the newest thing, the latest thing. Bigger and better. And they always want more. More drugs, more food, more money. America is a mouth that can never be fed enough." Ramon laughed at that. He pointed out the window. "Just like our friend out there. Pilar, you should see those things eat on a corpse. They're like dogs. They'll eat until their bellies burst open, and then they'll keep on eating. They can never eat enough. Just like our friends north of the border."

She finally turned away from the horror show on the other side of the glass. Ramon was smiling at her, his hands in his pockets, black hair shiny in the low light from the lamp on his desk.

"Since when are you a philosopher?" she said.

"It's not philosophy to give the people what they want, Pilar. That's marketing."

"So, what is this thing you're marketing? A virus of some sort?"

"No, better. A flesh-eating bacteria."

"You're joking?"

"Ask him," Ramon said, pointing at the window. "He can tell you I'm not. This bacterium is a mutated form of *Clostridium perfringens*, which is pretty common. It's used as the main ingredient in self-rising breads, for example. In fact, I'm told it's common enough as a cause of food poisoning that most people produce an antibody against it. But it can get really nasty if it gets ahold of you. Even the common variety can cause fatal infections, if left untreated. And it's what causes gas gangrene in dead bodies. You can't tell from here, but our friend in there is probably smelling pretty ripe right about now."

"Lovely."

"It gets better. Like I said, we've caused it to mutate. What we've got going on in there is strain of *C. perfringens* that's been genetically crossbred with *Lactobacillus rhamnosus.*"

"*Lactobacillus*? That's the stuff in yoghurt."

"That's right. Very good."

"I'm surprised you've heard of it, though."

"I just read the pamphlets, Pilar."

"So how does it work?"

"Well, apparently it has the ability to influence the neurotransmitters that regulate our physiological and psychological brain functions."

"And that causes this?"

"We hadn't planned on that. All I wanted was something that could piggyback off of a food supply and cause as brutal a death as possible. I wanted impact."

She looked once again at the zombie still beating on the glass. "Well, that's certainly impact."

"It's the monster America deserves."

"So tell me, what exactly are you planning on doing with this monstrosity you've made?"

"Oh, Pilar, you're disappointing me. You haven't figured it out yet? You brought me the perfect opportunity when you got Senator Sutton's schedule."

She frowned at him.

"You wouldn't seriously consider releasing this thing on a city, would you?"

"No, of course not. We couldn't control what would happen in a situation like that. If it wasn't contained early enough, we might very well end with something right out of *The Walking Dead*."

"You watch that show?"

"It's become interesting to me lately."

She nodded.

"Besides, releasing this on one of the senator's scheduled events would probably miss her. There's no way to ensure that she'd eat from whatever food we decided to piggyback the bacteria on, which is probably going to be cold cuts or bread, something like that."

"Then how . . . ?"

"What we needed was an enclosed environment," Ramon said. "We needed somewhere that was isolated and completely enclosed for several days at a time. That way, we could be certain we got to her."

She frowned at that. Where did he honestly expect to find circumstances like that?

And then it hit her.

"The cruise she's taking. You're going to release this on a cruise ship."

"Exactly."

It was brilliant. She could see that. She could picture it, a cruise ship gliding into the docks at Cozumel with thousands aboard. The psychological impact of that would be catastrophic, and Ramon Medina would come out on top. He'd be the king. No other cartel could touch him—they'd be too afraid to. The Americans would be the same story.

They'd be too afraid he'd release his little bag of horrors on one of their cities.

"You realize they'll vilify you worse than they did Bin Laden, don't you?" she said.

"Perhaps."

"They will. No question about it."

"Let them. As long as they fear me, they'll have enough sense to stay away."

She shook her head. "God, I hope you know what you're doing."

"I do, Pilar. I know exactly what I'm doing. But I need your help."

"Me? What can I do?"

"I need someone onboard that ship."

She laughed out loud. "Yeah, right."

"Pilar, I need someone on that ship to make sure the plan goes like it's supposed to. I need to know that the senator is dead."

"But, what about . . . ?" She gestured toward the zombie on the other side of the glass.

"You'll have all the information you'll need to stay safe."

"Her cruise is in two weeks. You expect me to master everything there is to know about this bacteria of yours in two weeks?"

"I didn't send you to Harvard for nothing."

She didn't know what to say to that. Pilar stared at the zombie and tried to fathom what was going on behind those dead eyes. The ghost of her own reflection stared back at her, much as it had done from the airplane's window, and she found herself happy, for now at least, for the walls she'd built up over the years.

"Pilar?" he said. "Please do this for me. I wouldn't trust anybody else."

Damn him, she thought. The bastard had to make it personal. He really knew how to get to her. She'd never been able to tell him no.

She closed her eyes.

"Fine," she said. "I guess I'm your girl."

CHAPTER 4

From the street, only two members of Juan Perez's team were plainly visible. At least to the untrained eye. That was good; that was exactly the way he wanted it. Exactly like Senator Sutton wanted it, too. She'd been very clear on that point. She knew Juan took his orders from the White House, and that she didn't have any choice in taking the protection his team provided, but she nonetheless made sure they knew how she felt about it. She didn't want to feel like she was living in a compound. And she would not give the cartels the satisfaction of knowing that they had driven her behind walls or that she was living in fear. As far as she was concerned, every moment she spent in the public eye was a slap in the face to the cartels, and she intended to get the most out of it.

It hadn't been difficult to meet her demands. The layout of her street and the surrounding businesses made it a snap, even for a small team like his. Her building was midway down Woodley Place, and there were discreet parking lots at the two large cross streets of Woodley Road and Calvert to the north and south, respectively. Every car turning onto the street (and it was a quiet street, so there hadn't been many) in the week since the attempt on her life at the Washington Hilton, could be checked and run through the NCIC databases without the driver ever seeing the agents who ran their plates. Additionally, the Secret Service had been able to lease an apartment directly across the street from the senator's building, and the Bank of America behind her had been kind enough to let them use a third-story office that covered the roof of the senator's building. The office had the added benefit of commanding a long view down the service alley that led behind the senator's apartment, which cut down on the number of posts he'd have to man and helped him stay under budget. Also, there was an Indian curry house down on Calvert that Juan had grown quite fond of, and a yoghurt shop up at Woodley Road that Tess liked. All in all, Juan was pleased with the setup. Nobody was getting in here without bringing down an immediate response, and his agents didn't have to work in crappy conditions to make sure that happened.

Satisfied, he went inside and met Paul Godwin, who, as usual, was on his cell phone.

"Okay," Paul said. From his stiff, attentive posture, Juan figured he was talking with the senator. "No, he just walked in. Are you ready for us? Okay."

He hung up the phone and he and Juan shook hands.

"Thanks for coming on such short notice."

"Not a problem," Juan said.

He nodded at the sling holding Juan's left arm. "How's the arm? Does that hurt?"

"It's all right," Juan said.

"I've never known anybody who got shot before."

"I don't recommend it."

Godwin forced a laugh, but Juan could tell how uncomfortable he was. "Sounds like good advice. Listen, that reminds me. She's been pleased with how well your team has done keeping a low profile. Considering how everything's been going after the shooting, you guys have really done a great job. We're concerned, you know, with her image. With the press being what it is, it doesn't pay to be a bad neighbor."

"I imagine not. Is that what she wants to talk to me about?"

"Not exactly. Here, come with me."

Paul gave a quiet courtesy knock on a white door that led into the rest of the apartment, waited a moment, and then opened the door and ushered Juan into a spacious sitting room. The floor was hardwood, the white wood-paneled walls adorned with paintings of Senator Sutton's ranch near Val Verde Springs, Texas. This sitting room was where Senator Sutton did most of her press conferences, and the room had been on the news enough recently that, upon stepping into it, Juan felt like he was entering a place he knew well, despite having never been, like the set of a favorite sitcom.

Senator Sutton rose to greet him. She was wearing a red pantsuit over a black blouse, and when she shook his hand, it was with the firm, self-assured grip of a woman accustomed to holding court.

"Won't you have a seat, Agent Perez?" She gestured to one of the white high-backed chairs opposite the corner of the couch where she always sat during press conferences. "We have coffee or tea. Soft drinks, if you prefer."

"I'll get it, ma'am," said Paul. To Juan, he said, "Black coffee, two sugars, right?"

"Uh, okay. Sure. Two sugars." Juan was lost as to how Paul knew his tastes in coffee until he remembered they had been at the table together for a while that night at the Washington Hilton. The man had spent so much time on his cell phone that night Juan hadn't thought he'd been paying attention. Clearly, he'd misjudged him.

Sutton already had a cup of tea on the coffee table in front of her, and she sipped it, waiting for Paul to come back with Juan's coffee. Juan glanced up at the paintings on the wall.

"Your ranch looks like a nice place," he said.

"Thank you. Wayne and I like it, too. You're from Del Rio, aren't you, Agent Perez?"

"Yes, ma'am." But he didn't elaborate. The house where he grew up looked quite a bit different from her ranch, and she seemed to sense that in his silence, for she didn't press for more details. They may have hailed from the same part of Texas, but they were still from different worlds.

Paul came back with his coffee, served in a fragile porcelain cup on a saucer that reminded Juan of a little girl's tea set. But when he drank it, his eyebrows went up.

Christ, he thought. The rich drink good coffee.

"I'm going on vacation," Sutton said.

The comment caught Juan off guard. "Oh?"

"Yes, a cruise, actually. To Cozumel."

Juan coughed on his coffee and had to put it down on the table between them. "Oh," he said. "Mexico. Really?"

Sutton glanced at Paul and chuckled. Paul was on his cell phone again. He didn't look up, but he chuckled, too, and Juan had the feeling he was the odd man out on a joke.

"I was going to ask your opinion of that," Sutton said, "but I can see that isn't necessary. You don't approve."

"Well, ma'am, I guess you're entitled to a vacation, just like anybody else."

"That's not exactly what I'm driving at, Agent Perez. I want your opinion."

"My professional opinion, you mean?"

"Of course. It's not every day I'm put under the watchful eye of a presidential security detail."

"Well, in that case, I think a cruise is going to be a logistical nightmare for my team. And two weeks is gonna be pretty tight when it comes to setting up cabin arrangements, and we'll have to contact the—"

Sutton held up a hand. "Agent Perez, let me stop you there. I don't want the Secret Service treatment on this. This is going to be a casual affair. My husband, and I, and of course, Mr. Godwin, if I can get him off his phone long enough to enjoy some Caribbean scenery."

He looked at Paul, who was still focused on his phone. No help there.

To Sutton, he said, "Ma'am, I think you lost me."

"Agent Perez, I know an awful lot about you, despite your sealed Army record. You spent five years in Delta Force. I read the action report for the silver star you won in Zacatecas." She suddenly smiled at him. "Don't frown like that, Agent Perez. I know that information is classified. I have clearance."

He nodded.

"I also know you were recruited by the CIA's Special Operations Group. Not many people get an invitation like that, but you turned them down. Why?"

Juan didn't hesitate. "I'm a soldier, ma'am. Not a spy."

"Yes, but you left the Army. Why? Why walk away from what I understand to be the most coveted spot in the Army?"

Images of his wrecked first marriage surfaced, along with a lot of guilt and regret, but he didn't let it show on his face. He sipped his coffee and said, "Deploying for months at a time isn't good for a marriage," he said. "I left to try to save mine."

"Ah," she said. "Well, fair enough. My point is I know that you've spent more time fighting the cartels than just about anybody else out there. You know them, and I respect that. I haven't fought them the way you have, but I've engaged them in my own way, and I've come to think of you as something of a kindred spirit in that regard. We both have the same enemy, and we both mean to stamp him out forever. So it's your professional opinion as an enemy of the cartels that I want to hear. Knowing them the way you do, how do you think they'd react to an American senator vacationing right under their noses?"

He leaned forward and took another sip of his coffee while considering his answer.

"I still think it's a bad idea," he said at last. "Why play games like that with your safety?"

"This is most assuredly not a game, Agent Perez. You need to understand that I am very serious about what I'm doing." She paused there, staring him directly in the eye. Finally, she said, "What I intend to do is make a statement the cartels will never forget. Not only am I going to ruin them financially, but I am going to rub their noses in it by drinking piña coladas in their backyard."

Juan nearly laughed. And he would have, right in her face, if what she was suggesting wasn't so offensive. The woman's sense of entitlement was shocking.

"You don't approve," she said.

Paul laughed without looking up from his phone. "I told you."

Juan didn't trust himself to speak, so he simply shook his head.

"Why?" Sutton said. "I want to know. I thought you, more than anyone, would understand why this is so important."

Go easy, he told himself. The ground can slip away from here if you're not careful.

"You're making a statement," he said. "I get that."

"But . . . ?"

"I've seen what happens when politicians make statements. I saw it in Zacatecas and I saw it Ciudad Juarez. When politicians make statements, innocent people end up getting killed."

"Killed?" she said. She looked genuinely shocked. "You're referring to that woman who was shot at the Washington Hilton last week. That was not my fault."

"No," he said. "Her death was not your fault. I'm not blaming you."

"Then what are you saying?"

"I'm trying to make the point that cruise ships carry families, senator. People take their kids on cruises. It's fine if you want to thumb your nose at the cartel in their own backyard, as you say, but are you prepared for the collateral damage that might bring with it? What happens if some cartel assassin opens fire on you while you're in a crowd? Could you really justify the importance of making a statement in a situation like that?"

She didn't answer right away, and as Juan sat there waiting for her response, he was certain he had gone too far. Agents, they taught at the academy, were meant to be seen and not heard. There were no politics when you were on the job, and those agents who spoke their mind usually found themselves looking for a new job.

But she surprised him with her response. "You made an odd career choice for a man who hates politicians, Agent Perez."

"I don't hate politicians, ma'am."

She held up a hand. "It's okay," she said. "I get it. I must say though, I didn't expect you to be as opposed to this as you so obviously are."

He smiled. He was tempted to remind her that he'd been raised on the poor side of Del Rio, and that things often looked different when seen from the bottom up, but he didn't take the bait. He'd made his point, and anything more than that would turn her against him. Instead, he pressed his advantage.

"Well, you're obviously committed to this. Can I at least make a suggestion about the kind of protection we put in place for this trip?"

"I told you, Agent Perez, I don't want the Secret Service treatment on this."

"I know. But I think there's a middle road that will work for both of us."

"Oh?"

"You said this trip is just you, your husband, and Mr. Godwin here?"

"That's right."

"Then may I suggest that Mr. Godwin bring his fiancée?"

Paul Godwin looked up from his phone for the first time since they'd all sat down together. He looked utterly perplexed.

But Senator Sutton was way ahead of him. "You're thinking of Agent Compton, aren't you?"

"I am," said Juan.

"Oh, I like her," said Sutton. "Paul, what do you think?"

Godwin nearly jumped out of his chair. "Absolutely," he said. "You bet. That'd be, uh . . . yeah, I like that idea. A lot, actually."

Juan smiled. Godwin didn't have much of a poker face. The man was clearly thinking how nice it'd be to share a cabin with Tess Compton, maybe even getting lucky after a couple of fuzzy navels up on the sundeck.

Yeah, good luck there, buddy, Juan thought. Put a

toe out of line with Tess Compton and she'll break you into little pieces.

"So, it's settled then?" said Sutton.

Still smiling, Juan turned his attention back to the senator. "Yes ma'am," he said. "I'll tell Agent Compton she's headed to Cozumel. I'm sure that'll make her day."

CHAPTER 5

Juan Perez's apartment was in a three-story brownstone in Arlington. Tess Compton got there after nearly two hours of slogging her way through late evening traffic. The trunk of her Honda Accord was loaded with new clothes, new luggage, three new bikinis, the kind of things a bride would bring on her honeymoon, which was the cover story she and Paul Godwin had worked out for their seven-day cruise to Cozumel.

She checked herself in the driver's side window of her car, and decided she looked okay. Good enough for government work, as her daddy used to say. Tess had been shopping all day—her first day off in ten days—and she was exhausted. It would have been nice to go home and take a shower, get some of this capital grime off her, but there was no time for that. Juan had said he wanted to meet with her before she left for Galveston in the morning, and as she was catching a plane at five a.m., it was now or never.

Juan buzzed her up and she let herself in the front door. She found him sitting on his couch, files and photographs spread out in front of him on the coffee table. He had a bottle of Victoria beer on the table—no coaster, of course—most of it gone.

He did like his beer, but it hadn't gone to his waist. Probably never would, either. Not a man like Juan Perez. He was a legend. At forty-four, he still looked like he could pass for twenty-eight. It was his Hispanic blood, she decided, that made him age so gracefully. He was still every bit as handsome as any man she'd ever seen outside of the movies, and though he stood only five foot nine, the same height as Tess when she wore heels, he still had the lithe athleticism of the Special Forces operator he'd been throughout his twenties. Ordinarily, on his days off, and there weren't many of those, he wore polo shirts tucked into khaki slacks, with leather shoes and a belt as black as his hair. But today he was in old blue jeans, ratty at the cuffs, white gym socks, and a faded gray T-shirt that hung on him in all the right ways. The change in his look, she knew, was because of the sling he had to wear after the botched assassination attempt at the hotel two weeks earlier. It hadn't seemed to slow him down, though. He was still turning in sixteen-hour days, still working late into the night on intelligence data from his contacts in Mexico and Texas. In fact, if it weren't for the dark rings under his eyes and the weariness she had started to see in his expression lately, certainly since San Antonio, she'd believe he was bulletproof. In the two years she'd been fortunate enough to work for him, she'd come to think of him that way. The invincible Juan Perez.

"How's the arm?" she said without sitting down.

"It's okay. Itches a lot." He motioned to the couch beside him. "Here, sit down. I want to show you something."

"You want another beer first?"

"You want one?"

"No," she said. "If I have a beer now I'll fall asleep. I'm exhausted."

"What are you exhausted for? I thought I gave you the day off."

"You did. I've been shopping." He looked confused, like what she'd said had made no sense at all. "Have you been to Penn Quarter lately? Shopping isn't easy."

He said nothing for a moment, as though seriously considering her question, and then shrugged. "Okay, sit down."

What a frustrating man, she thought.

She'd met Juan five years earlier, when she was completing her seventeen-week Special Agent Training course at the academy. A crack shot since her early teens, she was mesmerized by his skill on the weapons range, and when she learned he was former Delta Force, she went into fan girl mode. After her graduation, in a sort of schoolgirl crush that embarrassed her now, but that he, thank God, had never brought up, she e-mailed him several times, asking to be considered for his team.

His response at the time had crushed her. He told her that he didn't take on rookies, even talented ones like her, and that she needed some experience under her belt before she could expect to be taken as a serious contender. Looking back, she realized how practical he had been. Juan was always practical. Now that she knew him as well as she did, she found he could sometimes be a pain in the ass he was so practical.

Crushed, but not deterred, she'd kept tabs on him, and when his team was tasked with protecting a federal judge who was testifying before a Senate select committee, she managed to get herself assigned to the same detail. A man, a Montana survivalist by the name of Wayne Hodges, had come out of the crowd of protestors and tried to slosh a Mason jar full of pig's blood on the judge. Hodges was a big man, much bigger than Tess, but she'd managed to take him to the ground quickly, even made it look easy. She even kept the pig's blood from spilling. Juan was impressed. An offer to join his team followed. And a year later, she was his second in command.

She glanced over the paperwork in front of him. Working for Juan, she'd become something of an expert herself on the cartels, though of course her knowledge was only parroting his far deeper knowledge. He'd actually lived this stuff while down in Mexico. He'd fought these people on their home ground, in their own streets and alleys and living rooms. Juan Perez was their boogeyman.

But what she saw surprised her. The shooter from the Washington Hilton Hotel had been a low-level soldier with the Juarez Cartel, and his knowledge of the cartel's hierarchy hadn't gone above his boss's boss. They learned nothing of substance from him. This stuff, though, these pictures, she recognized several high-ranking members of the Porra Cartel. Cooperation among the cartels was unheard of, even when it was for their mutual survival, so seeing information on the Porra Cartel meant there was a third column in this game.

She pointed to one of the pictures, which showed a handsome man she knew as Ramon Medina playing tennis on a court lined by bougainvillea.

"Why are we looking at this stuff?" she said. "I thought we were focusing on the Juarez and Gulf cartels."

He shook his head. He looked troubled. "I am. For the shooting at the hotel. This, though," he said, pointing to the pictures, "I think this is something different."

He handed her a police report, a Charge and Disposition Report written by a detective with the San Antonio Police Department's Narcotics Unit, though the detective's name and badge number had been censored. That meant the detective was probably on loan to one of the major drug task forces in the South Texas area, most likely HIDTA, the High Intensity Drug Trafficking Area Task Force, made up of officers and detectives from twenty-eight different local, county, state, and federal agencies and charged with multi-jurisdictional authority to cover nearly all of South Texas. They'd worked with some of the HIDTA guys when they were figuring out how to handle the threat on Senator Sutton's life in San Antonio. There was a chance, she thought, that she knew the author of this report.

She quickly scanned the fourteen-page packet.

It began, as so many of these reports often did, with an alert beat cop. While on routine patrol on San Antonio's west side, the cop had seen a yellow panel van pulling away from a warehouse he knew to be abandoned. Thinking it was either a stolen vehicle or thieves scavenging the building for copper, he'd pulled them over. The driver was an American citizen, the passenger from Ciudad Juarez. Both were dressed in ostrich skin boots and pressed jeans and western-style shirts, like they were ready go out to the Tejano clubs. The officer separated them, questioned them, and got conflicting stories. He got some cover officers out with him and searched the van.

And found a rolled-up tarp containing the remains of at least two, but possibly three, dead bodies. The bodies had been burned and most of what was left had sort of melted together. SAPD's Homicide Unit locked the scene down and their Crime Scene Unit searched the warehouse. They found bloodstains on the pavement outside the back door, and more bloodstains inside, on the warehouse's main floor, but nothing else. The men in the van were arrested and questioned, but said nothing.

No surprise there.

Tess turned back to the front of the report and skimmed it again. Finally, she tossed it onto the table. "Okay, so what am I missing? It's a murder case, possibly cartel related because of the suspect from Ciudad Juarez. What else is there?"

Juan handed her a manila folder marked with the seal of the Bexar County Medical Examiner's Office. Inside were three autopsy reports. Skimming the first one, her eyes went wide.

"Traces of flesh-eating bacteria?" she said.

Juan nodded. "The samples were sent to the CDC in Atlanta for confirmation, but the tests are going to come back positive. My contacts in San Antonio are sure of that."

"Okay," she said. Then she shook her head. "No, I'm still missing something. I can see from those photographs over there that you're looking at the Porra Cartel for this. I assume that's why the task force in San Antonio sent this stuff to you."

"That's right."

"Okay. I still don't get it."

"That's because you're not asking the right question. Look at this setup. What's wrong with it?"

She glanced over everything again.

And then it hit her.

"The bodies. They were moving the bodies. Business as usual, they would have left the bodies in the abandoned warehouse. It probably would have taken a week or more for somebody to discover them. There had to be a reason they were taking such a chance moving the bodies." She whistled. "My God, they knew that bacteria was in them."

"That's what it seems like to me, too."

"So what does this mean? Do you think there's a cartel out there experimenting with a flesh-eating bacteria?"

He shrugged. "Maybe. But that doesn't really seem consistent with anything I've seen the cartels do. It's not their style, you know?"

"I wouldn't put terrorism past them."

"No, me either."

"So . . . what then? They got into some flesh-eating bacteria at that warehouse and their friends burned them and then decided to take the bodies somewhere to dump them?"

"I don't know," he said. "That sounds more likely than the first option, but that's still not saying much."

"No, it isn't."

He picked up a small stack of black–and-white photographs, surveillance photographs from the looks of them, and started tossing them onto the table like he was dealing cards. From the sag of his shoulders and the set of his mouth she knew he had been through these photographs hundreds of times and was frustrated with himself for not spotting what his gut told him should be there.

She picked up the photographs. The first three showed Mexican Federal troops wearing hoods and carrying machine guns, standing like proud hunters over a roomful of seized guns and cash.

But the next few photographs showed Ramon Medina, the head of the Porra Cartel, and a half dozen of his highest-ranking lieutenants. Many of the faces were familiar to her, though their names, in most cases, eluded her. It was hard to keep track, as those in favor came and went like rumors. A man could be a chief lieutenant one day, and a severed head in a duffel bag the next.

But Ramon Medina was a constant. He had ruled the Porra Cartel with an iron fist for almost twenty years. And these pictures, Tess realized, covered a good part of that career, for in the span of six or seven photographs she could see his transformation from street-hardened thug to Mexican aristocrat. Here was a photo of him as a young man, wearing a bloodstained white T-shirt and jeans, his hair a mess, his eyes crazy with rage as he screamed at three badly beaten men tied to chairs. Here was another of

Medina, arm in arm with a *narcocorrido* band. Another was the one she'd seen earlier of Medina playing tennis on a court surrounded by bougainvillea. Then there was still another of him dressed in a tailored suit, taking a beer from a young girl. And another, of him—

"Wait a minute," Juan said. He reached forward and snatched up the photo of Medina taking the beer from the young girl.

He sat there, staring at it, his face inscrutable.

"What is it?" she asked.

He shook his head. "My God, it can't be her."

"What?" She leaned over his shoulder, careful not to put her weight on his wounded arm, and looked at the picture. She didn't see anything strange about the picture.

Juan pointed at the girl. She had long dark hair that spilled like a wave over her bare shoulders and a bubbly, effervescent smile. She had the beer outstretched, offering it to Medina, her expression that of a seventeen-year-old girl in the midst of a terrible crush.

"Do you see her?" he said.

"Yeah, but . . ."

"Think, Tess. Remember, from the Washington Hilton? Think. Right before the shooting. Remember when Paul Godwin asked us if we needed anything else from him?"

She thought back to that night, playing the moment again in her memory. She saw Paul, clueless as ever, on his iPhone, like usual, asking if he had to stick around or if Juan was done with him. He had turned. There had been a woman there in a black evening gown, holding out a martini in each hand, a smile on her face that was more like an invitation than anything else.

"Oh, my God," she said.

"Get Paul Godwin on the phone," he said. "Right now. I want to know who this woman is."

"Yeah," she said. "Yeah, I think you're right."

She dialed Godwin's number. "How do you think all this fits together?" she asked.

"No idea," he said. "At this point, I have no idea."

CHAPTER 6

At eleven a.m. the following morning, Pilar Soledad was in a taxicab pulling up to Pier 23 at the Galveston Cruise Ship Terminal. Because she was traveling under her Monica Rivas persona, she was dressed in a yellow tank top, white shorts, and strappy silver sandals. She accented the look with silver hoop earrings, Gucci sunglasses, and silver bangles on her wrists. It was a nice look for her, breezy, summery, and showed off her legs. As Pilar, she would have pulled her hair back in a no-nonsense, efficient ponytail, but as Monica she had to pay closer attention to such things, and today her long black hair was in curly waves that she'd taken extra time that morning to get just right.

She took her phone out of her purse and checked the schedule for the senator's flight. They were on time, due at Hobby International Airport in ten minutes. Pilar was scheduled to board the *Gulf Queen* right at noon, and assuming that it would take a min-

imum of two hours, but probably closer to four, for
the senator and her party to get from the airport
down to Galveston, and then through the customs
line at the Cruise Ship Terminal, she figured she
would have just enough time to get herself aboard
and get what she needed to do done. It'd be close,
but she could make it.

She tossed her phone back into her purse and
glanced out the window at the *Gulf Queen*. At
256,000 tons, beautiful and gleaming white in the
Texas summer sun, it towered above the terminal's
facade. Besides its 2,400 staterooms and room for
6,400 passengers, the *Gulf Queen* featured twenty-
one decks, two casinos, dining rooms, dance halls,
cafés, pools and playgrounds, theaters, and even a
shopping mall and a skating rink. She was more
than the floating hotel the Caribbean Royalty Cruise
Line billed her as. She was practically a city unto
herself.

Which was kind of a shame, Pilar thought. Because in three days she was going to be nothing
more than a plague ship.

Up ahead, terminal employees were helping
buses and taxis to unload a lot of smiling, yet still
somehow anxious-looking American passengers.
That anxiousness, that chronic inability to relax,
Pilar realized, was a fundamental part of the American cultural identity. It followed them around like
the hum of a live electrical wire.

She glanced toward the front of the cab and
caught the driver, a white-haired, fat white man with
bad teeth and a sunburned face and neck, staring at
her legs in the rearview mirror.

She bristled. The man had been leering at her

since he picked her up at the airport and a part of her wanted to kick in the few front teeth he had left just to show him where he stood in life. Instead, she took the big floppy hat she'd brought and draped it over her bare knee.

Realizing he was caught, the man said, "This is you up here, ma'am."

She nodded. A few years ago she'd watched as three of Ramon's soldiers tied a rival cartel member's hands behind his back, sat him on a sidewalk in front of a garbage Dumpster, and cut his head off with a chainsaw. She remembered the way the blade had made its first bite into the man's throat, the way he'd thrown his head back against the metal Dumpster, and the way disbelief and fear had colored his pale face.

It wasn't hard to imagine this pig's face on that doomed man.

It wasn't hard at all.

The driver stopped the cab and popped the trunk and opened her door for her. She let him hold the door, but made as though she didn't see his outstretched hand. Frowning now, no doubt thinking she was just another one of those stuck-up Mexican nationals with too much money and not enough humility, the cabbie tossed her bags on a porter's handcart. Pilar said nothing. Instead—and she was kind of enjoying this—she took out a conspicuously large sheaf of bills and carelessly rolled off five twenties for him. "That should cover the ride and your gratuity, I believe," she said.

He looked at the bills with a mixture of greed and distaste. He'd figured out that he was being dismissed as a simple hireling, as though she had the power to buy and sell him, and she could tell how it galled him.

"Yes, ma'am," he said through gritted teeth.

"That'll be all." She turned to walk away, and with a lilt in her voice said, "Thank you."

Behind her sunglasses, her eyes were blazing with mischief.

Sometimes it could be so much fun to be a bitch.

The porter was a different story. He was younger, Hispanic, with a quick, alert gaze that Pilar knew well. As the cabbie pulled away, he made a show of asking for her boarding papers and scanning them with a barcode gun.

"Solo las dos bolsas, señora?" he said, abruptly switching to Spanish.

Excellent, she thought. Ramon had promised his best people to support her on this, and this young man here had just identified himself to her with the code that everything was right on schedule. Definitely a good sign.

"Sí," she answered back, using the prearranged signal. *"Es solo un corto viaje."*

"Muy bueno. Los otros paquetes ya han sido entregados."

She nodded. Inwardly, she let out a little sigh of relief. What Ramon promised, he delivered. He'd always told her that, and he'd never failed to follow through on his promises. But it was still good to know that the other parts of the plan were falling into place. She was almost ashamed to admit it, but as she was reading up on the bacteria to be used, and the logistics involved in introducing it into the cruise ship's deli meats and sushi and butter supply, she'd had serious doubts about Ramon's ability to pull the whole thing off. Actually, she'd been feeling more than doubt. If she was honest with herself, she was terrified. But now, with everything coming together, she felt better.

Walking quickly, she made her way to the passenger sign-in and customs registration terminals.

From here on out, she was going to be on a tight schedule.

Pilar was among the first passengers to board the *Gulf Queen* when the gangway opened at noon.

The ship itself was an extravagant maze of hallways, stairs, and levels leading off in every direction. Crew members in crisp white uniforms were everywhere, smiling and greeting the passengers as they made their bewildered way to their staterooms. But Pilar had memorized the layout and knew exactly where to go. She headed down to Deck 5, found her stateroom, and slipped inside.

On the bed was a monkey made out of twisted and folded towels. She smiled, despite the nervousness that had started to twist her stomach again, and set her carry-on luggage aside. The room was small, consisting of a double bed, a bathroom, a built-in desk, a small couch, and two chairs, all of it crammed into about 200 square feet.

But she didn't pay attention to the cramped quarters. She wasn't going to be spending a whole lot of time in here anyway. What really mattered was under the bed.

She got down on her hands and knees and said a silent prayer what she needed was actually there.

It was.

Secured to the underside of the bed with duct tape she found three nylon gun cases, one large and two smaller ones. She removed them all and put them on the bed. First, she unzipped the largest of the three. Inside was a German-made .40 caliber Heckler & Koch MP5, one of her personal favorites, and enough ammunition to fill the six thirty-round magazines tucked into the case's pockets. One of the other gun cases contained a pair of Glock 22 .40 caliber pistols and three fifteen-round magazines for each gun. Pilar was pleased with the setup. The fact that both the machine gun and the pistols used the same ammunition would give her some added flexibility when things started to get crazy.

Which was another thing.

These weapons were one of the two packages the porter down at the terminal had promised her were in place. The other was the perfringens and lactobacillus bacteria that Ramon's people had introduced into the deli meats and butter supply in the *Gulf Queen*'s kitchens. If everything moved according to schedule, and based on what she'd seen so far she saw no reason to believe that it wouldn't, by the early morning hours the first victims of the necrotizing fasciitis would start to turn. The models she'd seen indicated that the rest of the nearly 7,000 passengers and crew would be dead or dying by nightfall of their first full day at sea. And by the time they reached Cozumel, the *Gulf Queen* would be nothing but a nightmare that the Americans would be forced to shoot out of the water.

But before that could happen, Pilar had a lot to do, and that was where the third gun case came in. She opened it and found a credit card–style pass key that was supposed to open every door on the ship; a small plastic envelope containing two remote omni-directional listening devices that looked a lot like lithium watch batteries, but were in fact sensitive enough to pick up even whispered conversations all the way on the other side of a stateroom; and, of course, the small white paper sack she'd been promised. She took a deep breath that didn't make her feel any easier. This was real. This was actually happening. She'd done major operations for Ramon Medina before, many of them, in fact. She'd killed perhaps as many as a hundred men and maybe a dozen women, simply because he'd asked her to. But this was the biggest thing she'd ever had a hand in, and the idea that it was all coming together left her with a mix of dread and excitement that caused her stomach to turn like it hadn't done since those early days back in Ciudad Juarez. She was about to murder 7,000 men, women, and children in the gris-liest display of terror the world had ever seen, and for a second, she nearly ran to the bathroom to vomit from the enormity of it.

She forced herself to calm down. She couldn't function like this, and she was running out of time. Pilar closed her eyes, took in and released a few deep breaths, and then opened her eyes. Calmer now, she put the paper sack into her purse, scooped up her big floppy hat and sunglasses and pass key, then made her way to the senator's stateroom on Deck 7.

It was time to get busy.

CHAPTER 7

Tess was up late the night before, talking with Juan. And she was up early that morning to meet Paul Godwin and the senator and her husband for the trip down to Galveston. She was exhausted, and her first-class seat on the plane was so deep and comfortable she felt like she might melt into it. She'd been looking forward to sleeping a little on the ride down, because planes always put her to sleep. Instead, she'd been forced to listen to Sutton and her husband argue.

It started when he asked the flight attendant for the best single malt scotch she had.

Rachel Sutton had said, "Are you nuts? It's not even six a.m."

He'd said, "Okay, fine. A Bloody Mary then."

And from there the argument had gone round and round some invisible point in their past that was both a part of whatever this tension between them was and more than that. Things between them were complicated, Tess could tell.

"It's not his drinking," Paul said to her.

She looked at him.

"If that's what you're thinking, it's not that."

He was leaning in close to her, whispering.

"I wasn't trying to spy," she said, embarrassed.

"No, of course not. They can be kind of hard to ignore sometimes."

She nodded, and waited a moment for him to say more, but he didn't. She went back to looking out the window. The sun was coming up and she wondered where they were. There was a river down there, snaking its way through a brown landscape. Tracing its course out to the horizon made her think of how tired she was. Maybe she could sleep, even with them arguing.

"He was drinking pretty heavy when I first met them," Paul said suddenly. "That was during her first term."

"How long ago was that?"

"Oh, about thirteen years ago. I was right out of law school, all gung ho for the Democratic Party. I was gonna make a difference, you know?"

"Have you?"

He shrugged. "I guess it depends on how you measure it."

"So, you're world-weary now, is that it?"

He smiled.

"So what changed?" she asked.

"With me?"

"No." She hooked a thumb toward the seats behind them, where Rachel Sutton and her husband were doing their best to stare off in opposite directions. "With them."

"Ah." His smile softened a little. He had a nice smile, she thought, boyish, innocent looking. She supposed he was cute, in a way. He was certainly no Juan Perez, but he was okay. "Well, her career really started to take off. She works sixteen hour days, six days a week. Did you know that?"

She nearly reminded him that she'd been watching every move the senator made for the last month, but she didn't. Instead, she just shook her head.

"All that hard work paid off. She won election after election, all the while taking a larger and larger role in the party, and the more her career took off, the more his had to get put on hold. He had a thriving practice back in Del Rio, but he gave it up for her."

Tess didn't see the problem. "Makes sense."

"Well, yeah, to our generation. He's from a different time, though. Reminds me of my dad, kind of. The man never changed a diaper, never did the cooking. Except for burgers on the grill on Labor Day. You know the type? He was the breadwinner and all that. The man's place is to provide, the woman's to run the home. Dr. Sutton's the same way."

"Are you saying he resents her for doing well?"

"Yeah, pretty much. He's never come out and said so. I don't think he's even admitted it to himself. But I'd say that's pretty much the score between them."

"That's awful," she said. "That seems really sad to me."

He shrugged, but she could tell it bothered him, too. She wondered why he was telling her all this. It wasn't really her concern. She was here to do a job, nothing more.

But it's because it bothers him so, she realized. That's why he was telling her. He was like some grown-up kid watching his parents inching closer every day toward divorce.

Or maybe it was more one-sided than that. Maybe he was so fiercely loyal to Rachel Sutton that he tended to look at everything in her world through a lens of hero worship. Either way, it was going to be an interesting vacation.

She heard them talking again.

"Don't you dare shush me again," Dr. Sutton snapped.

The senator whispered for him to be quiet, but it didn't work.

"I don't care who hears, damn it."

"Uh-oh," Paul said. He stood up. "Excuse me." He took his iPad and a manila folder out of his carry-on, smiled at Tess, and said, "I was saving this for the ship, but I guess now's the time. Back in a sec."

He went back to the senator's seat.

Tess heard him tell Dr. Sutton he wanted him to look over a PDF on the iPad, something about rural issues in health-care reform. He said he needed a doctor's take on it. Then he handed the manila folder to the senator.

"What's this?" Senator Sutton asked.

"Notes on your speech to the National Urban League next month."

A moment later, he dropped down in the seat next to Tess. The arguing from the Suttons had stopped. She glanced back at them. Both were reading, absorbed.

"They're like children sometimes," he said. "You just got to keep them busy."

She studied him, and was genuinely surprised by how deftly he managed the older couple.

"You care about them a great deal, don't you? Her especially."

His smile wavered for just a second, as though he suddenly realized how much of his hand he'd shown her.

But then he recovered his grin. "Hey," he said, "it's what I do."

Tess got her first look at the *Gulf Queen* from the gangway. The sun was piercingly bright. Even with her sunglasses on, the sky was a washed-out blue. The breeze was hot and smelled like the ocean and oil. Against the late summer sky, the ship looked as tall as a building. It was impossibly huge.

"Oh, cool!" a boy shouted as he sprinted by her.

The boy, who couldn't have been more than ten, climbed the railing and pointed toward the bow.

"Look, Mom! Look at that!"

The boy's mother, a beleaguered looking woman in a red top and brown gypsy skirt, shouted for him to get down. She charged ahead and took him by the hand with a death grip that made him cry out. But it didn't seem to deter the boy any.

Tess was almost even with them when the woman

finally pulled him down. She smiled tiredly at Tess, who smiled back. Tess liked kids, even though she'd begun to suspect, much to her mother's frequently voiced disapproval, that she would never have any of her own. Looking up at the ship, then letting her gaze wander down the vastness of its lines, she certainly understood the kid's sense of awe. It was an impressive ship.

But then they stepped off the gangway and Tess's mind clicked into a different mode. Gone was the tiredness, the sense of childlike glee at the size of the ship. There was a crowd here, and her charge was wading into it. That meant she was back on the clock.

They entered the reception deck, which reminded Tess an awful lot of the nicer ballrooms in the capital's best hotels. The ceiling and the columns and the balcony along the far wall were white and gold and trimmed in highly polished hardwood. The floor was marble, with mosaic waves drawing the eye inward, toward a large central room featuring a larger mosaic of two dolphins chasing each other around a golden crown, the symbol of the Caribbean Royalty Cruise Line. Crew members in crisp white coats and black pants formed a reception line on either side of the entryway, all of them smiling and offering help with questions and directions. And at the far end of the receiving line stood two men, the captain and his first officer.

Tess had done research on both of them before leaving D.C. The captain was Mark Rollins, a Brit. He was tall, slender, white haired, dignified looking. He had done ten years in the Royal Navy followed by a good, if undistinguished career with Caribbean Royalty.

The man next to him was Anthony Amato, the first officer. He was an Italian out of Bensonhurst, dark haired, short, stocky, probably fifteen years younger than his captain. In his late thirties, Tess reminded herself. No military service in his background, but he had graduated from the Merchant Marine Academy and had a sterling service record during the six years he'd served in the Disney Cruise Lines and the ten he'd served with Caribbean Royalty.

But the fact that the two men were here waiting for them didn't bode well.

Tess turned to Paul Godwin, who was standing to her left, taking pictures of the entryway with his iPhone.

"You're seeing this, right?" she said to him. "I said I didn't want to make a production of our arrival."

"Huh?" he said. He looked at the reception line and nodded. "That? Nah, it'll be fine. Wow, can you believe this place? You see pictures of ships like this, but you never really get a sense of how *big* they are until you're standing inside them."

Tess sighed. What was the use? He wasn't listening to her. Neither was the senator. She'd told them, during their briefings, that to alert the Caribbean Royalty Cruise Line of their visit was to invite unnecessary attention. Ship captains were like hotel managers. Tell them they were getting a visit from a celebrity, especially one about whom whispers of the presidency were already starting to circle, and they turned into obsequious idiots.

Tess told the senator what would happen. The captain would greet them at the door. He'd make a fuss and the next thing any of them knew, the whole ship would know Senator Rachel Sutton was aboard. Any hopes of keeping a low profile would be out the window.

But, of course, she'd been overruled. The senator, Tess quickly figured out, had no intention of keeping a low profile. This was going to be her big slap in the face to the cartels, and she wanted to be seen. She wanted the cartels to feel the sting of her slap.

"And besides," Sutton had said, "it'll be rude to keep that from the captain. The man's no doubt proud of his ship."

Tess had held her tongue after that. At least they hadn't alerted the media.

Tess looked past Paul, to where the senator and her husband were standing. Passengers were coming aboard, families mostly, a few of the adults doing a double take when they saw the senator. People she didn't know kept getting between her and the senator, something that made Tess nervous.

She pushed her way through the crowd, raising an eyebrow from one man who couldn't quite figure out how to get out of her way until she practically shoved him aside.

Tess got next to the senator and gave a man a dirty look when he tried to approach Sutton. The man got the idea quickly enough and turned away, going back to his wife and muttering something Tess guessed wasn't flattering.

"Agent Compton," the senator said.

Sutton had been careful all that morning to address Tess by her first name, as they'd all agreed, and her abrupt shift back to her title made Tess stiffen involuntarily.

"Yes, ma'am?"

The senator leaned in close enough to be heard at a whisper. "I am not a sheep," she said, "and you are not a sheepdog. Do we understand each other?"

"I'm sorry, ma'am. I only wanted—"

"No," Sutton said, cutting her off from any further discussion with a flick of her hand. "I've got this. Everything is fine. You just need to back off and relax."

She looked like she was expecting Tess to challenge her, but Tess just nodded. It wasn't worth the argument, not if everybody onboard recognized Sutton at a glance, which they were obviously doing.

"Good," Sutton said. "Now, we have a captain to meet." She turned to her husband. "Come on, Wayne. Put on a smile."

"Senator Sutton," Captain Rollins said, extending his hand. "So glad to have you aboard."

There were greetings all around and Tess, out of habit, hung back a little. So did Paul. They stood side by side, and she caught him smiling at her. He knows the drill as well as I do, she thought. Alert and at the ready, but out of the way.

Then First Officer Amato broke away from his captain and joined Tess and Paul. "I imagine this will be a nice break for you, Special Agent Compton."

"How do you figure that, commander?"

"Well, this is one of the safest environments

you're likely to work in. Nobody comes aboard, after all, without us knowing about it. And plus, you've got help. I've got a full security detail for this voyage ready and willing to help you in any way we can." He flashed her a winning grin. "In fact, they're all around us right now."

Tess hesitated before answering, debating with herself about how to handle this. Amato and his team meant well, and she certainly didn't want to embarrass this man when he was willing to be on her side, but they were a bunch of amateurs, and amateurs had a way of getting underfoot. Still, they might be useful, to a point.

She said, "I see you don't have any women on your team."

Amato looked stunned, like he didn't know exactly how to respond to that.

"Well, uh, no. As a matter of fact, we don't. I guess you checked up on us."

"I did, yes. But that was just observation. It looks like you have an eight-man team, right?"

"Uh, that's right." Amato smiled uneasily. "How did you know?"

Tess pointed to two men leaning against the upstairs railing. "Those two up there. That man over by the buffet. And there, there, there, and those two over there."

Amato said nothing.

"Are any of your men armed?" she asked.

"No," he said, his voice almost a whisper.

She gestured toward her carry-on. "Well, in that case, I won't completely relax."

Captain Rollins was looking at her now. "Agent

Compton, do I understand you to say you brought a weapon aboard my ship? You're armed."

Tess smiled. "To the teeth, captain."

Later, as they walked to their staterooms, Paul came up beside her. "You enjoyed that, didn't you?"

"What?"

"Amato looked like somebody had shot his dog when you pointed out his security people."

"Hey," she said, mirroring the grin he'd given her on the plane, "it's what I do."

The four of them made their way up to Deck 7, passing casinos, delis, theaters, bars, and even an indoor shopping mall, all of it interconnected by a maze of hallways that seemed to go on forever.

Paul stopped at a junction and took out his iPhone. He'd downloaded an app for this, he'd said on the plane. Maps, show times, restaurant reviews—he had it all covered. He studied the phone now, looked left, then right, and started off to the left.

Tess cleared her throat and pointed right, keeping her hand down so the senator couldn't see.

"Uh, I think it's this way," Paul said and headed to the right.

The senator nodded. She looked impatient, like she couldn't get to the room fast enough. She and her husband were enjoying a temporary truce, Tess saw. They weren't happy with each other, that much was obvious, but at least they weren't yelling at each other anymore.

Paul fell in beside Tess. "Thanks for the help back there."

"No problem. They make these things like this to encourage exploring."

"Yeah, well, it makes me feel like I've been swallowed whole." He nodded down the long hallway in front of them. "Fair warning, though. We see some kid on a Big Wheel coming around the corner and I'm out of here."

She laughed. "Deal." She put a hand on his shoulder and was surprised to feel him go suddenly tense. At first, she thought she'd startled him, but then she saw him sniff the air and turn to watch a pretty girl in a floppy hat go walking down the hallway.

She cleared her throat again.

He turned to her. "What?"

"If we're going to be engaged you need to stop looking at other women."

He smiled, but it wasn't the winning grin she'd already grown to like. He looked distracted, like he was worried.

"Something wrong?" she asked.

"No, just . . ." He glanced behind them again, but the girl in the floppy hat was already gone. "It's nothing," he said. "I just thought I recognized her perfume."

They were at their cabin now. Tess opened the door and saw a monkey made of rolled and folded towels sitting on the foot of the queen-sized bed. "Hey, look at that," she said, pointing at a couple of chairs out on the small shelf that passed for their veranda. "We've got a view of the ocean."

"Yeah, that's nice," he said. But he was looking at the bed. "I thought we were going to get two twin beds."

"For a honeymoon?"

He didn't smile.

"Is that gonna be weird for you?" she asked.

"You mean, uh, sharing a bed? No, of course not."

"Uh-huh. Well, hurry up and get over it, okay? We're playing a part here and the housekeeping staff will talk if they see we're not sleeping in the same bed."

"You don't think they know the senator's here already?"

"Maybe. The service did make Rollins and his officers sign confidentiality agreements, though. Hopefully, if they're good to their word, we should be able to keep things on the down low. For a while, anyway."

"How long do you think that'll last?"

"At least until we put Mexico in our rearview mirror, I hope."

She opened her luggage and laid out her pool things, a black bikini and a wrap, some sunscreen, and an Atlanta Braves baseball cap.

He watched her emptying out her bag. "Can I ask you something?"

"You don't snore, do you?"

"Huh? No, it's not that. It's about that girl I met at the Washington Hilton the night of Senator Sutton's speech."

"What about her?"

"She was nice. Do you really think she's the same girl in the picture?"

She considered him for a moment before answering. She remembered his disbelief when she'd told him that his new girlfriend looked an awful lot like the serving girl for one of Mexico's most powerful drug bosses, the way he'd scoffed at her. She remembered the way he'd looked at the picture of the seventeen-year-old girl holding out a beer to Ramon Medina, the way a shadow of a doubt had darkened his expression.

In the end, he'd agreed not to see her again. He'd given over her phone number and had sat glumly through a humiliating debriefing in which he'd described every detail of his night with her.

Tess, for her part, had been sure that night. Maybe it had been Juan's certainty rubbing off on her. Maybe it was the thrill of working a high-profile team that made her see shooters in every shadow. Regardless, she was less sure now. It just seemed so unlikely, and really, she'd only seen this Monica Rivas woman for a moment, and that across a crowded room.

"I think it's best we play it safe for now, don't you?" she said.

"Yeah, I guess. It just seems so crazy. How could she be that girl? I mean, she went to Harvard."

That was true, Tess thought. They'd checked that. It had only taken a few phone calls. Her biography seemed airtight.

"Do you think maybe she just happened to meet him when she was younger or something? You know, like a random thing? Maybe she had no idea who he was."

She shrugged. "Anything's possible. Agent Perez

is researching her now. If there is anything to it, he'll find it."

He nodded, but didn't look convinced.

"Hey," she said. "Cheer up." She reached into her bag and pulled out a military-issued M4 machine gun. She tossed it on the bed on top of her black bikini. "We're on vacation, remember?"

CHAPTER 8

Back in her cabin, Pilar tossed her hat onto the bed, took out her iPhone, and keyed up the app that allowed her to listen in on the omnidirectional microphones she'd planted in the senator's room. Sutton and her husband were arguing about his drinking. Pilar listened for a few minutes, hoping to learn something of the senator's schedule, but they weren't talking about anything she could use. Just the same thing being said over and over again. She found it tedious and pathetic.

Such a powerful woman, Pilar thought, suffocating in such a boring marriage.

Bored herself, Pilar switched over to the microphone in Paul Godwin's cabin.

The conversation there was more interesting. Paul and the lady Secret Service agent were talking about sharing a bed. She thought of the lady agent that night at the Washington Hilton. She was blond, slim, elegant in her red gown and pearls. Beautiful even. And practical, too, from the lecture she was giving Paul on sharing the bed.

Pilar smiled sardonically at the thought of Paul that night she'd gone up to his room. She could still picture him, timid, his heart pounding when he touched her, his breath hitching when she touched him. Was he doing the same thing now, looking at that bed with the little monkey made of towels on it, his mind racing around thoughts of sleeping next to that pretty agent?

She would probably like that lady agent, if they ever sat down together and talked shop. Pity that would never happen. And come to think of it, she'd probably like the senator, too, under different circumstances. Men, she thought, they had no idea the foolishness women suffered out of a sense of duty. She sighed and opened her carry-on bag. It was a pointless train of thought anyway.

Paul was saying, "Huh? No, it's not that. It's about that girl I met at the Washington Hilton the night of Senator Sutton's speech."

Pilar had only been half-listening, but that got her attention. She stood up straight, all her senses focused on the phone.

They were talking about her. How had she come up? It'd been close as she was leaving their cabin. She'd passed right by him, probably close enough for him to smell her perfume. But he hadn't spotted her. She was certain of that.

So why were they talking about her? What picture were they talking about?

It wasn't good that the lady agent's boss was researching her, either. Her Monica Rivas identity was solid, and would stand up to even a Secret Service background check. It had gotten her into the Washington Hilton, after all, so she was pretty sure they wouldn't find anything. But why were they looking into her. What had set them off?

Well, there was no point in obsessing on it now. Besides, if they suspected something was wrong they wouldn't have come aboard in the first place. The best thing to do, she decided, was to just continue with the plan. The *Gulf Queen*'s meat and fish had already been dosed with the *Clostridium* bacteria and they were probably just a few hours away from seeing the first victims turn. Still, Ramon ought to know about this.

She used her iPhone to connect with the e-mail account she shared with Ramon, typed out a quick e-mail to him, and saved it to the drafts folder. The next scheduled check-in was twenty minutes away, so he'd see it soon enough.

Pilar took off her clothes and changed into a white bikini and tied a sarong around her waist. She plugged earbuds into her phone and tucked the iPhone into the top of her bikini bottom.

Then she went off to hack into the ship's computer.

CHAPTER 9

It was late and Anthony Amato, the ship's first officer, was dead. Pilar stood near the door to the officer's cabin and stared at the body. He was wearing just his boxers, the dark hair on his chest and arms standing out in stark relief against the white of his sheets. His neck was twisted so that his head hung over the side of the bed and his sightless eyes stared down at the floor. He was stocky, stronger than he looked, and he'd actually put up a pretty good fight when he realized she was trying to hurt him. It had surprised her. She'd had to pop him in the throat to get his hands off her. From there, she snapped his neck easily.

Still, she'd underestimated him, and that wasn't good.

She pulled her iPhone from her bikini bottom and went over to his desk. His left hand was on the chair next to the bed and she pushed it off before taking a seat at Amato's computer. She logged into the ship's computer mainframe using the pass codes she'd seen him use and then plugged her phone into the USB port.

A few moments later, a program designed to disable the ship's lifeboats began to run. From here on out, the boats could only be lowered manually, and with the havoc that was about to ensue, she doubted many of them would make it to the water.

Pilar unplugged her phone and quickly wiped down the surfaces she had touched. She had undoubtedly been caught by the ship's video equipment walking around with Amato throughout that afternoon, but that wouldn't be enough to connect her to his death. Should anybody happen to find his body, that is.

She took one last look around the room, then slowly opened the door and scanned the hallway.

It was empty.

She hurried to the elevators and rode up to Deck 20, where she would find the bridge and the communications center. The doors opened with a soft chime and Pilar stepped out. To her left she heard a woman talking quietly and Pilar looked that way. It was a young couple walking along the outside deck. The man was carrying a child, a girl of about four, her head on his shoulder and her eyes closed. The night breezes off the ocean were cool and sent a wave through the little girl's brown hair.

The little girl looked so pretty, so peaceful as she slept, and staring after them as they walked away, Pilar felt sick for what she was about to do. Policemen and rival cartel soldiers, those she killed without a second thought. Even the American tourists onboard this ship, the men and women, meant little to her conscience. But that child. What logic could she use to make sense of killing a beautiful little girl like that?

Memories of Lupe rose up in her mind with such suddenness that she gasped. He'd been about that little girl's age. She remembered holding his trembling body in the back of that eighteen-wheeler, the air so hot she could hardly breathe, the smell of all those dead bodies around them, promising him they'd be all right. And then he'd stopped trembling, and she'd panicked. "Lupe!" she'd said, the sweat from her face dripping into his open eyes. He didn't blink. He couldn't. He could only stare at her with that same wide-open, unknowable vacancy with which Anthony Amato had stared at the floor. "Lupe, no. Please no."

For a moment, she almost broke down. Had she done so, it would have been the end of her. She knew that. She would have gone back to her cabin and put a gun in her mouth. Or thrown herself overboard.

But she didn't. She forced herself to think of Ramon Medina instead, and that turned her insides to steel.

She turned away from the deck where the young family had disappeared into the darkness and made her way to the Radio Room. Earlier, while First Officer Amato still thought he had a chance with the woman he knew as Monica Rivas, he had given her a tour of the bridge. She was surprised to see that the radio room was unmanned, and she said as much. He'd told her that modern cruise ships duplicated most communications functions on the bridge, making the radio room largely redundant. By law, they were still required to have two operators on duty and to cover at least sixteen hours out of the day, but those shifts only came during the day and when they were close to port. During the wee hours of the morning, all communications functions were handled from the bridge.

That made Pilar's job that much easier. She used Amato's keycard to access the room and closed the door behind her. She would have to turn on the light to do what she needed to do, and that of course meant she ran the risk of discovery should a member of the bridge crew pass this way, but it was a chance she had to take. The radio room was small, about the size of her bedroom back in D.C., and dominated by the main console. She plugged her iPhone into its USB port and initiated the programs that would make the *Gulf Queen* deaf and dumb to the outside world.

She heard two men talking in the hallway outside and froze. In order to completely silence the ship she had to disable not only the main VSAT, or Very Small Aperture Terminal, broadband capabilities, but also the Global Maritime Distress and Safety Systems and the older style satellite-based radio/telephone system the ship used to communicate with vessels yet to be equipped with VSAT. Also, she had to disable the satellite emergency position indicating beacons, which could be released manually to float free of the ship and alert rescuers as to the ship's identity and location. It was a lot to do, and the program in her iPhone that hijacked it all was only twenty percent downloaded with an estimated eight minutes still to go.

The voices drew nearer.

Uh-oh, she thought. Time to act.

Pilar set the phone down and moved to the wall next to the door. If the men entered the room they'd see her phone right away and know that something was wrong. She'd have no choice but to kill them.

Then there was a flicker of light and shadow in the door's vent window and Pilar knew they were looking inside.

She saw the door handle wriggle up and down and she tensed, ready to attack the moment both men were inside the room. Then the door opened and a younger man in white uniform stepped inside. Through the crack at the door hinges she could see him glance around the room without going inside.

"Nobody," he said. "I guess they left it on."

"Better turn it off. Amato's gonna be pissed if he finds out they left it on."

"Yeah."

The young officer thumbed the light switch and closed the door behind him, leaving Pilar in the dark, still tensed for the attack.

She relaxed but didn't move.

She stayed there, in the dark, silent as the grave, until her phone chimed to let her know the program had finished downloading. Moving fast, Pilar unplugged it, wiped off everything she'd touched, and got out of there. She could hear voices from the bridge just a few feet away, and she was careful to pull the radio room door closed as softly as she could.

Then she got in the elevator and headed down.

The elevator stopped at Deck 11 and three chunky-looking girls in their early twenties got on. All three of them looked seasick.

One of them, a doughy-faced girl in an Alabama Crimson Tide shirt with red circles around her eyes, said, "You know which floor the doctor's at?"

"You mean the infirmary?" Pilar asked.

The girl nodded, her mouth pursing up like she wasn't sure if she was going to throw up or not.

"Deck four," Pilar said, and said a silent thanks when the doors slid open on 7.

She watched the doors slide shut on the three girls and frowned. It was starting already, a lot sooner than Ramon had said it would. If people were already showing symptoms, that meant the first to turn would be doing so in a few hours. Ramon would no doubt be pleased.

She hurried to her room and signed into the e-mail account she shared with Ramon. The program she'd fed into the ship's communications system gave her a twenty-minute delay, which was just enough to time to send off a quick report. After that, she'd turn on the cell phone jammer in her luggage, change into some battle clothes, and hunker down for what was coming.

She opened the drafts folder and was surprised to see a message waiting for her there. It was her time to send, not his. He had never broken that protocol before. A little worried, she opened his message.

My Little Viper,

I know this thing will be done by the time you read this and I'm proud of you. I knew even back when you were a little girl stealing from me that you were special, and look at you, all grown up. You give them hell now, you hear. You are my angel of death and I'm glad you love me.

R.

Pilar read the message through again, and one more time after that. *I'm glad you love me.* What the hell kind of thing was that to say to a woman? The man had no shame.

But he *did* know her heart. She hated that, but it was true just the same. She loved him. He owned her, body and soul, and she was drawn to him just as this ship was drawn to its own destruction. She could no more change the truth of that than undo the ghastly thing she'd just put in motion.

She erased his message and typed one of her own. A simple one, because she didn't trust herself to contain her anger in a longer one.

The message read simply:

It's done. It's started already.

CHAPTER 10

It was 4:30 A.M. and Juan Perez was parked in the street in front of the McAllen Produce Terminal just west of downtown San Antonio. Already trucks were moving into the lot and it was filling up with men going into work. The traffic didn't concern him, though. In fact, he was glad for it. A lot of vehicles coming and going made for good cover.

He was in a white '98 Toyota pickup he'd borrowed from his local contact in the FBI. It fit right in with all the other battered pickups coming and going. So far nobody had looked twice at him, but if they had they would have seen a man in jeans, boots, and a shabby, loose-fitting flannel shirt, somebody who looked just like every other guy out here going to work. His target was actually a meatpacking facility halfway down the block. After his conversation with Tess the night before she left for the cruise, he'd been thinking a lot about Ramon Medina and the Porra Cartel. They were big along the Texas bor-

der, especially around Ciudad Juarez, and he'd seen
some intelligence that they were trying to expand
operations, but even with that they were hardly the
major players. Still, they'd managed to put themselves center stage with the flesh-eating bacteria the
SAPD had intercepted the week before. It was a potential game changer if ever there was one. The recovered samples had been sent to the CDC and
tested, and the news was bad. Juan had the full report in the file resting in his lap, but it hadn't taken
much of a read to figure out they were dealing with
a major league bad bug. The stuff was highly re-
silient and dangerous enough to kill just about anything with which it came in contact. Its potential as
a WMD device put it up on everybody's radar; but
Juan had been able to make a case that the Porra
Cartel's involvement demonstrated a direct link to
the assassination attempt on Senator Sutton, and so
Mr. Crouch, Juan's point of contact in the White
House, had agreed to let him take point on the investigation, even over the objections of the FBI and
the Justice Department. Everybody wanted a piece
of the case, it seemed, but the White House had spo-
ken, and now it was Juan's case to make or break.

He'd tried his contacts in the South Texas High
Intensity Drug Trafficking Area Task Force to see if
they could locate properties tied to the Porra Cartel,
but while they'd been enthusiastic, they'd been little
help. Juan was actually kind of shocked to learn that
most of the task force's efforts were focused on
street-level interdiction, small-time distributors and
dealers. They occasionally went after mid-level
dealers who got too big for their britches, but that
was about it. They had no active interdiction pro-

gram to deal with the tens of thousands of commercial motor vehicles rolling through San Antonio every day. They had no forensic accountants doing background work on local businesses. They, really, had nothing much to show for their efforts. South Texas HIDTA was the kind of outfit that splashed it all over the news every time they busted a million-dollar load, but not the kind that made any real impact on drug trafficking. Worse still, they had completely ignored any sort of counterintelligence efforts. They'd done nothing to explore soft spots within their own unit, or to develop a deep understanding of the key players for the other side. And, of course, they'd done nothing to understand the long-range goals of the specific cartels. They were, not to put too fine a point on it, street cops messing with street-level players. And that meant he had to go to the FBI. It made him feel like a beggar with his hat in his hand doing it, and they'd made sure he knew his place, but in the end the FBI had come through with some good information. They'd found that the Cavazos Meatpacking Company was staying afloat on a wave of cash currency and managed to trace at least some of that cash back to a holding corporation in Ciudad Juarez, Mexico, known to be a front for the Porra Cartel. Their information jibed with the report Juan had received from the CDC geeks— that the bacteria would remain at its most viable and virulent level when it had a constant supply of meat to feed on—and so he'd come here, to this dark, badly paved road in the laborers' district of San Antonio, to do a little counterintelligence of his own.

He glanced at his watch: 4:37 A.M. Christ, he'd been at this since eight o'clock the previous evening.

He was exhausted. And his injured arm, while finally free of the sling he'd been forced to wear, was nonetheless tender. It ached no matter how he held it. He was thinking about walking around the corner of the deserted building across the street to piss when he saw a shiny black Suburban turn the corner and glide up to the front loading docks of the Cavazos Meatpacking Company.

He sat up.

There was no need for binoculars. Even in the dark, he could see well enough the three men coming out of the building to meet the Suburban at the dock.

Wincing at the pain in his arm, Juan reached over for the wand and receiver for his Krentz-Orbiter Directional Receiver. It was out of date and clunky, but nonetheless effective. It utilized a single forward microphone ringed by buffers that eliminated side noise, which in effect amplified the range of the microphone to as far as half a mile.

He wasn't anywhere near that range now, only a few hundred yards, in fact, and as soon as he turned the device on, he heard the voices from the loading dock coming in loud and clear.

There were five men there, speaking in Spanish.

With his free hand, Juan copied down the things they said on a yellow legal pad. He was careful to copy it out in Spanish, using their exact words whenever possible, so as not to miss anything. If they were talking in code, it wouldn't survive on-the-fly translation.

But it didn't take him long to realize they weren't using code. One of the men that had gotten out of the Suburban, a young guy dressed in black jeans, white shirt, and black blazer who appeared to be the one in charge, asked about a second truck and if they had drivers ready to move out. One of the men who had come from inside the building told him no, that the men had heard what was in the barrels and what it could do and none of them wanted anything to do with it.

The young guy got angry. He jammed his finger into the man's chest and told him to find somebody to drive it out of here in the next five minutes or he'd be doing it himself.

The man's two friends looked on without saying anything. They looked too scared to speak. Juan didn't recognize this young guy in the black blazer, but whoever he was these others were clearly afraid of him.

I'll find somebody, the man said at last.

Good, the younger man answered. I want that van in Nuevo Laredo by ten a.m.

Nuevo Laredo, Juan thought. Why on earth would they be going there? The Porra Cartel didn't have interests there. They operated out of Juarez, six hundred and fifty miles to the west. Nuevo Laredo was controlled by the Zetas. In fact, they had a stranglehold on Nuevo Laredo not even the Mexican Army had been able to break.

And then it hit him.

He looked down at the CDC report on the passenger seat and it all made sense. Back in 2003, Nuevo Laredo, which sat directly across the border from the Texas city of Laredo, was solidly in the hands of the Gulf Cartel. Los Zetas were the armed wing of the Gulf Cartel, its street fighters. At the end of Vicente Fox's presidency, the Sinaloa Cartel tried to take Nuevo Laredo from the Gulf Cartel. Los Zetas attacked and in four months of savage fighting cleared the Sinaloa Cartel from Nuevo Laredo, which they dominated from that point on. Then, in 2010, Los Zetas broke with the Gulf Cartel. The fighting escalated across all of northeast Mexico, and eventually culminated in the 2012 Nuevo Laredo Massacre that left more than seven thousand soldiers and civilians dead. Los Zetas emerged from that fight on top, gaining total control over the Mexican entryway to the I-35 corridor, the most lucrative drug trade route in the world.

To outsiders, the constantly shifting allegiances of the cartels were harder to follow than a soap opera, but to Juan the problem seemed simple enough. The Porra Cartel, which had proven itself to be lean and hungry these last ten years, was looking to take over control of the Texas border. It already dominated in Ciudad Juarez. If they succeeded in releasing this flesh-eating virus of theirs in Nuevo Laredo, they stood a chance of taking over that door to the U.S. as well. Literally nothing would stand in their way to becoming the most powerful drug smuggling operation in the world. Never mind that millions would die to make it happen. The Mexican Drug War had already claimed more than a million lives. What were a few million more?

Juan traded the eavesdropping microphone for his cell and called Detective Jason Rowe, a former San Antonio Police SWAT officer and his contact with the South Texas HIDTA Unit. As it rang, he stepped out of the truck and started walking toward the Cavazos Meatpacking Company. He was tucking the back of his flannel shirt out of the way of his Sig Sauer P229 pistol when Rowe's voice came over the line.

"Where are you?" Rowe said.

"About to go into the Cavazos building. Listen, something's happening. They're moving out of here. How far out are you?"

"I'm on the way to roll call, Juan. Wait a minute, did you say you're going into the Cavazos building?"

Juan broke into a trot. "Yeah."

"You can't do that, Juan. You don't even have a warrant, do you?"

"I'm going in exigent circumstances. This won't wait. I need you here right now."

"Listen, Juan," Rowe said, a note of desperation seeping into his voice, "just hang on, okay? Let me get some of the guys together. We'll be there in fifteen minutes, twenty tops."

"Won't wait that long. It's going down now."

"What do you mean it won't wait? What are you doing, Juan?"

But Juan couldn't answer. He'd already closed most of the distance to the loading dock. The men were moving inside now, and the young guy turned to check the street behind him. Juan quickly ducked out of sight behind a Dumpster and pulled his pistol.

"What are you doing, Juan? Come on, talk to me, man."

Juan waited for the men to slip inside the building before answering. "I think we found the first battle in a war," he said.

"A war? Juan, what in the hell—"

"I'll tell you when you get here. Just get here."

"Okay, wait, wait, wait. What is this about a war?"

"You remember that flesh-eating bacteria the

CDC told us about? Call Tom Parkes over at the FBI and tell him I found where they're hiding it, but it's going mobile right now. I need your people out here and Tom needs to get us a team equipped to lock down the bacteria."

Juan was less than ten feet from the loading dock when a young Porra soldier with a cigarette hanging from the corner of his mouth and a rifle slung over his shoulder stepped out of the dark alley next to the building.

The man stopped in his tracks, his eyes going wide.

Juan slipped his phone into his shirt pocket and veered toward the man. Before the soldier could react, Juan kicked the side of his knee, causing him to cave forward. Juan caught him, spun him around, and threw his right arm around the man's neck. The man struggled, tried to pull away, but his efforts were too little too late. Still clutching his pistol, Juan hooked his right hand over his left forearm, tightening his hold on the man's neck while simultaneously pushing with his left hand on the back of the man's head. Sleeper holds worked quickly when executed properly, and Juan was an expert. The man sagged to the floor, limp and unconscious. Moving fast, Juan pulled him back into the alley.

He could hear Rowe screaming at him over the phone. Juan pulled it out of his pocket and said, "I'm going in. Get here quick."

"Wait, goddamn it! You need to do this tactically. Be smart about this. Let us hit it the right way."

"You SWAT guys can be kind of chickenshit sometimes, you know that?"

"Juan, I'm fucking serious here. Do not go—"

Juan disconnected without waiting for the rest. He silenced the phone and slid it into his back pocket. If he knew Rowe, and he was pretty sure he did, the man would do everything he told him. And it wouldn't take him fifteen minutes to do it either. He and the entire rest of his unit would be on the way in five. With luck, they might even get there in time to pull his ass out of the fire he was about to start.

Hopefully, he thought.

Then he slipped through the door.

It opened onto a narrow hallway that led around a corner to his left. Juan pressed against the wall and listened. He could hear muffled voices coming from the bowels of the building. The hallway was cold. There was a faint odor of decomposition partially masked by a bleach smell. It was enough to raise the hairs on the back of his neck.

Somebody—probably the young guy, Juan figured—was barking orders. He sounded upset again. Juan reached into a pocket on the inside of his shirt and removed a pen-shaped digital video recorder. The device looked just like a normal black-and-gold ballpoint pen, but was actually a highly sensitive digital recorder capable of capturing up to forty minutes of video footage. He didn't figure on using even half that.

The hallway ahead turned right, so Juan moved to the left-hand side of the hall and slowly inched his way around the corner, his weapon up and ready. It was an operator's trick called pieing the corner. Doing it correctly maximized both cover and visibility. If anybody stepped into the hallway, he'd see him a fraction of a second before they saw him, and that would be all the time Juan needed.

The hallway went about twenty feet before opening up on either side to what looked like a warehouse floor. Juan could see the shadows of two men just inside the door on the left-hand side of the hall. Armed guards, he thought, almost certainly. That meant he had to hit the room hard and fast, not giving them a chance to react. He had no idea how this was going to turn out, but he did know the rules of engagement. His badge hung from a sturdy beaded chain around his neck. Juan pulled it out and let it rest on his chest. He'd have to identify himself, at least give them the chance to surrender, even though he knew that wasn't going to happen. He was about to step into a gunfight, and he was ready.

He checked his watch. Three minutes to five.

No time like right now, he told himself, and focused his breathing. In and out, slow and steady, like a metronome. During the selection process for Special Forces the doctors had discovered Juan had something called a metronomic heartbeat. Most people's heartbeats vary with what they're doing. Fast when they're stressed, like when they have a gun to their heads or they're about to jump out of an airplane, slow when they're sitting on the couch reading a book. Not Juan's though. His was steady nearly all the time, no matter what he was doing. The doctors told him it was because his brain produced a higher than normal level of a neurotransmitter called neuropeptide. They told him it was like the body's version of a Valium, mitigating the effects of anxiety and stress. It was a good thing, they told him, and a trait he shared with most of the successful Special Forces operators. And it was helping him now to stay focused and calm. He brought his pistol up and glided down the hall, rounded the corner and charged into the room yelling, *"La Policia! Abajo en el suelo! Al suelo!"*

Caught flatfooted, the two guards at the door fumbled with their weapons trying to get them up. One of them accidentally squeezed off a round into the ceiling. Juan didn't give him a chance to fire another. He shot the guard closest to him, putting a single round center mass in his chest. The man staggered backwards, but didn't fall. Juan lunged for him, grabbed the muzzle of the man's AK with his left hand, and pushed the rifle flat against the man's bleeding chest. With his other hand Juan fired twice over the man's shoulder, dropping the second guard to floor.

The first guard was making a choking sound. Already his eyes had turned up into his skull and he was shaking. That made him easy to control. Juan spun him around, using him as a human shield for the three gunmen moving in on him. The men opened fire just as Juan spun the first guard around, the bullets thudding into the man's back and causing his body to twitch and dance. Juan pushed the man toward the middle of the room and fired at a man running straight at him, hitting him in the stomach and in the face. The man fell forward onto his hands and knees, and then collapsed onto his belly.

"Matar a ese hijo de puta!" somebody shouted. Juan didn't see who, though it sounded like the young guy in charge.

Just the man Juan wanted to get his hands on.

To his left was a metal staircase leading to a catwalk that went the length of the room. There was a
narrow gap between the catwalk and the wall and he
ran for it, rounding the far side of the stairs just as
more shots zinged off the pipes that ran beneath the
catwalk.

"Se fue de esa manera," the young guy yelled
again. *"Cómo él, lo consigue!"*

About twenty feet down there was a gap in the
pipes. Juan reached that just as two men came
around the stairs. Had Juan been in their shoes he
would have hung back, where he could use the stairs
for cover. But these two were stupid. Not seeing him
right away, they rushed forward, and when Juan pied
around the edge of the stack of pipes he was using
for concealment, the two men found themselves
framed in the narrow funnel between the catwalk
and the wall. They were set up like ducks in a county
fair's shooting arcade. One man stopped and tried to
backpedal out of the funnel. The other brought his
gun up to fire. Juan shot him four times in the chest,
then put his sights on the second man at the foot of
the stairs and dropped him with three shots.

The slide of Juan's pistol locked back in the empty
position. He brought it up to his chest, ejected the
spent magazine, and retrieved another from his back
pocket, all while walking back toward the main floor.
He was in operator mode now, every action deliberate, smooth, and executed with practiced precision.
Juan had only taken the briefest of glances at the
main floor, but it had been enough to lock it into his
mind. There'd been the two guards at the door, and
the three men he'd killed by the stairs. That left a
man in a blue T-shirt and jeans that had been stand-

ing far off to his right by a long metal table and the young guy in the black blazer. The guy in the blue T-shirt had pulled a pistol, Juan had seen that, so when he came around the back side of the stairs, he was ready.

The young guy in the blazer was running toward the back of the main floor, toward some offices along the far wall. Juan scanned the rest of the floor and saw the man in the blue T-shirt ducking behind the table. There was some kind of pulley attachment just above the table and he was using that as concealment. There wasn't enough of him showing for a clean shot, not at thirty yards with a pistol.

But maybe . . . There was a six-inch gap between the table and the bottom of the pulley. Raising his pistol and fixing his sights on the surface of the table, Juan slowly squeezed the trigger. Bullets hitting hard surfaces such as concrete and metal at an obtuse angle tended to hug that hard surface. It was a trick he'd learned while street fighting in Ciudad Juarez years earlier, where shooting at targets hiding under cars was a necessary survival skill, and when the gun jumped in his hand he wasn't surprised to hear the shot zing off the table and then the man let out a startled cough. He stumbled away from the table, coming out from behind the pulley, and when he did, Juan saw the man's blue T-shirt had become a bloody bib from the wound in his neck. He collapsed to the ground without Juan having to fire a second shot.

Juan broke into a sprint and went after the young guy in the blazer. He'd already made it across the main floor and was disappearing into an office, but Juan was closing fast. He hit the door with his good shoulder and caved it inwards. The young guy was standing in a doorway on the far side of the office with a gun in his hand. He fired five wild shots at Juan's direction, but Juan was already diving toward a heavy oaken desk in the middle of the room. He hit the ground and rolled left, firing as he did so and driving the guy through the door and out into the hall.

Juan could hear the man's footfalls disappearing down the hallway. He climbed to his feet, hustled to the door and pied around the corner. The man had stopped at the end of the hall, his gun up and ready. But Juan had the jump on him and fired twice, both shots hitting the man in his right shoulder. He wanted this man talking, not dead.

The man screamed and fell back against the wall, leaving a long smear of blood there. His pistol fell to the carpet, and before he could reach down with his good hand to get it, Juan let out a yell and charged him.

The man turned tail and ran into the darkened recesses of the building. It wasn't hard to follow him, though. He was shot and panicking. Juan could hear him panting, whimpering really, and when he caught up to him, he pushed him headlong into a wall. The man screamed from the pain and then screamed again when Juan grabbed the wounded shoulder and used it as leverage to pull him to the ground. Working quickly, he pushed the man onto his stomach and wrenched the wounded arm behind his back, slapping a handcuff on the man's wrist a moment later.

He tried to pull the other arm back, but the man

was lying on it, squirming around like he was trying to reach something in his opposite side front pocket.

"Dame tus manos!" Juan yelled. *"Hacerlo ahora!"*

Still the man wouldn't release his arm. He kicked and bucked, tried to roll over and throw Juan to the side. Juan clamped his fingers down on the man's wounded shoulder and squeezed, causing the man to howl in pain, and still he wouldn't give up his free arm.

Then Juan felt him grab something and he thought: *Crap, a gun!*

"Soltarlo! Soltarlo!" Juan yelled. "Drop it!"

He clamped down again on the wound, digging his fingers into the bullet hole, tearing it. The man's screams echoed off the walls, and after nearly ten seconds of that he'd had enough and rolled over, freeing up his right arm, all his resistance gone.

Juan pulled the arm back, expecting to see a gun, and instead saw what looked like a garage door opener in the man's hands. The man's thumb was mashing down on the button so hard it had turned white.

"What the hell is this?" Juan asked.

The man laughed. There were tears running down his blood-spattered face, but he was laughing.

The crazy bastard, Juan thought.

"What have you done?" Juan asked him.

The man's laughter turned to a cruel sneer. *"No entiendo Ingles,"* he said.

Juan grabbed the wound again, this time sinking his thumb down to the knuckle in the wound.

Between the man's screams, Juan said, "Bullshit, asshole. You speak English just fine. Now what the hell did you do? Why were you sending that bacteria down to Nuevo Laredo? Where's the truck?"

The man couldn't laugh anymore. He tried, but he couldn't. He was panting now, his skin an ashen white.

"You want to know?" the man said.

"Yeah, I want to know."

This time the man did manage a laugh. A laugh that made him sound like one of the damned. "You want to know. I'll show you."

His head fell back on the carpet. He had all but passed out. Juan was about to go for the wound again when a door burst open not ten feet down the hall. A man fell out and collided with the opposite wall.

Instantly, Juan was on his feet, his weapon in his hand.

The man's head lolled on his shoulders. His arms hung limply at his side. Even in the low light of the hallway the man's face looked diseased, blistered and cracked. There were oozing wounds on his cheeks and his forehead. And when he stood up, pushing away from the wall, Juan could see he was missing an ear, his clothes bloody and shredded rags.

"What the hell?" Juan said.

From below him, the handcuffed man let out a sound that was supposed to be another brave laugh, but instead came out like a groan.

The diseased man staggered forward.

Two more men, both as diseased looking as the first, stepped out of the doorway.

"Stop right there," Juan said, surprised to hear the hitch in his voice. "I said stop. *Alto ahi!*"

The man lurched forward. His whole body trembled when he walked. He wasn't drunk. Juan could see that at a glance. But something was wrong with him. Seriously wrong.

"Acuéstese en el suelo con las manos detrás de la cabeza," Juan said.

The handcuffed man started to laugh. "You're fucked, *pendajo*! You wanted to know what we did, this is it. You hear me, man, you're f—"

The rest was cut off sharply.

As Juan watched, both horrified and captivated, unable to look away, one of the three diseased men fell on the handcuffed man and tore at his face with his hands and his teeth. It was savage to watch, an awful act full of blind fury and inexplicable rage. A cold chill moved over his spine. Juan backed away, shaking his head, not at all sure what he was looking at, but scared nonetheless.

A hand fell on his shoulder.

He spun around.

And found himself nose to nose with another of the diseased men. This one didn't have any lips. His eyes were leaking pus and his skin was peeling from his face. He opened his mouth and leaned forward to take a bite out of Juan's face, and when he did Juan got a whiff of something he hadn't smelled since leaving Ciudad Juarez all those years ago.

The odor of a body left out in the sun to rot.

He gagged and fell backwards. The man reached for him and Juan reacted instantly by grabbing the man's wrist and pulling him.

Hard.

The man went flying, and Juan was shocked by how little resistance he gave. He tumbled headlong into the path of the diseased men behind Juan and they all went over.

Like bowling pins.

There was a woman standing in front of him when he turned around. This one had gray, matted hair halfway down her back, the remnants of some kind of white smock hanging from her shoulders. Behind her were half a dozen more just like her, diseased and lurching forward, unsteady on their feet, the odor of dead things moving with them.

"Oh, shit," Juan said.

He turned around and saw the bowling pins rising to their feet. When the first man turned to face him Juan raised his gun and centered the front sight on his chest. *"Un paso más y voy a poner una bala a través de su corazón,"* he said. "I mean it. Not another step."

The man stumbled forward, his hands reaching for Juan's face.

Juan braced himself.

And fired.

The first shot knocked the man back on his heels.

But didn't stop him.

His head tilted forward, his hands came up again, grabbing at air, and he took another step. Juan fired twice into the man's chest, both shots hitting almost directly on top of the first. Little bits of flesh and burned bits of fabric flew from the entry wound.

Nothing.

The man staggered forward.

Unphased.

Seemingly oblivious to his pain.

Juan leveled his sights on the man's nose and fired.

Half his head exploded away, big clumps of scalp and hair smacking against the wall like a thrown wet towel.

And still the man staggered forward.

Juan lowered his weapon, stunned, and for the first time since his father's funeral all those years ago, a prayer rose to his lips: *"Padre nuestro que estás en los cielos, santificado sea tu nombre, venga tu reino . . ."*

But the man didn't stop.

Slowly, Juan raised his pistol, and this time his aim was true. The man's head snapped back, and he sank to the floor a motionless heap.

Juan glanced over his shoulder at the advancing horde and knew he couldn't go that way.

He didn't have much time either.

Forward and out, he told himself.

He aimed for what his sniper friends called the kill spot, that little indentation between the bottom of the nose and the center of the upper lip. Put a bullet there and the medulla oblongata vaporized in a pink spray that went out the back of the head and ended the victim's life before they could even blink an eye.

Both of the men in front of him went down with a single shot and a badly shaken Juan Perez staggered down the hallway until he found an exit.

He pushed the door open and blinding white lights hit him in the face.

Men were yelling.

He put up a hand to shield his eyes, his other hand holding his weapon down by his thigh.

A familiar voice yelled, "Hold your fire!"

The next instant, Detective Jason Rowe was at his side, saying something Juan didn't quite catch.

It felt like the world was swirling all around him.

"Hey," Rowe shouted into his ear, "you okay?"

Juan slowly shook his head.

He hooked a thumb back toward the building. "Nobody goes in there," he said, surprised at how smooth, how calm he sounded. "Not yet."

CHAPTER 11

Paul Godwin woke to the morning sun on his face. After spending the night drunk his head ached horribly. With a groan, he turned away from the light. Tess was there beside him, dressed in a white T-shirt that during the night had climbed up enough to show her black panties and a little bit of her smooth white belly. Very nice. He tried to remember if anything had happened between them. He had flashes of her laughing; of the two of them tumbling through the cabin door on a wave of liquor; of her changing into the T-shirt she now wore, blushing and then giggling when she realized she'd just gotten naked right in front of him. He couldn't remember anything else though, and his head hurt too badly to worry about it.

He spilled out of bed, bleary-eyed and ill, and staggered toward the bathroom. His iPhone was on the dresser, but he didn't bother to look at it. He'd have to meet with the senator before breakfast to go over the day's business, but he sure as hell couldn't do it like this. Not feeling like this. It felt like he was still drunk.

A moment later, Paul was swaying over the toilet in the dark. He glanced at his reflection in the mirror and saw a dark patch at the corner of his mouth. Leaning closer, he saw it was a bruise, crescent shaped, brightening to an inflamed-looking red just below his bottom lip. There was a little bit of dried blood there, too.

He touched it and it hurt.

"Hey, Tess?" he called out. No answer. He stepped back into the cabin. "Hey, Tess, do you know how I got this?"

She groaned. Opened one eye. Closed it. Groaned again.

"You still sleeping?"

She lifted her head from the pillow, her eyes glassy and rimmed in red. "Of course, I'm still sleeping. Oh, God." She dropped her face to the pillow. He heard her mutter, "I'm never drinking tequila again."

"Is that what we were drinking?"

She groaned again.

He was surprised at himself. Spring break his sophomore year at Yale, down in Panama City, there'd been what he diplomatically referred to these days as a "tequila incident." For years after he hadn't even been able to stand in the same room as a bottle of tequila without getting queasy. "I haven't had that stuff since college," he said.

"Yeah, I know. You kept saying that. You told the whole bar that."

"I did?"

"You don't remember?"

He shook his head. "No, not really."

"Do you remember trying to get me to sing karaoke?"

"No. Please tell me I didn't do that." He paused, then said, "I didn't sing, did I? Please tell me I didn't."

"You kept trying to get me to sing 'The Night They Drove Old Dixie Down.' You said a good Southern girl like me should know it by heart." She groaned again. "Oh, God, I think I'm gonna be sick."

"Sorry about that."

"Don't mention it."

After a pause, he said, "Hey, do you remember how I got this?"

She turned her head just enough to look at him.

He pointed to his busted lip.

"You hit yourself with the door when we came back here last night. Do you remember that?"

"I think I remember you laughing."

"I was laughing at you."

"Oh."

She rolled over onto her back and put a hand over her eyes. "How about aspirin? Do you have any?"

"I don't know," he said. "I don't think so. I sure could use some though. You want to go get some with me? They've got that mall. Should be able to find something there."

"No," she said. "I just want to stay here and throw up."

"Oh. Okay."

"But if you're going get some Alka-Seltzer, too."

"Okay, sure."

He got dressed—khaki shorts, a Yale golf shirt,

and Birkenstocks—grabbed his phone and his room card and headed out. He almost knocked on the senator's cabin door to tell her where he was going, but thought better of it. She was probably still sleeping. God knows she needed it. The night before, at dinner, Dr. Sutton was complaining of a bad stomachache. He looked pale and he was sweating a lot. Paul and Tess had helped the senator get him downstairs to the cabin and after they put him to bed, she'd come to the door with Paul and Tess and urged them to go out and have fun. He'd earned that much, she said, and she'd be all right. But she'd looked tired. There was a haggard air about her he hadn't seen since they were working so hard to get the International Asset Seizure Act passed. He remembered those days, when she first started to get beat up in the press, and how much bitter resistance she'd gotten from her own party's leadership. She'd weathered all that though, and she'd come out on top, but it had been really rough on her, and on her marriage. Perhaps, as they stood there in her cabin, whispering so as not to disturb Dr. Sutton, she'd known what he was thinking because she'd smiled—forced the smile, he thought—and said, "Really, I'm fine. You kids go have a good time. Enjoy yourself." She'd even joked with Tess about it. "Agent Compton, would you please make sure he enjoys himself?" Tess had nodded and wandered back out into the hall. "Go," she told him. "I'll be fine."

That was the last clear memory he had of the night, and it bothered him as he wandered down the hallway to the stairs. The cruise line had an iPhone app that was supposed to help him get around the ship, schedule dinners and shows and shore excursions, everything he needed, but it was hard to use. And apparently not working this morning. All he could get was the map, and even on that the You Are Here feature wasn't working. He'd never been good at maps, and he felt lost trying to use this one without the little red dot to guide him. He'd been wandering for twenty minutes before he realized he didn't know what deck he was on.

Then he noticed that he hadn't seen anybody else since leaving his cabin. He was standing on a patch of marble tile outside of one of the ship's restaurants. It was closed now and so it didn't surprise him that it was empty. But when he walked around the corner to a long hallway that ran nearly the entire length of the ship, he didn't see anybody either, and that seemed wrong somehow. It was early, but it wasn't that early. There should be people, right? At least one or two heading up topside for breakfast. But there was nobody, and the silence unnerved him.

He started up the hallway, growing more and more uncomfortable with every step. What was going on here? Paul tried to tell himself to keep calm, there was nothing to this, but when another five minutes went by and he still hadn't seen anyone, he couldn't make himself believe it anymore.

Paul was rounding the corner to the main stairs when he heard someone shouting in what sounded like a mixture of Italian and English.

He stopped at the mouth of the hallway, listening down the stairs.

Whoever was doing the shouting was coming up the stairs.

And fast.

"Hello?" Paul said. His voice sounded strained, the fear held in check, but only just.

The next instant a crewman rounded the landing below him at a full sprint. He glanced once at Paul and though it was only for a fraction of a second it was enough for Paul to see the fear in his eyes.

"Hey!" Paul said. "Wait."

But the man ran right on by him, rounded the corner and kept running upstairs.

"Hey!" Paul called after him.

Nothing.

He was gone.

Paul looked around, knowing he didn't want to stay where he was, and went up the stairs hoping maybe to run into someone else.

He didn't find the crewman. He did find the mall, though, and he thought for sure that there'd be people here. The place was always crowded. The shops were supposed to open early and stay open past midnight, but they were all closed. Paul glanced up, scanning the balconies above him. Nothing. The mall was four-stories high, every level lined with balconies for sightseers to look down on the action. Somebody should have been at one of the railings.

He walked through the garden at the center of the mall, too scared now to worry about the ringing in his head. Where in the hell was everyone? At the opposite end of the market, he stopped at the foot of the stairs and turned around, scanning once again the stillness of the ship, the hideous and unnatural quiet of it. Then that quiet was broken by the soft patter of footsteps on the carpeted stairs behind him.

He turned, relief swelling up in him.

And just as quickly turning to shock.

A girl was standing there, a beautiful dark-haired girl dressed all in black.

"Monica?" He blinked, unable to believe his eyes. "Oh, my God, what are—"

But he didn't get the rest of it out, for the girl's eyes opened wide and she wheeled around, sprinting back up the stairs.

"Monica, wait!"

He ran after her, calling her name. She wouldn't stop. He could hear her footfalls mounting higher above him, gaining ground on him. He made it as far as the second landing before his body rebelled. His legs turned to water beneath him. His head felt soupy. His stomach heaved.

Unable to keep it down, he vomited into a potted fern next to the wall.

When he could stand up again, his head was swimming. His skin felt clammy and cold with sweat. But he felt a little better. Just a little.

He turned to the stairs where Monica had disappeared and shook his head. That *had* been her. There was no question in his mind about that. And he was certain she recognized him. The surprise had been plain as day on her face. So why had she run? And what in the hell was she doing on this ship?

He tried to think of what to do next, but had no idea. The deserted ship, seeing Monica here; it was too weird. He couldn't wrap his head around it.

Finally, not knowing what else to do, he went down the stairs to Deck 4. His map said the infirmary was there. Maybe he could get some aspirin there.

And maybe some answers, too.

* * *

Paul found the woman's body a few feet from the elevators on Deck 4.

Her head was bashed in with something blunt, like a heavy piece of wood. Blood had puddled around her head, caking in her hair. She looked to Paul to be maybe fifty, maybe a little older. It was hard to tell because her face was all scratched up and her mouth was torn at one corner, the gash going almost all the way to her ear. Her clothes were torn, too, and there were more scratches on her neck and her arms.

He'd gagged, and nearly vomited a second time when he saw the blood, and now he was standing a few feet from her, shaking, sweating, his breath coming in short, ragged pulls. Paul closed his eyes and tried to get his head back together, and that was when he heard the sound of a man sobbing from a nearby supply closet.

He went over to the door as quietly as he could, careful not to step in any of the blood, and listened at the door. Whoever was on the other side of the door sounded more frightened than he was, if that was even possible. And in between sobs he could make out a prayer. *"Guardia de mí, oh, Señor, de las manos de los malos, me preserve de hombres violentos, que han planeado hacer tropezar a mis pies."*

"Hello?" Paul said.

The voice inside the supply closet went quiet.

"Hello? Are you okay in there?"

Nothing but more silence.

"The door's locked. Will you open it, please? *Abre la puerta, por favor.*"

After a moment, Paul heard the lock turn over.

"Voy a abrir la puerta ahora, ¿de acuerdo?" he said.

Paul didn't get a response so he pushed the door open. Inside he saw a man in a uniform, but it was the uniform of one of the behind-the-scenes workers, the ones that cruise passengers weren't supposed to see. Laundry, or Housekeeping, Paul wasn't exactly sure.

And at the moment he didn't care, for as scared as the man looked he was holding the broken end of a wooden broom handle—clutching it like it was the edge of a cliff, to be more exact—and it was covered with blood.

"Oh, my God," Paul said. "What did you do?"

The man looked at him then, and his gaze was haunted. That was all Paul could think of to describe it. That was the gaze of a man who had seen more than he'd bargained for.

Far more.

"¿Qué has hecho?" Paul asked.

The man shook his head, like he couldn't believe it himself.

"Ella me ataco," he said. *"Ella trato de morderme."*

Paul shook his head, certain he'd heard that wrong. She hadn't tried to eat him. Certainly not that. *"Mi español no es muy bueno,"* Paul said. *"¿Has dicho que ella trató de comer?"*

"Sí," the man said, nodding emphatically. The stick was shaking in the air between them, and Paul couldn't help but see the bits of scalp and clumpy bits still clinging to the tip. *"Yo no qué hacer. La*

golpeé con esto. Ella no iba a morir. La golpeé una y otra vez. Ella no iba a morir."

"She wouldn't die?" Paul repeated.

The man nodded. His haunted expression gave way suddenly to a desperate need to be understood. Yes, yes, he nodded. Yes.

Paul was frightened. It was finally sinking in that he was standing just a few feet from the man who had caved that poor woman's head in. And he was still holding the stick he'd used to do it. He had to hold himself together. He had to get that weapon away from him and get him to a ship's officer. But to do that, he had to look like he was in control.

"Give me the stick," he said, holding out his hand. "Give it to me. *Dame el palo.*"

"No." The man shrank back, clutching the stick to his chest. He was shaking all over. *"Ellos volverán, los muertos."*

"Los muertos?" Paul turned his palm up and thrust his hand in the man's direction. *"Dame el palo."* He wanted to hand the stick over. Paul could see that in the man's demeanor. He wanted someone to step in and take control. "My name is Paul," he said. "What's your name? *¿Cuál es su nombre?*"

"Pedro."

"Pedro, okay. Pedro, you need to give me the stick. *Dame el palo, por favor.*"

Neither man moved for a long moment. Then the man's face went slack and he held the stick out for Paul to take.

"Thank you," Paul said. He'd been holding his breath. He let it go now and stepped backwards into the hall. He motioned for the man to follow. "Come with me," he said. "Let's go get help. *Ven conmigo.*"

Pedro nodded and stood.

Paul took another step back. He put his hand on the door. "Come on," he said, motioning for the man to follow.

The man stepped into the hallway and Paul closed the door behind him.

And there was another man standing there. Paul lurched back, stumbling over his feet and bumping into the wall. The man wore the white uniform of a ship's officer, but the entire front of it was covered in what looked like bloody fish guts. His face was a ghastly mess, the lips bloated and torn, hanging from his mouth. Like the woman back at the elevators, his face and arms were laced with deep, bleeding scratches, and there were bite marks on his hands.

Paul didn't even get a chance to raise the stick. Pedro had stepped out of the way of the closing door and right into the man's arms. Both men tumbled to the ground, the officer coming down on top. Pedro pawed and slapped at the man, but the officer tore into him with the ferocity of a wounded animal. He pounded on him, scratched him, scratched at his eyes. Paul watched, horrified, as the officer clamped his teeth onto Pedro's nose and tore it away.

Blood spurted onto the man's face and onto the walls and Paul lurched again.

The officer looked up, locking eyes with Paul, blood dripping off his chin. Paul swallowed, and something inside him let go. His bowels turned to water. His legs felt like they could barely hold him.

"What's wrong with you?" he said.

The man rose to his feet, a low, stuttering growl rising from his ruined throat.

"Stay back. Leave me alone."

Paul could feel himself shaking so badly he thought he might fall apart. What he was looking at was impossible. People didn't do stuff like this. It wasn't real. It couldn't be.

But the man was coming after him.

Paul turned to run, but froze in his tracks. A woman, this one dressed like a passenger, was coming at him from the opposite end of the hall. At first it took a moment for Paul's mind to take her all in, for there was no way in hell she should still be on her feet, not looking like she did. There was no meat left on her right thigh, only tattered flaps of pink skin and strings of tendons hanging from her femur. Her left arm hung uselessly at her side. She was supporting herself on the railing with her other arm, pulling herself along inch by painful inch. Her mouth was an angry, vacant hole, and though she seemed to be speaking, she didn't make a sound.

Before Paul could move, the ship's officer was all over him, his cold, blood-sticky hands clamping down on his shoulder.

Paul let out a scream and pulled away. He still had the broken-off broom handle he'd taken from Pedro and he jammed it into the officer's face. Outside of the movies, Paul had never seen anyone so inexplicably violent. The man snarled and snapped like a pit bull, and though Paul had the pointed end of the broom handle digging into his throat, the man still raged.

"Get off," Paul said, grunting as he tried to turn the man away.

Instead, Paul pitched over backwards, the man coming down on top of him.

The pointed end of the broom handle sank into the man's neck. Paul heard it enter with a sucking sound, like a boot getting pulled down into the mud.

And still the man fought him.

He didn't even seem to notice the pain. He opened his mouth and blood welled up at the back of his throat, choking off any noises he might have made. But it didn't slow him down at all.

"Get off me," Paul said, and twisted the four or five inches of broom handle sticking out of the man's throat to one side.

The man fell onto his back, hissing and gargling as he struggled to get back on his feet. Paul backed away until he ran into a door. Without warning, someone slammed into the other side of the door, growling just as the ship's officer was trying to do, beating on the wooden door with his fists, trying to claw his way through.

Paul bolted. He didn't even look where he was going.

He just ran, his mind reeling.

Chapter 12

Pilar had been careful to stay in open areas, where there were plenty of directions to run, if necessary. She'd had her sidearm handy, just in case, though so far she hadn't needed it. She'd been moving through the ship since before dawn, surprised at how fast the bacteria had spread, how thorough it had been, and was impressed with what Ramon Medina had been able to accomplish. A lesser man would never have been able to pull off something so spectacularly destructive and wasteful of life. He really was a man endowed with a unique and terrible vision.

And then she'd seen Paul coming up the stairs. She'd been careless, daydreaming about Ramon, and that was bad. She'd walked right into Paul, and she'd been so startled by seeing him that she'd blanched and run rather than shoot him where he stood. If she could do it over again, he'd be dead right now. From here on out, she couldn't afford that kind of mistake. It would get her killed.

But she had learned something from the encounter. He'd called her Monica, which meant he was still in the dark about who she really was. That was good, but it was small comfort because it meant that Senator Sutton was almost certainly still alive. After all, if she were dead, he'd be with the body, trying to figure out what to do next.

And if the senator was still alive, Pilar would have to take the plan to the next phase. That meant she'd have to go back to the bridge and plug into the ship's computer system. That was going to make things far more difficult for her, but at this point it couldn't be helped.

She pushed Paul Godwin out of her mind and took the stairs up to Deck 20. Here too the decks were deserted. She saw a few crew members running around with radios in their hands, but none of them had any sense of discipline. They were lost, and from the look of panic on their faces she knew there was little doubt that the whole ship would be overrun by mid-morning. The crew was certainly helpless to do anything about it. And once she finished this last stage of the operation, she'd be able to sit back and let the zombies do the work for her.

She stayed in the shadows as she worked her toward the bridge, and she was almost there when she heard a little boy crying from a cabin off to her right.

Pilar stopped, turned, and stared at the door that was hanging open. Every nerve in her being was humming, telling her to stay away—just turn around and continue the mission. She was so close now, just one more hallway and she was there. But that little boy's voice called to her in a way that sounded so painfully familiar she was unable to turn away.

Pilar drew her weapon and kicked the door open. She walked into the cabin, ready to shoot anything that moved. The cabin was a big, spacious affair, and not even the overturned dresser and the bed sheets thrown to the floor could disguise the opulence of the place. This family had spent a king's ransom on their vacation. She went through the living room and into the bedroom, and all at once she realized what had happened here. The boy she'd heard sobbing was perhaps ten years old, maybe a little younger. He was cowering beneath the body of his father, whose face was a bloody wreck. The mother had collapsed on top of the father's legs. She must have tried to claw her way through the father to get to the boy, for she had obviously changed. The bib of blood down her front told plainly of that. Her forehead was bashed in, no doubt by the broken and bloody laptop computer by the father's side.

The father was just dead. He was, she figured, one of the three percent who simply died when exposed to the bacteria and failed to revive. If he hadn't turned by now, he wouldn't turn at all. He'd simply died, and left in his wake a cowering son so overcome with grief that he couldn't even move out from under the bodies of his parents.

Pilar had been prepared to turn around and leave. She'd seen a lifetime of children robbed of their parents. She'd lived that hell herself. She was already turning on her heel, admonishing herself for being stupid enough to come in here in the first place, when the boy said, "Why?"

She lowered her weapon. All at once she saw that

the boy was infected. His eyes were bloodshot, his face scratched and bloody. Clearly, the mother had gotten to him, despite the father's efforts. But he was still alive, and he was still capable of asking the hard questions. At least for a few minutes longer.

"Why?" he said again.

Pilar didn't hear a little rich white boy, though. What she heard was Lupe, twenty years ago, cowering in the heat of an eighteen-wheeler's trailer, asking why the world had to be so hard and cruel. What had he done to deserve a death like this? What could he possibly have done to deserve this?

Pilar raised her weapon and centered the front sights on the little boy's forehead.

He didn't flinch. He didn't look away. He didn't have to. It was Lupe's face staring back at her.

"Why?" he asked.

"I'm sorry," she said. "You have no idea how sorry I am."

"I don't want to die."

She almost put the pistol down. It was too much, far too much. But then he vomited blood all over the back of his father's corpse, and when he looked up at her, his eyes were yellow and bloodshot. He was still alive, but death was lurking in those eyes, biding its time.

"I'm sorry," she said again. "God, I'm so sorry."

She fired one round.

It took a long time for the echo of the shot to fade away, but fade away it did. She turned, utterly disgusted with herself, and made her way to the bridge.

There she plugged her iPhone into the ship's computer and called up the housekeeping subroutines. She cleared her mind, forcing herself to focus on the task at hand. It was one of the comic ironies of an operation like this that a mighty cruise ship, a floating testimonial of American opulence and excess, could be undone by those who cleaned the toilets.

Pilar accessed the housekeeping end-of-cruise command and forced the computer to activate it. She turned to the ship's security cameras, which showed long views of most of the ship's twenty-eight decks, and waited.

One by one, the locks to the cabin doors clicked, and the doors sighed open.

The program she'd accessed was designed to allow housekeeping unlimited access to the various cabins onboard ship once all the passengers had disembarked. Most, if not all, of the passengers had closed their doors during the night to tend to their sick loved ones. During the night, most of those sick passengers would have died.

Now, the dead were free to move about the ship.

CHAPTER 13

Tess went back to sleep after Paul left, but it didn't help any. When she woke, she was still sore, still groggy, still dreadfully hungover. It'd been stupid of her to drink like that, but tequila was Juan's favorite drink and for all the time she'd spent with him over the last few years she'd picked up a taste for it.

But good lord, did it have a way of sneaking up on her.

She rolled over and checked the clock on her phone. Paul had been gone for a long time. He might have caught some breakfast, but she didn't think so. The plan had been for them to all go up together once the senator and her husband got ready.

And he hadn't closed the door, either. What kind of idiot couldn't close a door? She pulled it closed and then went to the bathroom and peed and splashed some water on her face. Her eyes were bloodshot and there were dark circles on her cheeks.

Great, she thought. She was going to be hurting all day.

It was ten o'clock back in Washington, so she took her phone out to the balcony and tried calling Juan, just to check in. But her phone wouldn't connect. She was getting a signal. She had two bars. But every time she tried to call out, all she heard was static. Text messaging wasn't working either. Every number she tried came back with a Message Not Sent error.

"Come on," she said irritably. Freaking four-hundred-dollar phone and it wasn't worth a crap.

Tess went over to the desk and pulled out the list of shipboard contact numbers she'd gotten from First Officer Amato. Her room was equipped with a wave phone that was able to call any other wave phone on the ship. These phones never went out of range because they were for shipboard communication only.

She tried Amato's extension on the bridge and got nothing.

She tried his cabin. Again nothing.

The first couple of calls got her frustrated, but as she went down the list and got nothing, no matter what number she called, her internal alarms started to go off. Something was wrong.

From her workbag she pulled out her tactical gear and got dressed, secreting a few extra magazines for her Glock in the cargo pockets of her BDUs. Then she pulled her hair back in a ponytail and went across the hall to knock on the senator's door.

The hallway was deserted except for a man walking away from her down at the far end. That seemed odd, too. At this time of the morning there should be people coming and going every which way.

She knocked again.

"Who is it?"

"Senator Sutton, it's Tess Compton. Will you open the door please?"

"Just a second."

It took her a long moment, but Sutton eventually threw the dead bolt and then undid the chain and opened the door. Right away Tess knew something was wrong. Sutton looked like she'd been crying, and she was wearing the same dress she'd worn the night before to dinner. Her hair was a crinkly mess that stuck out in different directions like quills and her skin looked pallid and damp.

"What happened?" Tess said. "Are you okay?"

Sutton nodded. "It's Wayne. He's really sick."

"Where is he?"

Sutton pointed to the closed door of the bathroom. Inside, Tess could hear Dr. Sutton throwing up.

"How long's he been like that?"

"Since last night. It got really bad around two or so."

"Why didn't you call me?"

"It's supposed to be a vacation. I wanted you and Paul to—"

"I'm not on vacation, senator. I'm here on duty."

"Yes, I know, but—"

"Is your phone working?"

"Well, I don't know. I haven't tried to—"

Tess went over to the senator's desk and pushed her papers out of the way. She pulled out the senator's list of contact numbers from the desk drawer and started trying them, one after another, but got nothing.

"Where's your cell phone?" Tess asked.

"Um, over there," Sutton said, pointing to the bedside table nearest the balcony.

Tess scooped it up and started dialing. Same static as on her phone.

"Christ, I can't even reach Paul on this thing." She quickly went through some of the phone's other functions, got nothing but more frustration and tossed it on the bed. "Your Internet and texting are down, too. Where's your laptop?"

"In my briefcase." She pointed at the floor next to the desk. "There."

Tess quickly opened it and signed on, but the laptop was just as useless as the phones.

"What's going on?" Sutton asked.

"I have no idea. But I can't reach Paul. I can't reach my contacts in Washington. I can't even reach Amato or the captain. The wave phones just ring on and on." Before Sutton could respond, Tess crossed to the bathroom door. "Dr. Sutton, this is Agent Compton. I'm going to get the ship's doctor for you. What do I need to tell him about your symptoms?"

He mumbled something, but she couldn't really hear him through the door.

"He's had trouble talking for the last thirty minutes or so," Sutton said. "But he's been running a fever, vomiting, diarrhea, too, I think. He's been tearing up a lot, too. He said he thought it was food poisoning."

"All right. I'm going to have to go get the doctor. We need to have him looked at, and quickly. Are you going to be okay here? You'll lock the door?"

Sutton took a hesitant step forward, and put her hand out.

"What is it?" Tess asked.

"Do you mind, um, can I come with you?" Sutton glanced at the bathroom door. "I just can't listen anymore," she said in a whisper. "God, that sounds so bad, I know, but I just can't take hearing him like that."

Tess studied the woman. She was ripping herself up inside with guilt and worry. Their marriage, from the little Tess had seen anyway, had been on the rocks for a while now, but she still clearly loved the man.

"Sure," Tess said. "Why don't you put on something besides your dinner dress, though. You have a pair of jeans or something?"

"Oh, yes, of course."

Sutton changed into a pair of loose fitting khaki slacks, a blue blouse, and dark blue deck shoes and they headed out. They hadn't gone but a few doors down though before Tess realized there was something wrong besides the phones. A lot of cabin doors were standing open an inch or two, but there didn't appear to be anybody around.

Tess pushed one of the doors open and glanced inside. She held the door open so Sutton could see.

"Where is everybody?" Sutton asked.

"Shhh," Tess whispered. "I don't know, but let's try not to make too much noise."

Tess's instinct was to pull her weapon and move out like she was going through the shooting course back at the academy, but she didn't want to scare Senator Sutton; and besides, a part of her just couldn't believe that something was really critically wrong onboard the ship. How could it be? They'd only been at sea for one day. A bad phone connection and being unable to get online didn't amount to a catastrophe. The girl at the AT&T store had warned her she'd have intermittent cell phone coverage at sea anyway.

Still, she'd been an agent long enough to learn that when her internal alarms were going off, there was usually a reason. And she was on full alert as they got on the elevator and the doors closed behind them.

"Do you think he'll be okay?" Sutton said.

She was wringing her hands together, and for the first time, Tess could see the liver spots on Sutton's skin. Tess turned her attention to the lighted numbers on the elevator's control panel, the decks counting down from 8 to 7 to 6.

"Food poisoning is nothing to play around with," Tess said, as the elevator chimed at Deck 5 and the doors started to slide open. "But we're going to get him the help he—"

Tess stopped in mid-sentence. The elevator doors opened directly onto the main floor of the mall, and the place was packed with people. But there was something wrong with them. Tess realized that the instant the doors opened. One woman crossed directly in front of them, stopped, and turned in their direction.

Sutton gasped.

The left side of the woman's face was normal, but the other half looked like it had been caught in the gears of a machine. Her green dress was soaked in blood and bits of flesh dangled from the jagged edges of her wounded face.

The woman's lips opened to reveal a broken mouth of bloodstained teeth.

She growled at them and charged the elevator.

Tess pulled Sutton back and pushed the door close button. She pulled her pistol and leveled it at the woman. There were more people just as ghastly behind her running for the elevator.

"Hurry, hurry!" Tess said.

The doors started to close just as the woman reached them. She jammed an arm inside, but Sutton kept her finger down on the door close button while Tess kicked and pushed to get the woman away.

Then the doors closed and they started up.

"What in the hell was that?" Sutton said.

Tess shook her head, but when the doors opened again, this time on Deck 6, she had her weapon up and ready.

The landing in front of them looked deserted and they stepped out, Tess in front. But they'd only made it a few feet before a terrified man in a crewman's uniform came running through a set of doors on the opposite side of the landing.

The man nearly tripped when he saw them. He cried out, "Alive!" and ran toward them, his eyes wide and full of panic.

"Whoa!" Tess said. "Where are you going?"

The man babbled something in a language that sounded to Tess like Portuguese, but she couldn't understand a word of it.

"Speak English," she said, trying to grab the man and hold him steady.

He was covered in sweat. He twisted away from her, turned quickly to check the doors from which he'd just come, and then scrambled off across the lobby to the doors at the far side.

Tess and Sutton watched him go. He got most of the way across the lobby when the doors to which he was running burst open. Half a dozen men and women charged out. He screamed, and then the crowd fell on him, tearing into him with their hands and teeth.

"Oh my God!" Sutton said.

At the same moment, the doors at the opposite end of the lobby opened, and more people came out of there, every inch of their hair and faces and clothes drenched in blood.

Sutton screamed.

A man ran out in front of the others. He wore a blue sport coat, a sky blue silk shirt, and tan slacks. The clothes had obviously cost a great deal, but they were stained and ripped now. He ran at Tess and Sutton, arms outstretched. His mouth was twisted but his eyes showed absolutely nothing. They were dead eyes.

Tess raised her weapon and yelled at the man to stop.

He kept coming.

"I said, *stop*!" Tess barked, and then fired three rounds directly into the man's chest. The bullets straightened him up, but barely slowed him down.

Tess sighted in again and shot him in the face. The bullet blew a big chunk of blood, bone, and brains all over the floor behind him, but he still didn't go down. He staggered forward, only one arm raised now, his head tilted at a sickening angle, and Tess, despite her fear, lowered her weapon and gawked at the man.

"How in the hell?"

"Agent Compton!"

Tess looked over her shoulder. The crowd that had attacked the crewman were rising from his corpse and heading their way. The corpse behind them looked like it'd been eaten, even though it continued to twitch and writhe.

Tess raised her pistol again and fired another headshot, this one hitting the man right below his nose. A pink spray jetted out behind the man and he sagged to the floor in a heap.

"Agent Compton!"

"That way," Tess said, pushing her toward the elevators.

Sutton reached the elevator ahead of her and hit the up button. Tess put herself between the senator and the crowd forming around them. A woman pawed the air in front of Tess. She took a step back and shot the woman three times in the face before she fell to the ground.

Another woman stepped over her without a change in her expression and lunged for them.

Tess sidestepped her, grabbed the woman's outstretched arm, and threw her headfirst into the wall next to the elevator doors. She put a bullet in the back of the woman's skull before the woman even had a chance to rise to her knees.

"How we doing on that door?" Tess asked.

"Here it is!" Sutton said.

The next instant there was a chime and the doors sighed open. Sutton ran inside, motioning for Tess to hurry.

Tess stepped inside and jammed her thumb into the door close button again and again. "Come on, damn it, close!"

The doors closed just as the crowd was closing in and then they were alone inside the elevator, just the two of them, a quiet, summery arrangement for strings playing on the overhead speakers.

"What in the hell is going on?" Sutton demanded.

Tess shook her head.

"What was wrong with them?"

"I shot that man in the head and he kept coming after us. I blew part of his head off and it barely slowed him down."

Tess's anger faded, but her body still felt like it had electricity coursing through it. Her fingers tingled with it. Her face, even her hair, seemed to have been touched with an electrical charge. Only gradually did she realize how hard she was breathing.

"We're stopping!" Sutton said.

She backed into the corner farthest from the door, and would have shrunk into the wood paneling, if she'd been able.

Tess checked the control panel. Deck 10. They still had a trek to get back to their cabin on Deck 7.

She ejected the magazine from her pistol and slapped in a fresh one.

The elevator lurched to a stop, and Tess bladed off, ready to fire.

CHAPTER 14

The San Antonio Police Department had an elite group of homicide detectives called the Shooting Team. Their charge was to investigate all incidents where a police officer uses deadly force while in the commission of his official duties. They were the best of the best, with a proven track record of thoroughness and objectivity that had won the recognition and respect of advocacy groups with radically different political agendas, from the National Council of Police Chiefs to the Texas State Bar to the ACLU. With the exception of the Bexar County Sheriff's Office, which had its own version of the Shooting Team and therefore investigated its own incidents, the SAPD team also investigated use of deadly force by all of the thirty-eight other law-enforcement agencies working within the City of San Antonio limits. That statement of purpose was written into their General Manual and Standard Operating Procedures and was, in the main, unchallenged. But

Juan's shooting at the Cavazos Meatpacking building was a special circumstance, and from the beginning there were jurisdiction pissing matches.

After the shooting, Juan was put in an unmarked HIDTA vehicle and hustled off to the fourth floor of SAPD Headquarters. They put him in one of the interview rooms and told him he was free to use the phone or his own cell phone, whatever he wished, but he knew not to use either. All the interview rooms had hidden cameras to record anything said or done inside them, and he knew that SAPD was just waiting for an excuse to take over the investigation. And giving them anything on tape would be just that excuse. As a result, he'd sat quietly, drinking a weak cup of black coffee that Detective Rowe had brought him shortly after his arrival.

But the problem wasn't SAPD. Not completely anyway. Tom Parkes of the San Antonio branch of the FBI was furious with him for what he called "showboating" and "reckless fucking police work." Parkes had been on the phone with Washington most of the morning, and early on he'd stepped in to demand investigative dibs on the shooting. Currently, he and the SAPD were at each other's throats trying to determine who would be the first to eviscerate him. Juan had placed his own call to Mr. Crouch, his point of contact in the White House, but so far the man hadn't called him back. Until he did, Juan sat patiently, drinking his weak coffee and talking to no one.

About forty minutes after being deposited in the interview room, Detective Jason Rowe appeared in the doorway. Behind him, the main floor of the

SAPD Homicide Detail was in full swing. They had a hundred and ten detectives at work out there, and the phones wouldn't stop ringing. Rowe, dressed in a red T-shirt and jeans, his shirt pulled up to reveal the gun and badge on his right hip, looked way too stressed out for someone who'd only been at work for a few hours. There were black circles under his eyes and his lips were pale and cracked. He said, "You mind if we talk?"

"Not in here," Juan said.

Rowe's gaze shifted to a light switch in the wall, where Juan assumed the hidden camera and microphone where located. "It's not on," Rowe said. "The Feds made us shut it off."

"I'm not talking in here," Juan said.

"You really don't trust me, do you? I thought we were supposed to be on the same team."

"Would you, if you were in my place?"

Rowe stared at him for a second, like a schoolteacher not sure what to do with a brilliant but disobedient child. Then, with a jerk of his head, he motioned Juan to follow him out of the room. There was an open cubicle about twenty feet away, and they stepped in there, but neither man sat down.

Rowe said, "Listen, I think what you did was pretty fucking stupid."

"Okay."

"Okay, that's it?"

"What do you want me to say?"

Rowe was getting frustrated. Juan could see it in his eyes. "You can't just go into a warehouse without a warrant and blow the place to fucking kingdom come."

"I didn't blow anything up."

"You know what I mean. Don't be smart about it."

"I thought you said I was dumb to do what I did. Which is it, dumb or smart?"

"Really? Really? You're gonna fucking joke me around? Is that really what you're gonna fucking do?"

Juan didn't take the bait. He folded his arms over his chest and waited.

"Jesus," Rowe said in disgust. "You know, when we got the orders you were assigned down here, I looked you up. Army Special Forces, classified records, the works. I know you were assigned to Bragg, but there's nothing else about you on the books. What were you, Delta Force?"

"If I was, do you think I'd answer you?"

"No, I guess not." Rowe looked out across the crowded homicide office and shook his head. "You should have waited on us to get there."

"Are you here to criticize my tactics? Is that what this is about?"

Rowe shrugged in frustration. "You're not Delta Force anymore, man. This is the real world. People get hurt out here when you don't go by the book."

Juan leaned in and whispered, "Jason, you're a smart guy. And you're former SAPD SWAT. That says a lot. I have friends in the SEALs who have competed—and lost, by the way—against you guys at the Glock SWAT Olympics. So I know you're good. But let me tell you something about the cartels. They don't play by your rules. They don't even play by their own rules. They are animals, and if you believe they hold anything sacred, anything except power that is, then you already have one foot in the grave."

They stayed that way, staring at each other, for a long moment. Then Rowe looked away.

Finally, he said, "Is it true about that video you took?"

"I don't know what you're talking about."

"Goddamn it, Juan, enough of the fucking spy stuff. Is it true or isn't? They said you fought a bunch of zombies in there."

"I told you," Juan said, sounding calmer than he felt. "The cartels don't hold anything sacred."

Before Rowe could respond Tom Parkes stepped into the cubicle. He looked, as Juan's *abuela* used to say, madder than an old wet hen.

"What the fuck's going on here?" he demanded.

"I was bored," Juan said. "I needed to stretch my legs."

"We were talking about the SWAT Olympics," Rowe said.

"Oh, yeah?"

"Yeah," Rowe said.

"Great," Parkes answered. "Get the fuck out."

He stood aside so Rowe could leave. Rowe glanced at Juan, and in that look Juan sensed that Rowe was beginning to understand how serious all of this was. Rowe nodded, and left without another word.

Parkes watched him go, then turned on Juan. "What the fuck, man? You got a lot of nerve playing cowboy in my fucking city. You know that? Where the fuck do you get off?"

Parkes paused, waiting for a reply.

Juan didn't give it to him.

"You've got nothing to say for yourself? Nothing

at all? You know when you came here and asked for my help, I gave it to you. You know why? Because we're supposed to be on the same fucking team. That means you keep me informed about what you're doing and where you're going. You can't even show me that basic courtesy. Well, you've pissed off the wrong guy. I'm gonna fucking hang you out to dry on this. I mean it."

Juan stared up at Parkes without speaking, without blinking. Juan knew guys like Parkes well enough. Clean cut, built tall and lean like an Olympic swimmer, lantern jaw, the whole nine yards. Typical Marine turned FBI. Men like Parkes were good, solid cops, but they were American cops, and the violence with which the cartels conducted their operations was far and away outside their experience. Juan had faced those devils down, and after some of the shit he'd seen in Ciudad Juarez, and Nuevo Laredo, and Guatemala, and Columbia, getting stared down by a six-foot-two ex-Marine was not much of a threat.

Parkes, for his part, seemed surprised his height advantage didn't have more of an effect. Clearly, he was used to dominating other men. The fact that Juan simply stared at him, waiting for him to speak or get out, apparently unnerved him a little, for Juan saw the man's Adam's apple bob up and down.

Finally, Juan said, "Tom, I take my orders from the president, and those orders include gathering information any way I can. Your orders are to help me, not handle me. Is that clear?"

Parkes's face flushed with anger, but he knew where he stood in the grand scheme of things. He didn't like it one little bit, but he understood.

"Yeah, crystal," he said.

Juan let the hard edge come off his stare, and when he spoke again, his voice was quiet and relaxed. The point had been made, and Parkes had his say to save face. No sense in beating the guy up any more than was necessary.

"Did you find out anything about the missing truck?" Juan asked.

"Yeah," Parkes said. "I just got off the phone with a guy in the DEA. They found it in Galveston. Just outside the cruise ship terminals. It was abandoned."

"Abandoned? What about the cargo?"

"It's the truck all right," Parkes said. "They matched up registration. It was empty. No barrels or anything."

"Please tell they did a full scrub down of it."

"Of course, they did. Once we told them what we are dealing with, they brought in a CDC team. They won't have the official results for a few days, but right now it looks like the truck tested positive for the bacteria."

There was a chair to his left and Juan fell down into it heavily.

"What's going on, Juan? I'm sick of being in the fucking dark."

"I need my phone," Juan said.

"Your phone?"

"It's in the interview room."

"Oh. Oh, okay, sure."

Parkes went and got his phone and brought it back to him. Juan started dialing Tess's number.

"Who are you calling?"

"A friend," Juan said.

The call went immediately to voice mail.

Juan tried again, but got the same result.

"Crap," he said, and put the phone down on the desk in front of him.

"What is it?" Parkes asked. "Nobody's given us any information on this bacteria. What are we dealing with here, Juan? How bad is this?"

Before Juan could answer, Rowe appeared in the doorway to the cubicle. He had his cell phone in his hand.

"Hey, Juan, I need a word."

"We're busy," Parkes said.

"Fuck off," Rowe said, obviously enjoying the chance to stick it to Parkes. "Juan, they're saying it's the White House."

He held the phone out to Juan.

Juan took it from him and said, "Where can I go? I need to take this privately."

"Uh, sure," Rowe said. "Out in the hall, I guess."

"Thanks." Juan put the phone to his ear and said, "Mr. Crouch? Just a second, sir. Let me get to a private area."

Juan walked past the interview room, past the main lobby of the homicide office, where the lieutenant in charge of the unit was talking with an SAPD deputy chief, and out into the hall.

A pair of uniformed SAPD patrolman recognized him and tried to stop him.

"Sir," the older of the two men said, putting his palm up to Juan like a traffic cop. "You need to go back inside."

"Get out of the way," Juan said. He stared at the cop, not looking away, not saying anything more.

The younger of the two cops stepped forward. He

was in his mid-twenties, about Juan's height, with his uniform tailored to show off his biceps. Juan didn't give him a second look. He was the typical tough Hispanic kid the West Side of San Antonio produced in such profusion. They made good cops, but the kid was out of his league here.

Behind Juan, the SAPD lieutenant and the deputy chief stepped into the hallway. And behind them came Tom Parkes.

Parkes whispered something in the lieutenant's ear and the man said, "Let him go."

Reluctantly, the uniforms stood aside.

"I need the hallway cleared," Juan said.

There was a moment's hesitation, but then the lieutenant told everyone to clear out.

Parkes shot him an indignant look, but Juan turned his back on him.

When the hallway was clear, Juan put the phone to his ear and said, "Go ahead, Mr. Crouch."

"Why did you ask me to look into Ms. Monica Rivas's background?"

"Because of the picture I showed you."

"That's it?"

"Yes."

There was a moment's hesitation before Mr. Crouch spoke again. "Well, your instincts are good."

"Tell me."

"According to her passport records she left for San Antonio three days ago. We have no records of her movements since then, but I've had her apartment searched."

Juan figured he knew what that meant. If Crouch was moving pieces around the game board, that meant the NSA was involved, the National Security Agency, the experts on international intelligence and counterintelligence.

Juan knew enough not to speak, and just wait for the information.

"We have her official bio, the one your agency supplied after the attempted assassination on Senator Sutton. While it is true that she did go to Harvard, most of the rest of her bio appears to be false."

"Do you know who she really is?"

"You mean is she the girl in the photo? Yeah, it looks like she is. Facial recognition software shows a high probability. High enough for me to accept anyway. But we still don't know who she is."

"But it's logical that she's part of the Porra Cartel, right?"

There was a pause, and then Mr. Crouch said, "Yes, that sounds reasonable."

"The FBI just told me they found one of the trucks I'm looking for at the Cruise Ship Terminals in Galveston."

"Yes, I know about that."

"I think they're connected."

"To Senator Sutton? You've tried your contact on-board ship, I suppose?"

"I have. I haven't been able to reach her."

"I see. What do you want to do?"

Juan thought about it. The logical thing was to get to Galveston and look at it firsthand. That was the cop thing to do, to put all the pieces in place before taking action. But the operator in him had a different hunch.

"Can you get me on that ship?"

"Stand by."

Juan said nothing. He held the phone to his ear and waited. The man Juan knew simply as Mr. Crouch had a reach far beyond that of a normal White House staffer. Even with his Delta Force contacts, and his contacts working undercover in Mexico, there were limits to Juan's intel. But Mr. Crouch, who seemed to have direct access to the president, could go anywhere, hear anything, see all. He was the proverbial fly on the wall.

And so much more.

After a long wait, several minutes at least, Mr. Crouch came back on the phone. He said, "We can't raise the *Gulf Queen*. She's not answering on any of the regular channels."

"I need to be out there, sir. Can you get me on that ship?"

"You need intel first. I'm ordering a Predator drone to recon the vessel right now. Give this phone to the ranking SAPD officer you see."

"Yes, sir." Juan went back inside the homicide office. A dozen cops stopped what they were doing and looked at him, hostile glares everywhere he turned. He saw the deputy chief that had been with the homicide lieutenant earlier and handed him the phone.

The man listened without speaking.

Then he hung up the phone.

He called one of the uniformed cops over and pointed at Juan. "You get him to Lackland Air Force Base as fast as you can, you understand? Code Three."

The young officer, the same one that had been so eager to fight earlier, looked confused. "Sir, I . . ."

"You put him in your car and you run lights and

sirens all the way out to Lackland Air Force Base. You don't stop, you don't wait, you don't do nothing. You just get him there. Base security is under orders to guide you right to the runway. Understand?"

"Yes, sir," the officer said, clearly stunned.

The deputy chief turned to Juan and said, "I'm told there's going to be a T-38 standing by to take you where you need to go. I don't know who the hell you are, son, but apparently you've got some friends in mighty high places."

CHAPTER 15

Pilar was frustrated.

Frowning, she looked around the empty bridge. It was a narrow room some forty feet long, curved like a bow, just wide enough for the officers' chairs and some foot traffic. She'd had a crash course in operating the ship's various systems, and she'd already examined those and satisfied herself that all the automated systems were working perfectly. A ship like the *Gulf Queen* could cruise around the world on autopilot, so there was really nothing for her to do there. All she had to do was watch the security monitors outside Senator Sutton's door and wait for some indication she was dead.

Which was why she was frustrated.

For twenty minutes now she'd been watching the corridor, and so far nothing. The door was propped open, as were most of the doors on the ship by now, but so far nobody had stirred in the senator's room.

Someone was in there though. She could hear

them moving around through the bug planted in the room.

Maybe they had turned already and just hadn't figured out how to get out of the room. Some of the zombies were like that, stupid and docile. Frowning again, she figured she had no other choice but to go down there and see for herself. And that wasn't going to be easy.

She picked up her pistol from the engineering console and left the bridge. There was a service stairwell on the far side of the bridge, but she'd already checked that out and there were zombies trapped on the next flight down and she didn't want to have to face them if she could help it.

She went back the way she'd come, passing the room where she'd shot that little boy. There were scratching noises coming from in there, but she wasn't going to let herself get sentimental and go have a look. It'd been a stupid decision for her to go in there in the first place. She was smarter than that.

It was all the damn kids she'd seen, she decided. That was it. That was why she was tearing herself up inside. Going into this, she'd known there'd be children onboard. She'd known they were all going to die. She'd known that, academically.

The trouble was she hadn't internalized it.

That didn't happen until she came on board and saw them in their little dresses and suits, walking hand in hand with their parents. She'd once given orders for a group of seven men to be killed, and then watched without so much as a grimace as they were held down and their heads cut off with a chainsaw. Their pleas, their screams, the sucking sounds their throats made when a cut went badly—none of that had bothered her in the least. But children—oh, God! If there was a hell, no amount of prayer could keep her from it now.

Her, or Ramon Medina.

Time to go, she told herself. She could drive herself nuts like this.

She made her way to the stairwell, but stopped before going down. The stairs were of the switchback variety and she could see several landings below her. Two floors down a man in a T-shirt and bathing suit was looking up at her, his eyes locked on hers.

Her grip tightened on her weapon.

The man lunged up the stairs. More followed after him. Pilar couldn't tell how many, but it sounded like a lot.

She tensed, her pistol raised, waiting for them to round the stairs.

Their shadows bobbed on the walls. The stairwell started to shake. Echoes of their pounding footsteps resounded off the walls.

She took a breath and tried to steady the weapon. The first few were already coming into view, and that's when the first pangs of doubt swept over her. There had to be thirty or forty of them coming for her. The odds of landing a headshot on each one were astronomical. With a rifle, maybe, but never with a handgun. And even a headshot was no guarantee. Some of them took three, even four solid headshots before they went down.

But they were still coming, and they were close now.

"No, screw this," she said.

She lowered her weapon and ran back to the hallway outside the bridge. There she stopped. This was stupid. She couldn't go forward, couldn't go back. She was stuck.

Behind her, a zombie rounded the corner, then three more, five, nine. Pilar stared at the lead zombie. His hair still looked normal, like he'd just combed it. But his mouth was smeared with blood and his teeth were broken. His shirt was torn open at the neck and his chest was black with dried blood. There wasn't a hint of the man he used to be in his eyes, no humanity whatsoever. With that awful, empty look in his eyes, he ran for her. She squared her shoulders, raised her pistol and blew the top of his head off.

The zombie stumbled, sagged to his knees, but didn't fall. He looked up at her, half his face missing now, and his mouth moved like he was trying to chew up the distance between them. Three other zombies pushed him down, rolling him into the wall like a big wave does a poor swimmer. That was all she needed to see. She didn't stand a chance out here. Certainly not armed with only a pistol.

Which meant there was only one place left for her to go.

She turned and looked at the room where she had shot the little boy.

Karma is a brutal bitch, she told herself, and stepped into the room.

She closed and locked the door behind her, then closed her eyes and tried to pull herself together. This was going to be hard. Bodies hit the door behind her, causing her to flinch. She closed her eyes again and thought of what she had to do to stay alive. That had always been her strength, surviving.

But when she opened her eyes what she saw took her breath away. The little boy was crawling across the floor, pulling himself along on broken fingernails.

Pilar tried not to look at him as she made her way to the balcony and pulled the drapes apart, but something crashed behind her and she wheeled about.

The little boy had pulled a flower vase down from a side table. He was trying to climb over the table to reach her, and watching him, Pilar felt her stomach turn.

"Go away," she begged him.

The only response he could manage was to slap the floor.

The pounding on the door was growing louder. She looked from the door to the little boy, raised her pistol at what was left of his face, but couldn't bring herself to pull the trigger. Not again.

"I'm sorry," she said. "I guess I'll always let you down. I guess that's my fate."

She went out to the balcony and looked over the edge. Four stories below was the deck of a restaurant. In between, was a sloping wall of black windows. The angle was steep, but doable.

Behind her the door burst open, and Pilar went over the side.

She slid down the windows and dropped onto the restaurant deck. Two older women screamed and stumbled over each other to get out of the way, then stopped, holding each other, as they stared at the gun in her hand.

She ignored them. There was a door at the front of the restaurant, and Pilar headed for it.

"Don't go out there," a man said.

Pilar ignored him, too. The few people hiding there moved in her direction, all of them muttering for her to stay away from the door. They'd piled deck chairs up against it and run a broom through the handles to brace it closed.

"Hey," a man said as she started pulling chairs out of her way. "Hey, don't do that!"

He made a move to stop her, but froze in his tracks when she stuck her pistol in his face.

"Who are you?" he asked.

Pilar pulled the last of the chairs away.

"Where are you going?" the man said.

Another woman came forward. "Aren't you going to help us?"

Pilar threw the broom out of the way and pulled the door open. Milling around on the deck beyond were four zombies. They all stopped and looked at her.

"No," she said to the woman. "You're on your own."

"But you have a gun," the man said. "We could die here if you don't help us."

"Then you'll die." She pointed at the broom. "Better put that back when I'm gone."

Then she stepped through the door and started shooting.

Thirty minutes later, she was standing at a railing overlooking the mall. Earlier, when Paul had surprised her down on the ground level, the place had been deserted. It was anything but now. Zombies crowded nearly every inch of it.

She leaned on the railing and studied the crowd. There were four, maybe five hundred zombies down there and they made her think of Ramon. His vision had done this. His mad, horrible, beautiful vision had done this, and she marveled at the man. From a two-bit drug dealer working the back alleys of Ciudad Juarez he had made himself the most dangerous man in the world. He had raised the dead, and with them, now possessed the power to bring the Americans to their knees. He truly was the lord of chaos.

But the senator was still a problem that needed solving. She'd hoped to see her on the video feed, but that hadn't happened. She still thought it might, though, and so she'd pushed the ship's security cameras to her iPhone. Ramon wanted proof she was dead, and pictures if possible, so he could exploit them later in the media. Capturing Senator Sutton as a zombie on the monitors would be the absolute best-case scenario. And it might still happen. The bug she'd planted in the senator's room was still delivering audio to her phone, and she could hear the noises of someone inside the cabin bumping into things and staggering around. All they had to do was step into the hallway so the video cameras could pick them up.

She heard a noise behind her and turned. At the far end of the hall stood a woman in a black dinner dress. She spotted Pilar and staggered forward on bloody legs and broken ankles.

Pilar was about to shoot her when she heard shots from somewhere down below. She leaned over the railing, scanning the other levels until she saw a muzzle flash.

It was the lady Secret Service agent.

And she had the senator with her.

They were on the level right above the mall's main floor, and the agent was doing a pretty respectable job of holding off the crowd that had gathered around them.

"That's not good," Pilar said. Not only had the senator survived, but now she had armed protection; and from the looks of things her protection knew what she was doing. She was making consistent headshots, so she was obviously cool under pressure. That was going to be a problem.

But first she had to deal with the zombie in the black dinner dress.

It was getting close. It'd be an easy kill for Pilar. At this distance, with a handgun, she could put a bullet in both eyes, guaranteed to knock the thing down and keep it down.

But firing at the zombie would be stupid right now. It would give her away, just as the lady Secret Service agent had given herself away. Right now Pilar had the advantage of surprise working for her, and she intended to get all she could from it.

As the zombie limped into range, Pilar did a spinning back kick, her heel catching the woman in the solar plexus and knocking her back against the railing. Before the zombie could straighten up for another attack, Pilar rotated ninety degrees, hopped slightly so that her body coiled like a spring, and then released that energy through a side kick. The blade of her right foot caught the zombie in the throat and sent her sailing backwards over the railing, falling down four stories to the main floor below.

Pilar watched it go over the edge, then scanned left, and scanned right.

Nothing.

She was alone up here.

Good, she thought, because it was time to move.

The way she figured it, the senator and the agent would have to make their way up here to Deck 9 or 10 in order to cross over to their cabins. That gave her a few minutes head start. They'd be heading back to their cabin, Pilar figured, because the lady agent would want to lock her charge up in a secure area. That was fine, because when they got there, they were going to find a little surprise waiting for them.

Ten minutes later, winded from sprinting most of the way, Pilar was standing in the hallway outside the senator's cabin. The senator's husband, the drunk, was standing in the middle of the room, swaying badly. He looked drunk still, but he was never going to taste alcohol again. He was covered in bloody vomit, his face gray like ash, but there was no aggression to him. He was one of the empty ones, the ones too addled to be aggressive. He just stood there swaying, looking at her blankly. He had knocked over some of the furniture, but other than that he looked completely harmless.

Pilar had expected to find a zombie in the cabin. Something had to be causing the dull thuds she'd heard on the audio. A pity it was this jerk, though. But it served him right. Any man who put a woman through the kind of hell he'd dished out for Rachel

Sutton deserved a little misery, even if it was of the post-mortem variety.

"Too bad it has to end," she said, and shot him in the face.

She stood over him, her gun trained on his head, waiting for him to move, but he didn't. He was truly and finally dead.

She holstered her weapon, and got ready for the senator and the agent to come back. She couldn't help but wonder though what kind of zombie Ramon Medina would make.

CHAPTER 16

SAPD Officer Manuel Garza led Juan out to the parking garage and pointed at a patrol car. "That's mine," he said.

Juan went to the front passenger door, but the cop stopped him.

"No," he said. "You ride in the back."

Garza gave him a challenging look, but Juan only shrugged and got in the back. It wasn't worth making an issue of it.

The officer had the car going before Juan even had a chance to find his seat belt. As soon as they cleared the parking garage, the officer hit his lights and sirens and smoked up the tires getting them through downtown traffic. He took a corner hard, throwing Juan into the door and then grinning into the rearview mirror.

"Sorry about that," he said.

"No problem," Juan answered, still holding on to his patience, but only just.

The officer got them to US Highway 90 West and picked up speed. They shot by the other cars on the freeway, the police car heaving like a ship at sea over the uneven surface of the road. At one point, Juan glanced at the speedometer to see the car was topping 120 miles per hour, very close to the Crown Victoria's top speed. He almost said something, but Officer Garza was showing off. Anything he did say would only encourage Garza more.

Garza's attitude changed though when they turned into the main gates at Lackland Air Force Base. Traffic trying to enter the base had been directed to the curb. Armed Security Forces police were manning the gates with a fleet of police cars standing by and at least thirty soldiers with rifles flanking the gates.

"Whoa," Garza said. "Is all this really for you?"

"Looks like it," Juan said.

A Security Forces E7 with a rifle flagged them down. Officer Garza lowered his window and the airman leaned in, checking the backseat.

"Are you Special Agent Juan Perez?"

"I am."

The airman spoke into his radio and then gestured to Officer Garza. "Follow those cars there."

Their escort led them directly to the flight line, where a dozen F-16s waited in a silent row. "Oh, that is so cool," Officer Garza said. "I see those things flying out of here all the time, but I've never been this close to them before. They're beautiful."

"That they are," Juan said. The patrol car's back doors wouldn't open. "Hey, you mind letting me out?"

"Huh? Oh, yeah, sorry."

Garza got out and opened Juan's door. As Juan

got out, Garza stared all around, his eyes shining with wonder.

"This is so cool," he said. He turned his attention on Juan. "Hey, listen, about earlier . . ."

"Don't mention it," Juan said. "Thanks for the ride."

An aircrew chief and a man in a pilot's G-suit came over to them. The chief handed Juan a helmet. "See if that fits, sir. It needs to be snug but not uncomfortable."

Juan tried it on and nodded.

"Excellent," the man said. "This is Lt. Colonel Decker. You'll be flying with him today."

Juan extended his hand. "Good to meet you, colonel."

"You, too, Agent Perez. Are you ready to go? My orders are to get you to Truax Field ASAP."

"Yes, sir, I'm ready."

"Outstanding." He pointed to a T-38 Talon standing by on the flight line. "That's us there."

The aircrew leader tapped Juan on the shoulder and held out a parachute. The man tried to help him with it, but Juan didn't need it. He slipped into it easily and pulled the straps down snugly with a practiced motion.

"You've worn one of those before, I see," said Decker.

"I've jumped out of a few planes in my day," Juan said.

"Well, hopefully you won't be jumping out of this one."

"Amen to that. Do I sit in the back?"

"Unless you know how to fly it, yeah. When you climb the ladder, you'll see a rail on the right side of the cockpit. You can hang your helmet on that while you get in."

Juan climbed the ladder and hopped into the backseat. The cockpit was small, but at five-foot-nine and a hundred sixty pounds, Juan had little trouble fitting into it. The crew chief helped him strap in, threading his shoulder straps, crotch straps, and parachute key onto the lap belt.

"Pull that tongue over there on your right side and click it in here," the chief said. "Good." He pointed to the pull straps hanging off of Juan's chest. "Now tighten everything down."

When he was snug in the harness, the crew chief handed him his helmet. Juan kept his hands out of the way as the man connected his oxygen hose and his communications gear. Then the crew chief tapped Juan's helmet. "You're all set," he yelled. "Thumbs up if you're good to go."

Juan stuck up both thumbs.

"Colonel Decker," the crew chief said, yelling forward. "Package is tied down."

"Roger that," Decker answered.

Juan heard him going over his preflight inspection, checking switches and whatever else he was doing up there. Then the right engine spooled up and a moment later the left. Then Decker reached up and closed the canopy. The red lights on Juan's instrument panels went out. The cockpit began to pressurize and Juan felt it in his ears, like someone was stuffing cotton in them.

The next time Juan heard Decker's voice, it was through the earphones built into his helmet. "Agent Perez, we're about to take off. This is going to be rough so hang on. If the Gs get to you, just grit your teeth and tighten your ab muscles. If you pass out, don't worry, it's only temporary."

"Great. Looking forward to it."

"That's the spirit. Okay, hang on."

Decker pointed them toward the runway, got the all clear from the tower, and let go of the brakes. A second later, a roar filled the cabin as Decker activated the afterburners and the plane lurched forward.

Riding in the police car had been unnerving. Officer Garza had deliberately thrown him around the backseat, trying to make a point. He'd brought the car up to its full speed for the same reason, and had almost succeeded in making Juan seasick.

But the police cruiser fell a good deal short of the performance envelope of the T-38 Talon, and when the plane started down the runway, Juan felt the acceleration all the way down his spine. The pressure was only the beginning though, for as soon as they lifted off the tarmac, Decker turned the airplane straight up and they took off like a rocket, the city spiraling away below them. Juan had seen pilots in Iraq and Afghanistan doing the same thing after takeoff. He'd been told it was to keep them from getting hit by surface-to-air missiles. It always looked like fun to him, from the ground. But sitting in the backseat, it was a different story. He felt his eyes rolling up into his head. He could barely breathe, and he wasn't sure if he passed out or not. It was hard to tell.

"You okay, Agent Perez?" Decker asked, and Juan figured that he must have passed out, judging from the humor in the man's voice.

"Yeah, right as rain," Juan said, a little shakily.

"Outstanding. It gets smoother from here on out."

Juan was still trying to catch his breath. Eventually, he managed to say, "Okay. That's fine."

Decker laughed. "Okay, then. Second star to the right and straight on till morning."

They touched down at the Naval Air Station in Corpus Christi less than thirty minutes later, a little after ten o'clock in the morning. It was an overcast day for Corpus Christi, but still hot, and the smells of the Gulf and the sand and the gas fumes from the airplanes were almost overpowering. They had a car waiting for him. A Navy lieutenant came up to him from the car and said, "Are you Special Agent Perez?"

"I am."

"This way, sir. Commander Sanger is waiting for you."

Juan waved at Decker, and then followed the young lieutenant to the waiting car. The installation was a sprawling complex of cracked concrete airfields broken up by palm trees and air hangars. Built in 1941 to train naval aviators, its mission had expanded over the years to include training for the Marines, Air Force, and the Coast Guard, not to mention air force pilots from allied nations around the world. As a result, the buildings they passed carried an odd assortment of affiliations ranging from Navy, Air Force, the Marines, even, Juan was glad to see, a few for the Army.

"This is us up here, sir," said the lieutenant, pointing to what appeared to be a worn-down World

War II hangar. There were no signs to indicate what was inside, just weeds around the foundation and peeling paint on the walls.

The lieutenant led Juan inside through a side door and Juan was surprised to see that much of the hangar had been converted to office cubicles. There had to be a hundred people in here at least.

"Looks like the drone program's expanded a lot since I was in," Juan said.

"When did you get out?"

"About twelve years ago."

"Yep," the lieutenant said. "The program would have been just getting started then. These days, we fly missions all around the world."

"All controlled from right here?"

"Everything in our group, yes, sir. That's about three thousand missions a year, mainly over Latin America, but we control some of the missions flying over Afghanistan and the Persian Gulf here as well. Ah, this is Commander Sanger here."

Glen Sanger was short and slight of build, with bad acne scars on his cheeks, and Juan's first impression was that he was looking at a NASA flight engineer rather than a commander in the U.S. Navy. His handshake was a limp fish and for a moment Juan thought he was going to have to wade through a bunch of nerdspeak to get the information he needed, but there was a trace of a West Texas twang in Sanger's accent. It was subdued by a college education, but still there. And he was surprisingly direct.

"Agent Perez, what kind of horror show are you running?"

"Excuse me?" Juan said.

"I'm talking about what's happening on that ship. What in the hell is going on out there?"

"I thought that's what you were supposed to tell me, commander. What have you seen?"

Sanger looked past Juan to his young lieutenant. "You didn't brief him?"

"No, sir," the lieutenant said. "I haven't said anything to him about it. I thought you'd want to do that."

Juan turned his attention back to Sanger. "Well?" he asked.

"It'd be easier to show you."

Sanger led him to a cubicle where a big biker-looking guy with graying black hair sat in front of a bank of computer monitors. The Predators had just come into play during Juan's final days in Delta Force, and he remembered watching video feed from some of the first generation Predators they'd used while supporting CIA operations in Latin America. The Predator feeds were almost always grainy and poorly focused. And there was a choppiness to them that could give you motion sickness if you stared at them too long. Those early drones were severely limited in both range and time over target. They could usually manage a four-hundred-and-fifty mile outbound journey, remain over a target for twelve to fourteen hours, and then return. Good, but not great.

He'd been told that the drones had made significant improvement since then, both in terms of the intel they returned and their time over target capabilities. The current generation of drones, from what he'd been told, could stay over a target area for upwards of forty hours, and that after making an outbound trip of seven hundred and fifty miles or more. And from what he was seeing on the monitors, there was no doubt the quality of intel had improved even more than he'd been led to believe.

He leaned forward, studying the screen.

What he saw was an immense cruise ship, dead in the water, leaking smoke from half a dozen places along its length. He could see a few shapes moving along the deck, but couldn't make them out.

He pointed to one of the forms. "Can you get me a close-up of that?" he asked.

"Sure," the biker guy said.

The feed zoomed in on the figure. "Oh, God," Juan said. The man in the center of the monitor was hobbling down the deck on a leg that looked like it had been stripped of the flesh down to the bone. Juan could barely tell the color of the man's clothes because they were so stained with blood. But his face was what surprised Juan the most. There was no emotion there, no pain. He just trundled on down the deck, oblivious to the world, and even to his own misery.

"What in the hell is going on?" Commander Sanger asked. "You tell me, Agent Perez, what the hell is that?"

"Something you'll wish you'd never seen," Juan said.

He pulled out his cell phone and dialed the number that put him through to Mr. Crouch.

After two rings, it was picked up.

"Mr. Crouch, this is Agent Perez."

"Go ahead."

"I'm watching the drone feed now. The ship is infected, sir."

"Okay, stand by."

Juan stood there, watching the burning wreck of the *Gulf Queen* and the living dead wandering her decks for four minutes. No one in the room spoke. They all stood staring at Juan, waiting, hoping to hear what was being said on the other end of the phone.

After almost four minutes, Mr. Crouch returned.

"I've arranged with SOCOM to send a detail your way. We have a Delta Force unit working on an oil rig hostage recapture drill out at Hurlburt Air Base. I'm diverting them your way."

"Yes, sir. Thank you, sir."

There was a weighty pause before Mr. Crouch answered.

"Listen, Juan . . ."

The change of tone in Mr. Crouch's voice made Juan take notice. The sudden familiarity had an ominous ring to it.

"Yes, sir?"

"I want you to know my recommendation was to blow that ship out of the water. We can't afford the infection that's onboard that ship to reach a civilian population."

"Yes, sir," Juan answered, nearly choking on his reply. He was thinking about Tess. He couldn't stop thinking about her, how she'd been so eager to impress him that she'd jumped on this assignment.

"But I've got my orders," Mr. Crouch went on. "You've got your team. You extract Senator Sutton and any other of our people you can, and then abandon that ship. Thirty minutes after you board her, I'm going to send in a pair of F-15s to make sure that ship never sees port again. Thirty minutes. No more, no less. And I won't call off the birds for any reason."

"I understand, sir."

"Good luck, Agent Perez."

Juan started to respond, but Mr. Crouch had already hung up.

CHAPTER 17

Paul was still running on fear, blind with adrenaline, when he stumbled onto the Lido Deck. The blinding sun and the hot wind off the ocean hit him in the face like a slap, and all at once the reckless panic that had driven him to run for his life left him and only the cold, jittery numbness of shock remained.

He turned, scanning the deck.

A few pieces of trash, cocktail napkins and Styrofoam cups and bits of bloody clothing, had been blown by the wind against walls and chaise longues. Some of it floated in the pool. But aside from the trash, the deck was empty and relatively undisturbed. Row after row of chaise longues stood in orderly, undisturbed rows, like soldiers on parade. All the bar stools were neatly tucked up against the bar. Everything looked normal. Or close to it. That surprised him. After what he'd seen below, he figured destruction would be general all over the ship. At the very least, he thought passengers would have assembled up here in the hopes of signaling for help.

But he was alone.

He turned toward the green-blue sea and realized they were dead in the water. The sea was glassy; the sky calm with only a few tattered gray clouds high in the atmosphere. It was a beautiful day, and it was completely at odds with what he'd just experienced. Shouldn't the horizon be crowded with battleships and hospital ships on the way to help? Shouldn't the sky be smeared a coal black by smoke? He remembered the images he saw of that Italian cruise ship that had crashed and partially capsized, the way it had listed in the water and the way other ships surrounded it like lions on a fresh kill. Weren't disasters like this supposed to bring every available ship to help out? Wasn't that some kind of sailor's code or something?

Confused and frustrated by his own mounting feelings of helplessness, he turned away. Not knowing what else to do, he took his phone from his pocket and tried to call Senator Sutton. At the least he could tell her to get Tess and stay in her cabin with the door locked.

But the phone wasn't working. It wouldn't connect. He tried the e-mail and all he could get was the old stuff he'd already read. There were no new messages.

The Internet was down, too.

He was scrolling through apps randomly, desperately begging the phone to work, when a commotion on the opposite side of the pool caught his attention.

A veranda cast a shadow over the chaise longues and the bar and part of the pool and he leaned forward, straining his eyes against the dark.

Something was moving in the darkness over there, and while he couldn't make it out, he knew he didn't want to face it.

Paul ducked into a bar and knelt down out of sight.

A woman ran out of the shadows, obviously terrified, stumbling over chairs, nearly tripping headlong into a column next to the pool. She was panting, breathing hard, looking behind her every few seconds like hell itself was on her heels.

"What are you doing?" he muttered. "Run, lady. Get up and run."

She pulled herself up on the post and started around the pool, coming Paul's way.

"Oh, no," he said. "No, no, no. Stay over there."

But she kept coming. She was almost directly in front of his hiding spot now, less than ten feet from him, when a crowd of zombies ran out of the shadows, searching for her.

She saw them coming and sagged to the deck, her sweaty hair hanging over her face.

"Run," Paul said. "Please don't give up. Run."

But she was in a place his words couldn't reach. She was beyond exhaustion.

Paul stood up, and almost called out to her. He wanted to, but his fear was crippling. His mouth went dry. When he tried to speak, his throat felt tight, like he was choking. In the end he lost all his nerve and sank back into the shadows behind the bar, trembling and ashamed.

The zombies were coming around both sides of the pool. Some of them running, others hobbling along on busted legs, but they came on fast, and soon the woman's whimpers turned to screams.

"Help me!" she yelled. "Oh, God, please help me!"

The first few zombies to reach her fell on her, clawing at her face and arms.

She wasn't forming words anymore, just guttural screams and grunts, each one making Paul flinch. He hated himself for being such a coward.

Once, he mustered the strength to open his eyes.

He wasn't sure if she could see him or not, but she was staring right at him, her gaze locked even as her body jerked and danced from the zombies pulling on her.

Paul squeezed his eyes shut and clapped his hands over his ears.

It didn't do any good. He could still hear them tearing her to pieces.

Paul stayed behind the bar, arms wrapped around his knees, huddled as small as he could make himself, rocking back and forth and trembling, for several hours. The sun was almost directly overhead when he finally stood up and took in what had happened. The woman he'd been too scared to help was pawing at the wooden deck. She was trying to move, but there wasn't enough of her left to do it.

How could she still be alive? Her torso had nearly been torn in half. There was blood everywhere . . . on the deck, the chairs, the edge of the pool. It was everywhere. Her guts were spread out behind her like a spilled bag of yarn. And even still, she was moving.

Paul let out a gasp of disgust, and the woman turned her head his way. He turned his head almost immediately. The woman's face was pale and spattered with blood. The lower jaw was nearly gone. From her upper lip down to her collarbone she was one continuous open wound, little jagged bits of skin hanging on the edges like crudely torn paper.

When he looked back, she was trying to crawl in his direction. Her eyes showed no pain whatsoever, only a vacant, bottomless yearning, and every inch she slid through her own blood, every snap of breaking fingernails was an indictment of his cowardice. He could have saved her. He could have. He was sure of that. If only he'd been able to make himself move, or at least call out to her, he could have hid her with him. She'd still be alive.

My God, he thought. *That's it. They're dead. They're zombies!*

It was the only thing that made sense.

And the fact that that made sense made no sense at all.

He felt his stomach starting to turn. Bile rose up in his throat and he forced it down, but that made him feel worse.

He had to get out of there. Not just to be away from the wreck of a woman still clawing her way across the floor, but because of this new thing, this idea that the world had become so messed up, so very wrong, that it could have zombies in it.

With his mind reeling, he stumbled out of the bar and back below decks.

* * *

He had to find Tess Compton. Had to. The truth of that was solid in his mind. It was, perhaps, the one solid thing upon which he could focus. She alone had the guns, the training. She alone could save him.

And Senator Sutton would be there, too. He felt certain of that. Tess could protect him, and Rachel Sutton could tell him what to do.

That was what he wanted, he realized, someone to take charge, to tell him what to do. He was alone out here, exposed, forced to rely on his own resources, and that scared him even worse than what those deranged people up on deck had become. Even more than what that half-eaten woman had become.

Staying in the shadows whenever possible, he made his way aft, and down. He was on Deck 8, three levels up from the main level of the mall, when he heard the unmistakable rattle of gunfire.

He ran to the railing and looked down.

And gasped.

The main level of the mall was a writhing carpet of bloody faces and mangled hands. There had to be hundreds of those zombies down there, all of them packed together and pushing, fighting against each other. The sweet-sick stench of vacated bowels and blood rising from the knots of the dead made him gag. It almost made him forget about the gunshots he'd heard.

But then he heard two more shots, and saw movement near the stairs, on the level just above the mall's main floor.

He was about to call out to them, but movement above and to his right caught his eye.

It was Monica!

"My God," he said. "It can't be. . . ."

She was holding a pistol. Where in the hell had she found a pistol?

She was looking away from the railing, toward the stairs on her level. He followed her gaze and saw a zombie in a black cocktail dress hobbling toward her on broken legs. Monica didn't seem surprised though, or even worried. She kept her pistol down by her side and waited for the zombie to close the gap between them; and when it looked like the zombie was too close, easily within striking distance, Monica spun around in the air like in those kung fu movies and kicked the zombie in the chest, knocking her back against the railing.

The zombie never had a chance to react, for the next moment Monica side-stepped into another kick that caught the zombie under the chin and sent it flying backwards over the railing.

Paul watched it sail down to the writhing horde below, and his face twisted with disgust as the zombies fell upon one of their own, tearing the body to shreds.

But when he looked back at the next level up, Monica was gone.

He looked everywhere.

"Where did . . . ?"

He looked down again, trying to find Senator Sutton and Tess, but they were gone, too.

"Senator Sutton?" he yelled. "Tess?"

He instantly regretted it.

The horde below suddenly went still, and as one turned their faces in his direction. Their faintly luminescent eyes shone like stars in the summer sky.

A few started to run up the stairs, coming his way.

"Oh, no," he said. "No, no, no."

He turned toward the stairwell on the opposite side of the landing. He took a few steps that way and then stopped. Paul could hear footsteps, and lots of them, charging up the stairs.

And something else, too.

Guttural panting and growls.

"Oh, no, oh, no." *What do I do?* "Come on, come on. Think."

Already some of the faster zombies were on the level right below him. If he was going to make a break, it had to be now.

Right now.

He broke into a sprint, running for the open corridor that continued on to the left of the stairwell. Paul was thirty yards from the mouth of the corridor when two zombies started up the last flight of stairs.

"No!" he said. He was panting, barely able to breathe. "No. Not gonna make it, not gonna make it."

But he knew he had to. He had to clear those stairs or he would die here, torn to pieces like that woman up at the pool.

"Not gonna get me!" he shouted, and lunged ahead.

The zombies, as though in answer to his challenge, extended their hands, clutching for him.

Paul turned on the speed, running with everything he had. One zombie crested the stairs and then a second, and a third appeared behind him. They turned from the stairs to the mouth of the corridor just as Paul got there and lunged for him.

The lead zombie grabbed Paul's shoulder and spun him around. Another flew into him like football tackle, causing Paul to crash against the windows on the left side of the corridor. Paul, two of the zombies, and the heavy gold curtains on the windows all came tumbling down.

Paul landed on one of the zombies, his knee coming down hard on the man's back. It was a lucky landing, for it allowed him to stay upright. He slapped the curtain away from his face and scrambled forward, breaking contact from his attackers just as more zombies charged off the stairs.

Screaming, running for his life, Paul took off down the corridor. His lungs were burning. His heart was pounding. The muscles in his legs were on fire. His body was screaming at him to stop, to just quit, but he didn't dare.

He glanced over his shoulder and saw the corridor behind him was crowded with zombies, all of them running after him. Desperate, lost, hardly able to breathe, he rounded a corner and nearly tripped over a man sitting in a puddle of his own blood and vomit. Paul jumped over the man's nearly severed legs, ducked his shoulder, and rammed a woman who was reaching for him with a badly damaged hand.

He didn't let her slow him down. The lead zombies were pawing his back, pulling at his shirt. Even over the growls of his pursuers he could hear his Birkenstocks slapping on the floor. He seemed to be standing still, like he was caught in a dream where he pumped his legs harder and harder but never moved.

Just ahead of him was a housekeeping cart. He

reached it just ahead of his pursuers and pulled it
down. Those right behind him went tumbling forward, hitting the ground hard. The zombies were
fast, some of them anyway, but they were still unco-
ordinated and when they went down it was hard for
them to get up again. The first few to fall were still
trying to climb to their knees when those behind
them trampled them.

But even more were coming now. He could see
their eyes glowing in the dark of the corridor.

At the opposite end was a large open area. It was
poorly lit, but from what he'd seen of the ship so far
he knew areas like that tended to open onto other
areas, which might provide a way out. If he got there
far enough ahead of his pursuers maybe he could
find a place to hide. It was a slim chance but the
only one he had.

He ducked his head and ran, ignoring the pain.

When he reached the end of the corridor he
chanced a look back. He'd put a good amount of distance on his pursuers. But he wasn't sure it'd help
him. He had just entered the lobby of the ship's
theater. There was a bar directly in front of him,
done up in blue plastic and brightly polished steel,
and beside that a set of glass doors marked simply:
ENTRANCE.

But to the right of the bar was a curved hallway. A
small sign on the door read: RESTROOMS.

And he noticed something else.

The smell of the sea.

An exterior access, he thought. A way out.

He ran for it, passing the restrooms and stopping
at a fork in the hallway. Straight ahead was a stairwell leading down to the stage access. To the right

was the exterior access he'd hoped to find. He could see a small section of the deck and railing, the sea beyond it dappled in mid-morning sunlight. Paul was about to run for the outside when he saw a man hobbling into view on a leg that appeared to have been nearly denuded of flesh and muscle. Nothing but bone and a few sodden clumps of flesh and tendons clinging to the bones remained.

The man stopped, turned, and stared at him for just a moment before coming after him.

Behind Paul, the zombies that had chased him down the hall were entering the theater's lobby.

He was all out of options.

Paul ran down the stairs, praying to God with every step that he wouldn't run into the waiting arms of some zombie hiding down here in the dark. And then, all at once, faster than he was really ready for, he emerged into a room full of mannequins and outfits on hanging racks and props of all sorts and sizes.

The prop room, he thought. It was crowded with stuff, lots of nooks and crannies. Not a bad place to hide.

Paul ducked behind a rack of baseball bats, all of them marked by a sign that read: COBB PERFORMERS ONLY. He didn't dare try to close the door. The zombies were out there, and they were looking for him. If he tried to close the door, the movement would attract their attention and he'd be done for.

Instead, he ducked behind a mannequin dressed in a vintage Detroit Tigers uniform and slowly, silently, took down one of the wooden baseball bats and held it close.

A woman came through the door, her hair dark and matted with blood. Behind her was a man whose clothes had been stripped from his body and his torso opened up and hollowed out like the belly of a canoe. The two of them wandered through the prop room, looking for him. The man, for a moment, looked right at him before moving on.

As they moved toward the opposite side of the room, where the door was, Paul let himself breathe a little easier. They were leaving.

Until his phone went off.

Damn it! It was his twelve o'clock alert, reminding him of his regular appointment with Sutton. He pulled it out of the cargo pocket on his pants and tried to silence it, but it was too late. The zombies turned and headed right for him. They'd spotted him.

"Stay away!" he pleaded with them.

They reached for him, knocking down racks of clothes and one of the mannequins.

Outside, in the hallway, Paul could hear more zombies coming his way.

His cell phone chimed again and in his desperation he threw it at the naked man with the exposed ribs. It bounced off his face, distracting him long enough for Paul to get in front of the man and swing the bat at his head.

"Leave me the—" he said, breaking off with a grunt as the bat connected with the man's skull. There was a sickening, wet crack that Paul felt all the way up his arms, and the man sagged to the ground.

Paul stood over him, horrified, chest heaving. "Oh, my God," he said, running a hand through his hair. "Oh, my God."

But there was no time for him to take it in. The woman was already running through the racks of clothes, coming for him.

He turned the bat sideways in a port arms position and pushed it into her neck, forcing her chin up, using both hands to keep her face away from him. She tried to claw at his face, but with all the racks of clothes blocking her all she managed to do was pull a bunch of dresses to the floor.

Paul gave her a hard shove with the bat and took a step back. He saw his chance to strike and he took it. He swung for her face with everything he had, slapping the meat of the bat on her cheek with a blow that sent her teeth clattering across the floor like tumbling dice.

The woman fell back against a table, but gave no other indication that she was hurt. Her stare never wavered, never changed. She just stood up again, her mouth a bloody mess, her teeth smashed, and came at him again.

Paul raised the bat over his head and brought it down on her forehead like he was chopping wood. The blow caused her to fold. Her legs collapsed beneath her and she sank to the floor and didn't move.

But she was still looking at him. He had killed her—or had done whatever happened to these people when they stopped moving around—and the look in her eyes was still the same. Death made no difference.

He was already mentally frayed about the edges, but that vacant stare unhinged him. More of those zombies were coming in from the hallway, but he was so rattled even the threat of more fighting didn't cause him to react right away.

It wasn't until he heard them knocking about just outside the door that he moved. There was a rack of old-fashioned baseball uniforms to his right. He slipped behind them and waited, trying not to scream, as a dozen or more zombies came through the door, hunting for him.

CHAPTER 18

The elevator lurched to a stop, and Tess bladed her shoulders off in a shooter's stance, ready to fire. "Stay behind me," she said over her shoulder.

Sutton managed a thin squeak of a reply as she nodded.

Tess turned back to the door, drew in a deep breath, and waited. If she saw anything on the other side she was going to slap the close door button and take their chances on another floor. And when they did finally get off, no more elevators. She didn't like feeling this uncertain of what she was stepping into.

But then the doors slid open . . . and it looked clear.

She waited, scanning the landing, straining her hearing to the hallways beyond.

"Is it safe?" Sutton asked.

"I'll check. Hold the door open for me."

Reluctantly, Sutton put her finger on the open button.

Tess nodded to her. "It'll be okay. I'll give you the signal to step out."

Tess stepped out of the elevator, checking her left, then her right with two quick twists. Their cabins were along the port side, two floors down, and she went that way, scanning the corridors there for movement. She saw a man and woman midway down the hall that led to their cabins, but they were spread out and she felt certain she could put them both down without endangering the senator at all. She just hoped that nobody would pop out of the open cabin doors along the way.

She went back to the elevators, where Sutton waited. The poor woman looked positively ill.

"You ready to do this?" Tess asked.

Sutton nodded.

"Okay. Now there are two of those people between here and the stairs. We need to get past them and then take the stairs down to seven to your cabin. I want you to stay behind me, and I mean right behind me. Got it?"

Again, Sutton nodded.

"Good. We're going to get to your cabin, lock the door, and I'm going to try to find a way to signal for help."

"How are you going to do that? I thought you said nothing works."

"We'll keep trying. I'll burn bed sheets off the balcony like smoke signals if I have to. We'll find a way. Just make sure you stay right behind me."

"Okay."

"All right, let's go."

The two people in their corridor had spotted Tess and were already advancing on them when Tess rounded the corner. Of the two, the woman moved faster and Tess sighted in on her first.

The woman's mouth hung open, and when she raised her hands toward Tess, the fingers looked mangled. Her chest was covered in blood and what looked like bits of half-eaten food. When the woman got about ten feet away Tess fired, hitting her on the bridge of her nose. Her head snapped back and she dropped to the floor.

"Is she dead?" Sutton asked.

"I think so."

They advanced on the body uncertainly. The woman looked still enough, but after seeing that one man take a direct shot to the head and keep on going, Tess wasn't taking any chances.

Keeping herself between Sutton and the body, Tess circled around the fallen woman. She didn't move. Didn't even twitch. Tess was about to turn and shoot the man who was hobbling toward them when she saw movement in a doorway directly in front of her. It was a woman trying to reach her way around the door.

Sutton gasped, but Tess was already on it. She took a step forward and kicked the door as hard as she could. It smashed into the woman's face and sent her sprawling back into the room.

"Time to move," Tess told Sutton, and they broke into a run for Sutton's cabin.

As they neared the man, Tess opened fire, hitting him five times in the face.

He was still reaching for them even as he fell to the ground.

By the time they reached Sutton's cabin, doors were opening all down the length of the corridor.

Tess saw at least five people step into the hallway as she was struggling to get the access card into the slot on the door.

"Is it broken?" Sutton asked. "Oh, God, hurry."

"I am—"

The door lock turned green and Tess pushed the door inward, noticing several things almost at the same time.

The first was Dr. Sutton, covered in blood and dead against the foot of the bed with a gunshot wound to the back of his head.

The second was a woman standing on the far side of the bed, the same woman she'd seen holding a martini out to Paul Godwin at the Washington Hilton.

And the third thing she noticed was the gun coming up in the woman's hand.

Tess fired six shots as the woman dove to the right and rolled toward the desk. The slide on Tess's pistol locked back in the empty position and she quickly ejected her magazine and slapped in a new one, but before she could fire again, the woman leveled her sights on Tess and opened fire.

There was a burst of white light shot through with orange and gray and then Tess's world went black.

CHAPTER 19

For their briefing, the mission commander, Major Jim McBride, chose a hangar near Corpus Christi Bay, where the Chinooks they were going to fly out to the *Gulf Queen* could flare off and out to sea without attracting a lot of unwanted attention. The two teams, twenty-two men in all, were seated in folding chairs in the middle of the hangar floor, facing a big screen TV up at the front of the room. McBride stood in front of the TV. Juan stood off to the side with one of McBride's lieutenants, a much younger man who was on his second operation with Delta. In the crowd, Juan saw a few familiar faces, men like Rick Carter and Gabe Drake and Tom Hoffman, all of them E8s now. He'd been on many, many ops with those guys, and every once in a while he'd catch them smiling at him, pointing at him and cracking jokes. The rest of the guys were all E6s and E7s, a lot younger, but still with the look of seasoned operators. They wouldn't be on Delta otherwise.

Juan remembered briefings like this, right before Go Time, how focused everybody was. But at the first mention of zombies, the mood lightened. Most of the guys cracked smiles. A few made jokes. That didn't bother Juan, though. He knew they'd tighten up once the video feed started.

McBride told the room to shut up. "This is Special Agent Juan Perez of the Secret Service," he said. "For this mission, his call sign's going to be Sierra 1."

"Yeah, more like Fag 6," Drake said.

A chuckle went around the room. The ribbing was actually a backhanded compliment, and Juan was grateful for it. In the teams, FAG meant Former Action Guy. It was a term of endearment usually reserved for guys on the teams who had transitioned over to the CIA or the NSA, and it carried with it the connotation that this guy is cool, he gets it, he's one of us. It let everybody in the room know that one of their leaders considered Juan totally capable. Nobody was going to have to carry him on this mission.

McBride went on without acknowledging the interruption. "Some of you have already heard the threat on this op, and what you heard is true. If you are attacked by passengers, you are to treat them as hostiles and respond accordingly."

More chuckles went around the room.

"So this is seriously like Left 4 Dead?" one of the younger guys said. "We're going on a zombie hunt?"

Everybody laughed again. They thought it was preposterous, of course. Twenty-four hours earlier, Juan would have thought the same thing. But of course the truth was that they were going in against what could possibly be the worst biological plague the human race had ever seen. And they'd be doing it with nothing but Nomex flight suit gloves and body armor.

"I think you're gonna find this a little more intense than a first person shooter game," McBride said. "We're going to avoid contact with the compromised passengers whenever possible. If you do have to engage though, stay focused on shot discipline. Conserve your ammo and focus on head-shots."

"Yeah, but it's just zombies, right?" somebody asked. "No vampires or werewolves?"

Another wave of laughter went through the room.

McBride smiled, too, then stepped out of the way of the TV and hit play on the remote. The footage from Juan's pocket digital recorder came up first, and the room went silent. Juan watched what his pocket video camera had captured earlier that morning as he worked his way through the Cavazos Meatpacking facility. He relived it all, right up to the moment he encountered the first zombie.

That was when he turned his attention on the crowd watching the video, gauging their reaction. He saw them nod as he doubled-tapped the men in the hallway, and then nodded himself as the men watching the video leaned forward, their expressions turning to confusion when the man didn't go down.

But it wasn't until Juan shot the chunk out of the

man's head and he still kept coming that they started making noise.

"Oh, no way," one of them said.

"Holy shit," another answered.

The man on the video tottered forward, hands outstretched, and one of the younger guys laughed. "It is. It's a total fucking zombie hunt," he said.

Juan watched them slap each other on the shoulders and chatter about what was playing out on the screen, and in that moment he missed being part of the teams more than ever before. He was forty-four years old now, at the very top of his field, and yet he knew at that moment that he had never been happier than when he'd been in the teams.

The guys in Delta were treated like kings. He remembered their compound at Fort Bragg. They had it all— a full gym, two swimming pools, luxury housing. They had the finest armorers in the Army, willing and able to make any custom modifications an operator could want. They had on-call nutritionists and the Army's finest doctors and weight training coaches. They had access to more perks than a pro sports team. All they lacked were the scantily clad cheerleaders. Why anyone would walk away from that was a mystery.

Or at least it had been to the guys Juan worked with.

But it had been pretty simple, really. Juan was married at the time to the girl he'd dated most of his senior year in high school. Madison Kramer was her name, and for about six years they did okay. He'd recognized little things at first, signs they were drifting apart, and if it hadn't been for the constant deployments, being gone four months at a time, maybe they could have worked on it, gotten back to how it had been when they started out.

But of course that didn't happen. In real life, people just don't change.

At the end, he didn't even know her anymore. She was drinking a lot. He thought she was probably doing drugs, too, though he'd gone through the house and never found any. But she had the look, the weight loss, the apathy, the circles under her eyes.

He loved her, though. Truth was he was totally crazy for her. Realizing he had to quit the teams if he had any chance of saving his marriage, he did just that. He thought about joining the Marshal's Service, but a recruiter convinced him to come over to the Secret Service instead. He made it through the academy with flying colors, and Madison went to counseling. For a while, things had started to look up, but they didn't stay that way. She began to drink again. He saw the fogged-over, drugged-out look come back. He came home after a four-day trip to Philadelphia and found her sitting on the couch in her T-shirt and panties, cigarette burns on her thighs, and there wasn't a trace of the girl he'd known in her eyes.

"What the hell are you into?" he'd asked her.

But the answer didn't matter, because it was all lies at that point anyway. That was the end right there.

She said she wanted a divorce.

It crushed him, but he gave it to her.

Three years later, she was dead. Too much meth in some little town in Ohio he'd never heard of before.

And for that he'd given up his life in the teams. It

had all made sense at the time. But now, seeing his life that could have been, the logic behind the choices he'd made was hazy with regret.

But that was the past, and right now the briefing was winding down. They'd switched from his video to footage from the IRS platform, the drone circling the *Gulf Queen*. The ship was really starting to burn. It was leaking smoke all over the ocean.

McBride hit pause on the remote, and the room's attention shifted back to him. He said, "Remember: This is not a stand-up fight. If you have an option not to engage, take it. But if you do have to engage, headshots are the order of the day. And from what you saw there it may take several headshots to put one of them down." He turned to Juan. "Agent Perez, you have anything you want to add?"

"No, sir," Juan said. "You got it. Headshots if you have to, but only if you have to. The more noise we make, the more they'll come running."

"Okay," McBride said. "Anybody else?"

"Yeah, I got a question," one of the younger guys said. "What are we gonna do with that ship once we get the target out of there? I mean, if it's got all those zombies on it, who's gonna take care of that?"

McBride didn't hesitate. "We have a pair of F-15s standing by. Once we call out jackpot on the target, they're gonna sink her."

Instantly, the smiles and the joking faded and the room went quiet.

There hadn't been any instructions on rescuing other survivors, just the senator, and every man in the room knew what that meant.

"Okay," McBride said. "That's it. We'll have grid sheets for you in a few. Study the ship's layout, and memorize Senator Sutton's face. We move out in an hour."

And just like that the briefing was over.

The guys filtered away, each one to his respective ritual for getting his gear prepped for the mission. Then McBride and Rick Carter pulled Juan aside.

McBride said, "Agent Perez, Rick here figured you wouldn't have any of your own gear. Is that right?"

"I'm afraid so," Juan said. "I've got my Sig, but that's about it."

"Okay. Is that the sidearm you want to use?"

"Yes, sir."

"Fair enough. That's a good weapon. Okay, Rick, you gonna get him taken care of on his assault kit?"

Carter gave him a big smile. "Oh, yeah."

"Good. You guys make ready. We're burning daylight."

Carter hit Juan on the shoulder. "Come on," Carter said. "Brother, have I got a surprise for you."

Juan stared at him, confused for a moment, but Carter's grin was huge and it was infectious. He liked Carter a lot. In fact, of all the guys Juan had served with back in the day, he'd shared the most in common with Carter. Juan was Hispanic, born and raised in the poorest barrios of Del Rio, Texas. Carter was as white as Wonder Bread, but he'd come up from Seattle's hardscrabble Rainier Valley area, raised poor just like Juan. The two of them had come up together through the Rangers, making Delta on the same rotation, and had covered each other on a lot of missions since then. They understood each other, always had.

"What have you got?" Juan asked.

Carter led him over to one of the teams' supply vehicles and pulled down a heavy duffel bag. "Go ahead," he said. "Check it out. Papa's got a brand-new bag."

Still smiling, Juan opened it. Inside, he found a couple of sterilized Nomex flight suits. Operators never wore name or rank or even country of origin insignia on their uniforms, and these were no different.

"I didn't know if you'd gotten fat while servicing the first lady," Carter said, "so I brought you a couple different sizes."

Juan felt like a kid on Christmas morning. When the teams operated out of a regular facility, each man was assigned a walk-in locker about the size of a closet. Everything he would need for tailoring an assault kit to a specific mission was stored there. But on operations like this one, they had to bring all their gear like this, in duffel bags. Juan looked around the room and saw others laying out their gear as well, each one of them as superstitious as a baseball player about to step up to the plate.

Juan glanced back at Carter. "Go on," Carter said. "You haven't seen the good stuff yet."

He was right. The real treasures were buried deeper still in the bag. Juan pulled out two pairs of gloves, one to wear during the assault and the other a pair of heavy leather mitts for when they fast-roped down to the deck. He found a helmet and boots, a ballistic vest, a holster for his Sig, just about everything he was going to need for the operation.

And then, he saw it.

"Oh, shit," he muttered.

"Yeah, I thought you'd like that," Carter said.

Juan reached in and removed an old friend. It was the M4 with the customized ten-inch barrel that he'd used on countless raids. He didn't even need to test the five-pound trigger to know it. You spend that much quality time with a weapon, you know it immediately, even after twelve years.

He met Carter's gaze. "But . . . how?"

"It was still in the armory," Carter said. "I asked if they still had your paperwork on file and they did. The armorer had to look around for that, but he came up with it. I cleaned it myself to make it ready."

Juan let out the breath he was holding. "He sure did," he said. "Rick, thanks, man. Really, thank you for this."

"Don't mention it. Let's just hope you can still shoot straight."

CHAPTER 20

The zombies wandered through the prop room for an hour before they gave up looking for him and started to wander off. Paul stayed still the entire time, trying to keep his breathing quiet.

But standing still for that long was hard on his back. His legs were sore, too. Finally, he couldn't take it anymore and shifted his weight just a little, and when he did his knees cracked.

To Paul, it sounded like a gunshot, and he tensed every muscle in his body, bracing himself for the attack he felt certain was about to come.

But it didn't.

Thirty seconds went by. A minute.

Nothing.

Curious, he pried the uniforms apart just a crack, just enough to show a tiny slice of the room beyond.

It looked empty.

Spreading the uniforms a little more, he stuck his

head out and looked around. It was empty. The zombies had moved on.

He let out a sigh of relief and stepped out of the clothes rack. He thought about what to do, where to go. He could go back up the stairs, maybe, take his chances with the exterior access. But he didn't like that. Outside, most of the decks ran the length of the ship. That was a lot of distance, a lot of straight lines. It'd be hard to hide and easy to spot him. So that was out.

So was staying here, in the prop room. It was close in here, too close, and he was beginning to feel claustrophobic.

Besides, what he really needed to do was to find Senator Sutton and Tess Compton. That was his best bet of getting out of this madness alive.

Which meant that his only remaining option was to go through the theater and take his chances in the interior corridors. He didn't like that much, but it was the only choice that made sense.

He went through the door marked for STAGE ACCESS, crossed from backstage to the stairs at the far side of the stage and started down into the rows of empty seats. With all the lights off, there was an eerie sort of stillness about the place, and it gave Paul the creeps. He wanted to get out of there as fast as he could.

But he had only taken a few steps toward the top of the theater when he heard a woman sobbing.

He stopped in his tracks. He waited and listened.

Yes, he could definitely hear someone crying.

"Hello?" he called out.

Again he waited.

The sobbing had stopped.

"Hello?" he called out again. "Is somebody in here? I'm not one of those things. I won't hurt you."

Off to his left there was movement. He climbed a few more steps, craning his neck to see around the seats.

"Hello?"

A woman stood up. No, a girl, Paul corrected himself. Barely out of her teens.

"Are you okay?" Paul asked. "Are you hurt?"

He took a step toward her, but she quickly backed away and he stopped. She looked even more shaken than he was, and that leveled him out a bit. Made it easier to think.

He said, "My name is Paul Godwin. I'm not—I don't want to hurt you."

She was trembling, hugging her chest. Her face had a red, mottled look to it, like she'd been crying for a long time. Her hair was damp around her face and he figured that was from tears, or maybe sweat. It was hot in here. She was staring at him, not blinking at all, but he couldn't read anything in her eyes except fear.

"Are you hurt?" he asked.

She shook her head.

"What's your name?"

"Kelly."

"Kelly," Paul repeated. She was dressed in a crew outfit, he realized. Her white blouse and black slacks meant she was part of the Hospitality Staff. But maybe she knew what was going on. Maybe she knew what passengers were supposed to do. "Okay," Paul said, talking slowly, with a forced calm that he most certainly did not feel. "Good. Are you here by yourself, Kelly? Is there anyone with you?"

She nodded.

"Oh, there is? Okay, good. Um . . ." He looked around and then back at her. He shrugged.

"It's okay," Kelly said. "You guys can come out now."

Paul looked around, confused. In the low light the theater seemed very close, the air stuffy and stale. But then he caught movement out of the corner of his eye. It was a little girl, standing between the seats a few rows away. Another little girl stood up behind her, and another a few rows off. More and more of them were popping up all around him, until at last he counted twenty-three of them.

Paul's heart sank.

He looked at Kelly and said, "Children?"

She nodded. "Will you help us, please?"

Paul looked around again, all those children looking at him, waiting. Christ, he thought, kids. So many kids. And all he wanted was for someone else to take charge, to tell him what to do.

"Please," Kelly said. "Help us."

CHAPTER 21

Pilar rolled over with a groan. Gingerly, she touched her ribs where the lady agent's shot had grazed her. She winced at the pain.

Her fingers came away bloody.

It wasn't a serious wound, but it hurt like hell. It burned. She closed her eyes and ordered herself to master the pain.

"Just force it down," she told herself. "Force it down."

A few shallow breaths and she had it.

Or was close anyway.

She stood up slowly, wincing again.

The lady agent was facedown in a puddle of blood on the other side of the bed. She wasn't moving. Pilar watched her neck for signs of a pulse, however faint, and saw none.

"Good," she said. "That's one problem solved."

But the senator was gone, and that was what really mattered.

Pilar stepped around the bed and stood over the lady agent's body. She tilted her head to one side, studying the scene. Something was wrong.

The pistol, she realized. It was gone.

That was more bad news than she needed. The senator must have taken it. Definitely not good.

Not that the senator knew anything about how to use a weapon. She was one of the few politicians from Texas to talk favorably about gun control and had, on a number of occasions, mentioned that she disliked guns with a passion. But she was armed now, and even if she didn't have any experience as a shooter, that was a wrinkle that Pilar just did not need.

She knelt down to make sure the agent was dead, but before she could check for a pulse, a man bumped into the doorway. He ran for her, and Pilar barely had time to squeeze off a shot. His head snapped back, and it stopped the man's advance, but it didn't put him down. Pilar moved into the open area at the foot of the bed so she had room to maneuver. There was a jagged hole where his left eye had been, and the other eye looked sealed by dried blood, but he clearly had no trouble following her movements. He staggered forward, like his legs wouldn't work right, and then broke into a run.

Pilar sidestepped him, and the man tumbled headlong to the floor.

Before he could get up, Pilar put another round in the back of his head, spattering blood all over the floor and the curtains.

Two more zombies, both of them girls in their early teens, ran through the door. But Pilar was ready this time. She held her pistol with both hands now, arms forming an isosceles shooter's stance in front of her chest, and double-tapped them both before they'd even made it through the entryway.

The slide on her pistol locked back in the empty position, but she didn't reload. She needed to listen, to take stock of her tactical situation.

She could hear footsteps somewhere down the hall outside, lots of them, and coming her way fast. She was about to have company, drawn no doubt by the sound of gunfire.

Pilar ejected her empty magazine and reloaded with her last one. Fifteen rounds left. She was going to have to make them count.

She went to the doorway and scanned the hall. A crowd of the dead was coming her way. She could see their eyes luminescing in the dark, a by-product of the bacteria controlling their bodies.

"I'm going to need my rifle," she said.

The corridor was safe to her left, so she headed that way. First, she was going to head down to her cabin and get her MP5.

Then she was going to find Sutton and finish this once and for all.

CHAPTER 22

Paul Godwin couldn't believe his bad luck. A theater full of ten-year-olds and their babysitter, who wasn't that much older, and all of them were looking at him, waiting for him to tell them what to do.

He let out a long, slow breath.

A few of the children were sobbing quietly.

Others just stared at him with glassy, vague looks on their faces. Shock, he figured. Of course, it wasn't like they didn't have good cause to be in shock. He had been there himself just a few minutes earlier.

"What are we going to do?" Kelly said.

He focused his attention on her. She was cute, with short brown hair and an oval face and a little nose that turned up just slightly at the end. A little mousey looking, but cute. She wasn't hugging herself anymore. She'd relaxed her arms a little. They were still crossed defensively under her breasts though, and he could tell by the little furtive glances she cast around the theater that she was scared and barely holding it together. She was hiding it pretty well at the moment, for the kids no doubt, but he could tell.

He motioned toward the stage, away from the kids. "Let's go talk over there?"

"Yeah," she said. "Good idea. Okay, kids," she said, raising her voice just enough for them all to hear, "you guys get back down, okay? We're going to talk for just a bit."

The kids fidgeted, but none moved.

"I want my mom," one of the little girls said.

"I know, Isabella. Please, everybody just duck down out of sight, okay?"

One by one, the kids went back to hiding between the seats and Paul started toward the stage, Kelly following along behind.

Paul leaned against the leading edge of the stage. "How did you get stuck with all these kids?" he said in a whisper.

"I'm one of the actors here," Kelly said. "I teach a drama workshop for the kids on the days we're not performing. These kids were dropped off this morning at six. I haven't seen any parents since things started getting all crazy."

"We have to get these kids back to their parents. You can't take care of them. Not with all this going on."

"Don't you think the parents would have come to get them if they could?"

That stopped him. He didn't have a response to that.

"Those zombies are all over the ship. And a few

of the parents I saw this morning looked like they were sick. I don't think there are going to be any parents coming."

"Do you guys have any sort of contingency plans for this?"

"For this?" she said. "For zombies? You're kidding, right?"

"I—No, I know you don't. . . . I mean for, hell, I don't know, emergencies. You know, getting kids back with their parents when the ship's in trouble. Surely, you have something like that."

She nodded. "All the kids have wristbands. You probably saw that."

"Yeah, I think so."

"All the kids under twelve have to wear them. They've got their muster stations imprinted on them."

"You're talking about putting them on lifeboats. Getting them off the ship."

"Not exactly. In case of general emergencies there's a central Child Pickup Center on Deck 4. Our procedure is to take the kids there, and if the parents don't show, it's my job to make sure I get them on a lifeboat."

"I don't know. That's three decks down. A lot can go wrong. Are you sure you're not better off here? I mean, I didn't see you guys at all. I walked right by you."

"We were supposed to feed them breakfast and lunch. They haven't eaten. They haven't even had any water since this morning. We can't stay here."

Paul sighed. He looked up at the theater seats and shook his head. "Well, I guess you gotta do what you gotta do. But I think that's a really bad idea. You ask me, you should keep these kids here. There's a sink and a bathroom upstairs. And they can go a few hours without eating."

He was going to say more, but her expression had gone sour.

"What?" he said.

"You're not going to help us?"

"Well, I—"

"Oh, my God. You'd really walk out on twenty-three children. Are you for real?"

A few heads were popping over the backs of seats. Paul could see their eyes burning in the low light.

"Keep your voice down," he said. "Please."

"Why? So no one will know you're a chickenshit coward?"

"Hey!"

She glared at him, and though she'd pissed him off, they both knew she was right. He started to speak, but there was nothing he could say that was going to change the truth. She'd known him for less than five minutes and she'd already found him out for what he really was.

"I'm sorry," he said. "I really am."

He turned to leave.

"Just like that, you're going to walk out of here?"

He couldn't look her in the eye. "I'm sorry," he said again.

"I know who you are," she said to his back.

That stopped him. He turned around.

"You're here with Senator Rachel Sutton. I saw

you with her yesterday. What are you, like her family or her—"

"I'm her aide."

"What is that, like a secretary?"

"I'm her chief of staff."

"So . . . her secretary, basically."

"Yeah," he said, not wanting to argue any more, not wanting to do anything but get the hell out of there. How she'd gone from whining for his help to indignation to taunting in such a short period of time was beyond him, but he didn't want to stick around any longer.

He turned away again, this time determined to leave, and started walking toward the prop room.

"But if she's here, they'll come after her, right? They'll try to rescue her."

He didn't respond, just kept walking.

Kelly ran after him and grabbed his arm. He stopped, stared at her hand on his elbow, and then finally met her gaze.

"They'll try to rescue a U.S. senator, right?"

"She has a Secret Service agent with her."

"He's got guns with him, right? Maybe he could protect us."

"The agent is a she, and yes, I'm hoping she can protect the senator until some kind of rescue party comes. I don't know about the ship's communications system, but I haven't been able to use my iPhone since I woke up this morning. It's like it can't get a signal."

"I heard somebody talking about that earlier," Kelly said. "The Wave Phones aren't working either."

Paul nodded. The Wave Phones were for onboard use only, so that guests could call other guests on the ship. If they were out, and his phone and Internet were out, things certainly didn't look good.

"Paul, can I ask you something?"

He sighed again. "Yes, what is it?"

"Do you think this is happening . . . because of the senator?"

"What do you mean?"

"Those cartels, they tried to kill her in San Antonio last year. And then again a few weeks ago."

"Are you suggesting the cartels turned the people onboard this ship into zombies in order to kill Senator Sutton? That sounds, I don't know, a bit extreme. Why not just shoot her?"

"I don't know," she answered. "But doesn't it sound like a lot of coincidences piled on top of each other? First, she's here, on this ship. Then the zombies. Then your phone and the ship's communications system. That's a lot of things to go wrong, isn't it? I mean, what other explanation could there be?"

"For zombies?" he said. "Good God, I don't know. A couple hundred. Thousands maybe."

"Yeah, but they've tried to kill her twice already."

"With guns. Not by turning six thousand innocent people into zombies. How would the cartels even do something like that? Why would they do something like that?"

"I told you I don't know. I'm just thinking out loud. Maybe they're trying to do something like 9/11. You know, strike fear into the heart of America or something. I don't know."

"Yeah, well, I don't either. But I refuse to believe that this is Rachel Sutton's fault. I can't accept that."

"I didn't mean—"

"It's fine," he said, cutting her off. "Listen, you do whatever it is you gotta do to keep these kids safe. And good luck with that. Me, I'm outta here."

"No," she said. "You can't leave us here like this."

"I told you, I'm not—"

One of the kids screamed, her voice amplified by the theater's acoustics. Paul spun around and saw one of the little girls running between two rows of seats, a woman hobbling along behind her.

"Oh, crap," Paul said.

Beside him, Kelly let out a sound of helpless terror.

The little girl was just a few steps ahead of the zombie. Other kids were screaming, scrambling over the seats and running for the stage.

Paul ran up the stairs, the bat held high and ready to strike. The little girl cleared the seats and ducked down the stairs, nearly knocking him over. She got behind him and her screams turned to whimpers. He flinched from shock as a snarl sounded next to his right shoulder and, lurching to one side, nearly screamed as the woman's face filled his rapidly tunneling vision. She moved so fast.

Adrenaline took over as he began to swing the bat. She clawed at his face. Paul pushed her arms aside and swung wildly, hitting her in the chest and the stomach and the hip, but doing little good. It was enough to create some distance though, and that was what he needed. When she came at him again, he was ready. He swung the bat for her head and caught her with a glancing blow on the chin.

The zombie went tumbling into the rows, landing with her neck in the narrow gap between two seats.

Paul didn't hesitate. He jumped from the stairs onto her back, jamming her neck deeper into the gap. Her snarls turned to a gasping, choking sound. She put her hands on the seat backs and tried to push herself up and out, but she was jammed too deep.

Paul circled around her, the bat gripped tightly in both hands.

"You bitch. Fucking die!"

He swung the bat down as hard as he could, again and again, turning her head to a mashed bloody pulp, even as her body continued to twitch and dance under the blows.

When he pulled the bat back from what he'd done, a large, hairy section of the woman's scalp slid off into the seat beside her.

He turned and looked at Kelly and the children down by the stage. His chest was heaving from the exertion.

But she wasn't looking at him.

She was staring up at the top row of seats, her eyes wide. He followed her gaze and saw a bald man with bite marks all over his scalp coming through the lobby toward the stairs. He made it to the top row of seats, locked eyes on Paul, and started running down the stairs, arms out ahead of him.

Paul's heart was thundering in his chest. His breath shuddered and his hands felt numb as they gripped the bat. Sweat was rolling down his forehead now, popping out all over his arms, but he paid it no heed. There was no pain, not yet anyway. His palms were slick with sweat and he rubbed them on his shirt so he could grip the bat better.

To Kelly, he said, "Get the kids through the prop room back there. Go!"

"What are you doing? Run!"

"I'll be right behind you."

She said something else, but he didn't hear her.

The zombie was charging down the stairs. Paul turned to face him, asking himself what in the hell he thought was doing.

When the zombie was just a few steps away, Paul dodged to one side and swept the bat across the thing's knees. The bones shattered with a loud crack and the zombie went tumbling down the stairs, landing in a heap at the bottom.

Paul headed down the steps, and strangely, all he could think about was that New York Yankees gang The Furies from *The Warriors*, a movie he'd seen at least a dozen times growing up.

The zombie pulled itself up to its knees just as Paul reached the last step. "Warriors," he said, half singing it, "come out to pla-ay." He took steady aim and swung for the fence.

The sound of the bat striking the man's head echoed all around the theater, as did the thud of his body hitting the floor.

He turned and scanned the theater. Where there was one of those things there had to be more. But to his surprise the place was empty and quiet, the darkness pooling under the mezzanine deck halfway up the stairs. It occurred to him then that he could run for it. He could leave now and go try to find Senator Sutton and Tess and wait for somebody to come and save them. But if he did that, he might as well toss himself overboard, because he'd never be able to live with himself.

And just like that, he knew he'd sealed his own fate.

He turned and followed Kelly and the kids through the stage door.

CHAPTER 23

Getting from the senator's cabin to her own, two decks down, was relatively easy. It would have been easier still if Pilar hadn't needed to conserve her ammunition, but she had only the one magazine left and she'd used two rounds just getting down the stairs and another seven taking care of the zombies clustered in the hallway near her own cabin. One of the zombies, a man whose belly had been torn open and emptied from the base of his sternum to the waistband of his underwear, had taken four direct headshots all by himself. That in and of itself wasn't anything special, except that through it all, he'd had an awful grin on his face. Even with his scalp splattered against the wall behind him, that grin had remained. Her fourth shot had finally put him down, but it hadn't gotten rid of the grin, and it hadn't completely stilled him either. He was still twitching like an electrified frog on the dissection table when she closed the door to her cabin and tossed her nearly empty pistol on the bed.

She stopped there and ran her hands through her hair. Christ, what had she come here for?

She looked down at her pistol and for the life of her couldn't remember.

This wasn't like her and it scared her.

Why couldn't she focus?

Think, she told herself. Come on, focus. It's right in front of you.

She'd shot the lady agent. She'd made her way down here. But why?

Ah, the rifle! Of course, the rifle.

She let out a long sigh and tried to get her head back in the hunt. It was hard, though. She felt nervous, jittery, rough around the edges. It'd been a long time since she'd felt this scared, this uncertain of herself. She didn't like it. Not a bit. There was a time in her life when she'd felt sharp as a knife, like she could do anything, like no one could get the jump on her. And for a time, back in Ciudad Juarez, that was true. But since then, and especially since she'd come aboard the *Gulf Queen*, that confidence had wavered. Now, she felt fragile, like a delicate piece of spun glass. A strong wind might shatter her to pieces.

Pilar closed her eyes, but that was no help. In her mind she saw the slums of Ciudad Juarez, miles upon miles of burned-out abandoned buildings and clapboard shacks and hungry children fighting dogs for scraps of trash and the constant echo of gunfire. She had gone to Harvard, and dined at parties that cost $30,000 a plate, and still the memories of Ciudad Juarez haunted her like ghosts from a battlefield.

"Please," she muttered, begging herself to be strong. "Please."

But when she opened her eyes, the little boy from the cabin upstairs was there, clawing his way across the carpet of her little room.

"Why?" the boy asked, his question punctuated by the icicle snapping of his fingernails. It sounded like there was gravel in his throat.

"Get away," Pilar said. She put her palm up, shaking her head. "Go away."

"You let me die," the little boy said.

Pilar's eyes popped open. That was Lupe's voice. Even after twenty years, she knew it from the first syllable. She raised a hand, and extended it out to the boy.

"Goddamn it, you bitch, why did you let me die?"

She drew her hand back.

It wasn't the boy from upstairs. It was his ruined body, his face, but the eyes that stared back at her were the same that had found hers all those years ago in the back of that eighteen-wheeler.

She closed her eyes again, trying to push the image away.

"Why won't you look at me," Lupe said. "I trusted you. You promised you'd take care of me. You said you would, you said so. You lied to me."

"No," Pilar said. She squeezed her eyes shut even tighter. "No, you're not real. I know you're not real."

"You let me die. You let me *die*!"

It was too much. She opened her eyes, scooped up the pistol from the bed, and fired all in one motion, but the bullet put a hole in an empty spot on the floor.

Her ghosts were gone.

For now.

But it was a long time before her body stopped shaking, and before she was able to pull her MP5 from her luggage.

She cried the entire time she was loading it.

CHAPTER 24

Paul ran into the prop room and found Kelly and some of the bigger kids taking down bats to use as weapons. The equipment looked huge in their hands. None of them stood a chance against one of those zombies, but the fact that they were picking up weapons was probably a good thing. At least they weren't giving up. He supposed that was something.

The bodies of the two zombies he'd killed before entering the theater were still there, the man still twitching. Paul bent over him and stared into the man's ruined face. The eyes were barely recognizable, but Paul could see one of the eyeballs still trying to track him. What propelled these things, he wondered, made it possible for them to continue on like this?

Not at all like the movies, where the easy headshot did them in.

What were they?

He closed his eyes and tried to push away the thought that all of this was happening because of Senator Sutton. He didn't want to believe it, and he could even tell himself that it was pure nonsense, but, if he was honest with himself, he had doubts. Strong doubts.

It was seeing Monica that did it, really. Tess had told him that she and her boss thought Monica was somehow connected with the cartels, and while he didn't want to believe that either, there were just too many coincidences piled on top of each other.

"Did you do that?" one of the boys asked.

Paul opened his eyes and studied the boy. He was a good-looking kid, a bit small for his age maybe, but with an open, trusting face.

"I did," Paul said.

"Is it hard?"

"Is it . . . you mean, was it hard to do?"

The boy nodded.

"I had to do it. It was him or me."

Paul wasn't sure if the boy had heard him or not. He was looking at the body, a look on his face like he might get sick at any moment.

"Try not to look at it," Paul said.

"It?"

Christ, the kid was almost crying. What was he supposed to do with that?

"You called him 'it,' " the boy said.

"I . . . what?"

"Do you think it hurts? What happened to him, I mean. Do you think it hurts?"

"I don't know," Paul said. In truth, he hadn't even thought about it. He supposed not, but that didn't seem to be what the kid was driving at. The questions the kid was really trying to ask, Paul felt wholly inadequate to answer.

Instead of trying, he smiled at the boy, patted him on the shoulder, and then went over to Kelly and asked if she was ready to move out.

She nodded.

"How are we gonna keep these kids together?" he asked. "If they split on us, we'll lose a few."

She frowned at that, but didn't look worried. "They won't split up. They move as a class when they're at school." She clapped her hands softly to get the room's attention. When the kids were looking at her, she said, "Okay, we're going to line up, same as you do when you go to lunch at school. Mr. Paul here is going to go out first. He'll be our line leader. Stay together and stay behind him. I'll be the back of the line. Okay? Everybody ready?"

The kids didn't look ready, Paul thought. Not at all. But it was going to have to happen, like it or not.

They moved up the stairs and out onto the deck. It was midday now and the heat and the smell of the ocean were a refreshing change from the dark, stale air of the theater below. He motioned for the kids to follow him as he moved toward the rear of the ship. He'd been playing on his phone through the entire muster drill, but he remembered that most of the lifeboats were toward the rear. From here, they were going to have to travel half the length of the ship and go up two levels, and all of it without being seen or heard, which he thought was pretty unlikely. Between their feet scudding on the deck and their sniffles and sobbing and coughing, they couldn't help but make noise.

Paul's thought was to get them on the far side of the mall before reentering the ship and heading up the stairs. The deck was deserted, which was good, but then they reached the ship's English-themed pub, the Lamb and the Rose, and Paul's heart missed a beat.

The pub had a huge window facing seaward upon which somebody had written the words ALIVE IN-SIDE—PLEASE HELP US with some kind of white greasepaint. Even before he looked, he knew from the noises he heard inside that the words were no longer true.

Inside, three men and a woman were feeding on the corpses of perhaps ten people. It was hard to tell because a few of the bodies had been torn apart.

How was that possible? How could people tear each other apart, literally limb from limb, with their bare hands?

From behind him, one of the kids gasped.

Paul turned to shush the boy, but it was too late. When he looked back at the pub, the zombies were staring at him, blood and viscera dripping from their mouths.

"Oh, no," Paul said. He turned to Kelly. "Run! Get them out of here!"

Some of the kids were already running. Kelly pushed the stragglers along and they hustled past Paul just as one of the zombies crashed through the pub's glass doors. The others were right behind it. Paul swung the bat at the first zombie and caught it on the chin. It wasn't enough to kill the thing, but it knocked it off balance and gave Paul the chance he needed to run.

The kids were rounding a corner up ahead and

Paul followed. There was no way they were going to outrun the zombies though. With a quick glance over his shoulder, he knew that. He was already catching up with the kids, but the zombies were right on his heels.

He gave it one last burst of speed, his sandals slapping on the deck, and rounded the corner. The corridor led back into the ship. The last of the kids, two little girls, were going around another corner just ahead of him. Paul followed after them, his lungs feeling like they were going to burst.

Kelly was up ahead, ushering the kids through a white metal door.

It was some kind of kitchen, though from which of the ship's twenty-three restaurants he had no way of knowing. In the blind panic to get away from his pursuers he'd gotten himself hopelessly turned around.

"What are we doing?" he asked Kelly.

The room was dominated by three long metal prep tables, each one stacked with clean white plates and coffee cups.

"Under there," Kelly said, and before Paul could tell her he didn't understand, she opened some of the metal cabinets beneath the tables and motioned for the kids to climb in.

Paul ran to a second table and started doing the same thing. The kids moved fast, but still he could hear the zombies outside, getting closer.

They burst through the door right as he was pulling one of the cabinet doors closed on himself and a little boy. Paul strained his hearing, trying to figure out where the zombies were, but all he could hear was the pounding of the blood in his ears and the ragged pulls of his breathing. He couldn't quite catch his breath.

Just outside the cabinet door he could hear the faint tap and slide of shoes dragging on the tile floor.

The little boy next to him was trembling.

"They're going to kill us," he said. "I don't want to die. I don't want to die." He let out a loud groan.

The footfalls stopped.

Paul put his arms around the boy and squeezed him tightly. "Shhh," he whispered. "It's just like hide-and-seek."

The boy nodded against Paul's arm, but he was still shaking.

"Just be quiet," Paul said. "Pretend it's hide-and-seek."

Paul swallowed the lump in his throat and pulled the kid tighter. Outside, he could hear the zombies moving again, hunting for them.

CHAPTER 25

They might have been man and wife; Pilar really couldn't tell at this point. Not with all the damage that had been done to them. The zombies had chewed them up badly before they died. But Pilar imagined that they were husband and wife. She found something comforting in that. Creepy, yes, the way they stood there side by side, still wearing the tattered remnants of matching clothes, like being dead hadn't changed their vacation experience much; but it was nonetheless comforting to imagine love holding on even when life couldn't. He was tall, maybe six-foot-four, and she was short, just a little over five feet. They were probably a cute couple in life. Now, covered in blood and with bite marks all over their bodies, they stood in front of the salmon bar at the Great Northern Café. It was funny, actually. The two zombies, so plain, so average, typical middle-class Americans, were standing there looking at mounds of raw salmon, perhaps the same contaminated fish that had caused them to turn into zombies in the first place, and all they could do was paw at the glass. Just average Americans, hoisted on their own tasty petard. Ramon, Pilar thought, would be pleased.

Pilar, however, was screwed. The man and wife zombies weren't all that big of a deal. She could have sprinted right by them. The problem was the large crowd of zombies filing in through the door behind them. She'd been doing fine, making her way without having to use her weapons, when she rounded the corner just outside the café. A man was facedown on the floor at the foot of some stairs, and from the trail of blood on the steps it wasn't hard to figure out that he'd just tumbled down them. She could have avoided him, too, but something about him caught her attention. Ramon had told her that the same chemical reactions the bacteria used to stimulate the medulla oblongata, making postmortem movement possible, also inhibited the onset of rigor mortis. But . . . not in this zombie. It looked stiff, like every movement was bought with consider effort. She had taken out her iPhone and captured a quick video of the man, because she figured Ramon would want his scientists to see it. But when she was done with the video, she'd looked up to find herself surrounded.

A crowd of them had come around from the back of the stairs. Another smaller crowd had come up behind her. She looked forward, back, up the stairs, and realized they had closed in on her without making a sound. The only place to run was into the Great Northern Café, and so she'd sprinted into there.

Now she was hiding in the kitchen with a clean shot on the cute couple over by the salmon. From this distance, with her MP5, she could pop them both with an easy headshot.

But that probably wouldn't kill them, at least from what she'd seen so far. It usually took two or three, unless of course it was at point-blank range. All of which was a moot point anyway because the cute couple had brought along about seventy of their closest friends.

Unfortunately, she was running out of time. She had to find the senator, kill her, and then get off this damn ship before the authorities figured something was wrong and sent a force out to take care of the problem. But before she could do any of that, she had to get out of this kitchen without getting killed.

Somewhere onboard a fire had broken out. Every once in a while, she caught a whiff of smoke through the air vents, and that wasn't good. She'd turned off the fire alarm systems when she'd hacked into the ship's security and housekeeping programs, but even still, where there was fire there was smoke, and at sea nothing brought help faster than a ship on fire. Sooner or later, she figured, somebody was going to see that smoke, and they'd come running.

Which meant she had to get out of this kitchen.

She looked around for something she could use to clear a path out the door. There were knives and heavy cast iron pots everywhere, but nothing she could use to cut a hole through the crowd.

Except maybe that, she thought as her gaze wandered over the Viking gas range.

She looked inside the cabinets and on the shelves until she found what she was looking for—a case of Lysol disinfectant spray. She could make some serious use out of that.

Working quickly but quietly, she laid out sixteen cans on the prep surface next to the range. She checked the pilot light to make sure it was still burning, and then grabbed the biggest knife she could find and punctured all the cans.

No telling how long it would take for the whole thing to go up, she thought. Best to move fast.

She ran to the opposite side of the kitchen, where the zombies seemed to have clustered. Large crowds of them could be a lot like water. They moved fast when headed in a straight line, but when left to their own devices, they had a tendency to cluster in groups and just sort of stop, like a backwater on a river. They had clustered that way up near the front of the restaurant, and Pilar smiled when she saw the two married zombies right there in the thick of the crowd, still side by side.

There were two doors into the kitchen: one up near where the backwater had formed, and another toward the back. She went over to the door nearest the zombies, opened it, and whistled.

Pilar didn't wait around to see what would happen. She didn't need to. The crowd surged toward the door, even as she ran to the opposite side of the kitchen and ducked behind a table. She clapped her hands over her ears and opened her mouth wide to equalize the pressure just as the kitchen exploded.

The explosion threw her against the wall, and left a ringing in her ears. Her head felt like it was about to cave in. She had to blink several times just to keep her vision from shaking.

She stood up on wobbly legs.

The room was full of smoke. Debris was everywhere.

So too were the zombies.

Most had been knocked to the ground. Very few appeared to be seriously damaged from the blast—aerosol cans didn't make that big of an explosion, after all—but nearly all of them were sprawled out on the floor. Only a few still kept their feet, and those were turned every which way, clearly disoriented.

It wasn't much, but it was the window she needed.

She was still seeing double as she sprinted through the maze of bodies and out the front door of the café. Pilar headed up the stairs the rigor-afflicted zombie had fallen from, found a quiet little observation deck overlooking the foyer in front of the café, and dropped down against the wall.

She took out her iPhone and blinked at it, trying to read the display so she could go back to reviewing the security feeds. She had a minute, maybe two, to get her head back in order before the sound of the explosion drew even more zombies into the area. Best to use the time she had wisely.

"Now where are you?" she said at the screen.

She thumbed through one screen after another—corridors and casinos, shops and cafés—and found nothing.

Until she reached the bridge.

There, sitting in the captain's chair, distraught and apparently in shock, sat the senator.

Pilar had to laugh. When you were afflicted with the kind of narcissism that drove people into politics, where else would you sit but in the captain's chair?

So this was going to be easy.

All Pilar had to do was go get her.

CHAPTER 26

Rachel Sutton knew what she'd find even before she stepped onto the bridge. There were mangled bodies of crew and passengers alike nearly everywhere she looked, and many of them were still moving. The body of a young Indian crewman, his radio operator's headset still hanging from the back of his bleeding head, partially blocked the doorway to the bridge, and she had to step over him, grimacing at the smell of his opened stomach and ripped bowels. She wandered in a daze, like a woman just coming to after surgery, toward the captain's chair and sank down into it heavily.

She felt so lost. Not angry, or hurt, or even grief-stricken, but completely and irredeemably adrift.

Wayne was dead.

Her husband of thirty-eight years was dead.

She kept trying to grasp the enormity of it, but her mind was on a loop, always coming back to him on the floor by the foot of their bed, staring up at nothing. Rachel had only glimpsed him there in the few moments before the shooting started, but in those moments her entire world had crumbled. Tess Compton and that woman had started shooting. Tess had been hit and fell to the floor. The other woman had rolled out of sight, and it looked like she had been hit, too. Seeing a chance to get away, Rachel had knelt down and retrieved Tess's gun from the floor, and in that moment she'd seen Wayne there at the foot of the bed, the hole in the back of his head as big as her fist.

What in the world was she going to do? What could she do?

Never had she felt this alone, this uncertain. For so long she'd been in control, the woman everyone else looked to for answers, and now she couldn't even make herself believe this was actually happening.

It wasn't until the tears started that she got mad and forced herself to concentrate. Fear helped to her focus, a little. She was in trouble. A lot of trouble. She was on a ship full of zombies, hunted by a cartel assassin, and the only protection she had was lying dead in her cabin. If she was going to get out of this, she needed to focus.

She sat up in the chair and smoothed the wrinkles from her slacks. You can do this, she told herself.

The ship appeared to be drifting. There wasn't much she could do about that. She had as much of a chance of successfully steering this ship as she did of fixing its engines, which felt like they had stopped.

And there wasn't much she could do about the fires that seemed to have broken out in several places.

She couldn't even figure out the fire alarms.

But maybe she could call for help or something. They'd shown her the radio, somewhere around here. She walked down the line of computer stations, reading the controls, looking for something, anything, that seemed related to the radio. She didn't think it'd be this hard to find.

Then she found something that caught her eye.

A security monitor.

She picked up the remote control and experimented with the buttons until she found the ones that controlled the video feed.

It was like watching a slideshow from the filming of a horror movie. Where there weren't fires, there were zombies, and blood on the walls and bodies on the floors. Here and there she saw people, actual living people, huddled in cafés and libraries; a man walking down one of the decks, swatting the air around his head like he was swarmed by bees and muttering to himself; people were jumping from the railings, falling into the sea; a young mother, her expression one of vacant-eyed horror, holding her sleeping daughter in her arms.

It was the mother and child that did it.

That was Rachel Sutton's moment of crisis.

She stared at the mother, at that horribly empty look in her eyes, and she realized that all of this, the zombies, the fires, the death, was because of her. Perhaps the cartels had done this, found some way to engineer whatever kind of attack this was, but they had done it because of her. All these people, the dead and the living, were as they were because of her.

She closed her eyes and swallowed.

When she opened them again, the monitor was showing a long view down one of the decks, the yellow lifeboats all hanging like enormous potted plants along the left side of the frame.

Of course, she thought.

Maybe, if she could get there, maybe get a few others to go with her, maybe then she'd be able to look at herself in the mirror again.

It was worth a shot.

At least she'd be doing something. Anything was better than sitting her, stewing in her grief and shame.

"I'll do it," she said.

She picked up Tess's gun, such a heavy, awful thing, and left the bridge.

CHAPTER 27

With her beloved MP5 in hand, Pilar found moving through the ship a snap, relatively speaking. The rifle offered better control, better accuracy, and more takedown power. Pilar climbed the crew stairwell toward the bridge. The mall, and most of the other areas accessible to the passengers, had become as hectic as a beehive, and many of the security cameras now showed only a blurry mass of faces and writhing bodies. But the crew stairwell was almost empty, and she'd only had to use a few rounds to work her way up to this point, just a few decks below the bridge.

She was close now, and she had a decision to make. The video feed on her iPhone showed the senator still sitting in the captain's chair. She looked physically and emotionally broken, like she wasn't going anywhere without a good reason, and that was the crux of Pilar's problem.

Between Pilar's position and the bridge there

were about two dozen zombies, most of them crewmen. Where they'd come from she had no idea, unless they'd been on the way before they turned, made it this far, and just sort of stayed here after they died . . . another of those backwaters like the one she found down at the Great Northern Café.

That made sense to her. The bridge was the symbol of authority onboard ship. It was the same way of thinking that brought the senator up here, no doubt. But what was she supposed to do about with all these zombies? That was the question before her.

With the MP5 she could probably shoot her way through. At a full sprint, and with a few carefully aimed bursts she could make it. She'd be on the bridge in forty-five seconds to a minute, nothing to it. The trouble was that would allow the senator an opportunity to hear the shots and react. Maybe she would think it was help coming to rescue her, but Pilar knew she couldn't rely on that kind of assumption. Despite the fact that she'd dared to take on the cartels, Senator Sutton wasn't a stupid woman. A far more likely response would be for her to run the other way, toward the public stairwell. If she took it, she'd probably be gone in all of three seconds. If there were too many zombies for her to risk the stairwell, she'd probably do what Pilar did earlier. Go into a stateroom and lock the door. That would leave Pilar in the unenviable position of having to figure out which stateroom she was hiding in, and then to force entry, all the while having to deal with zombies coming at her from both sides.

Pilar scanned the landing just above her, where the zombie crew had gathered. There were three ways off the landing. They could go up or down, or they could follow a side corridor down to the officers' cabins. Pilar figured she would need about fifteen seconds to get up the stairs and kill the senator. It was doable.

But it wouldn't come cheaply.

She took out her iPhone and tried to think of another way. But there wasn't and she knew it. Working quickly, she removed the Otterbox so the phone would slide easily across the deck. She went to her music, called up Vicente Fernandez's "*Volver, Volver*," her favorite, and turned the volume up all the way.

Then she crawled to the top of the stairs, careful to stay just out of the zombies' line of sight, hit play, and threw the phone toward the officers' corridor. It slid like a hockey puck across the tiled floor, the opening trumpets of the song sounding clearly down the hall.

It worked. Nearly all the zombies turned at the same time toward the sound, and as the trumpets gave way to the lonely beauty of Vicente's baritone, the zombies started that way.

That's it, she told herself. Go, go, go!

Jumping to her feet, her rifle at the ready, she charged up the stairs, passing right by two zombies that hadn't moved down the hall yet and entered the bridge.

But it was empty.

The senator was gone.

"What the hell?" she said.

Pilar raised her rifle. There wasn't any place to hide on the bridge. She could see all of it at once. So where was Sutton hiding? And how had she known to run? Pilar hadn't given her time to do that.

But the senator was most certainly gone.

Pilar moved down the curve of the bridge, weapon at the ready, finger flexing on the trigger.

The bridge was clear all the way to the opposite end. And there Pilar saw what had happened. Down at the end of the corridor, near the passenger stairwell, a large group of zombies were turning and heading down the stairs.

"You crazy bitch," Pilar said. "You went down the stairs."

Pilar couldn't believe it. Running through a crowd of zombies like that took guts.

Or a death wish.

Pilar didn't think the senator had either.

"Why would you do something like that? What were you thinking?"

Pilar went to the captain's chair and tried to put herself in the senator's mind. She might have heard the music from Pilar's phone. Maybe. Pilar could hear Vicente's voice even now, thin and distant, but still rising triumphantly above the mariachi horns. But that wouldn't have caused her to run the way she did, would it?

"No," Pilar said. "There's something else. But what? What am I missing? Ah!"

The security video feed next to the captain's chair was locked onto one of the gathering platforms for the lifeboats. Another showed a café on the same deck, port side. There were people inside, maybe as many as forty of them, all huddled together in the dark.

"You're going to try to save them, aren't you?" Pilar said at the video monitor. "That's what you're going to do. You're going down there to put them on a lifeboat and get away."

Just like a politician, Pilar thought. She'd turn a tragedy into a PR opportunity; probably brand herself the hero of the wreck of the *Gulf Queen*. It made Pilar sick just thinking about it.

"Once, you would have done the same thing," came a voice from behind her.

Pilar spun around, weapon up and at the ready.

Lupe was standing there in the doorway, dead and covered with blood. Flies swarmed around his face, crawled over his eyes.

"Not the fake hero part," he went on. "That's not your style. But you would have tried to save those people. You probably would have done it, too."

Pilar shook her head. She squeezed her eyes shut and told herself it was just some six-year-old child, some unfortunate little boy that had died and found his way up here. But when she opened her eyes again it was still Lupe. And he was coming at her, hands outstretched, like he wanted to hug her.

"Stay away," she said.

He was almost on her now. With an awful numbness in her chest she swung the rifle's butt stock at Lupe's chin and knocked him facedown into the captain's chair.

Before he could get back up again, she threw the seat belt over his back, secured it, and pulled the strap as tight as she could make it, pinning him facedown in the seat, his body bent the wrong way.

She turned away from him, back to the security monitors.

"What are you going to do?" Lupe asked.

She ignored him. Tried to anyway. Pilar forced herself to think like the senator. When she got down to the lifeboats—assuming she made it that far—

she'd have to lower the boats manually. It wouldn't be hard to do. The manual controls were designed so that even the passengers could use them, if need be. Pilar would just have to keep her from doing that.

"You're going to drop all the lifeboats," Lupe said.

"That's right."

"Why?"

Pilar didn't answer. She went to the ship's emergency protocols on the computer and found the programs that controlled the lifeboats. With the first officer's passwords she'd taken before she killed him, it wasn't hard. But it did have to be done in stages. The computer only allowed four boats to be released at a time. But after a few keystrokes the process was underway.

"Why are you doing this, Pilar?"

"Shut up," she whispered. He wasn't real. This was all in her head. She knew that. She knew that, damn it. But it was so hard hearing his voice again.

"You never would have done something like this when I knew you. There are children down there. They couldn't have done anything to you. There's no way they deserve something like this."

"I said shut up."

"Why did you change, Pilar? What happened?"

She jammed the rifle into the little boy's ear. "Shut up! Shut the hell up. Right now!"

"You don't want me to shut up. You wanted me to come to you. You want to hear this."

Her lips were trembling. "I wanted no such thing."

"It was no accident you played that song down there. Do you remember, back in Juarez, when we'd sit on the wrecked cars up in the hills above the shacks and watch the tire fires burn? Remember that? You used to sing that song to me."

"Please stop," she whispered. "Please."

"Why did you change? Something went hard inside you. Why?"

"You know why."

"Because I died? Is that it?"

Pilar said nothing.

"Dying is what we do, Pilar. It's part of us, like laughing, and singing."

"Stop it," she said, almost spitting the words out. "There is no such thing as dying, only giving up. If you live or die, that's your own choice. You make up your mind to live and nothing can kill you. Nothing but disease or something you can't control. That's what I did, Lupe. That's the choice I made. After they pulled me from that truck where you died, they put me on a bus and sent me back to Juarez. They dumped me on the street with the drugs and the gangs and the men who wanted to turn me into a whore. You want to know what happened? You're right. I was ten years old. I was a child, but something went hard inside me, something that refused to bow. My neck will never bend. Nobody owns me."

"Not even Ramon?"

"Not even Ramon," she said, and pulled the trigger. And then, at a whisper: "Not even my own ghosts."

The boy's head burst all over the seat, clumps of his scalp dripping down the side of the chair.

She watched the boy's body go still, unaware of the tears on her face, unaware of anything but her loneliness and shame and desperate need to finally feel at peace with all the killing, all the death.

"Oh, my God, Lupe. I'm so sorry."

She sniffled, and only then did she hear the sound of footsteps running up the stairs.

"Damn it," she muttered. The sound of the shot had attracted all those zombies from down below. She was about to have a whole lot of company.

The first few burst through the door, pushing one another out of the way as they flooded onto the bridge. Pilar started shooting. The zombie closest to her, a short, plump man in white shorts and the bloodstained remnants of a blue Hawaiian shirt, was running at her full speed. Pilar's first shot hit him in the chin. Another man coming up fast behind him pushed him forward and soon both were on her, their hands pawing at her. Pilar's next shots knocked them both down, but didn't stop either man from moving. They crawled toward her, reaching for her, even as others trampled over them.

She focused on single, deliberate headshots, making every bullet count. Bodies started dropping. She fired through one thirty-round magazine, reloaded and emptied a second even as more zombies charged through the door. Nearly to the end of her third magazine, she began to retreat. The bodies were piled high in the narrow walkway. Some were draped over chairs. The bridge's windshield was spattered with blood and clumpy bits of muscle and bone and hair. The smell of gun smoke and blood was thick on the air. And still more zombies were coming through the door.

Pilar turned to run down the corridor where the

senator had disappeared, but stopped in her tracks. Three zombies had already come around the corner from the public stairwell at the end of the hall.

More were behind them.

"Ah, damn," she said.

She tried a few cabin doors close to her, but they were all locked.

She was trapped, zombies coming at her from both sides.

Pilar swung her magazine pouch forward and checked her remaining cache. She had five thirty-round magazines left and nowhere to run. She had no idea if it'd be enough, but it wasn't like she had much of a choice. She popped in a fresh mag, took a deep breath, and went to work.

CHAPTER 28

Rachel Sutton walked down the stairs from the bridge, pausing only long enough to catch her breath and, occasionally, to duck back into the shadows to let a zombie stagger by.

They weren't that hard to avoid, which kind of surprised her. Curious about why she kept seeing zombies mentioned everywhere, even from veteran senators who started using terms like zombie banks and zombie markets, she'd actually watched a zombie movie late one night while working up notes for a meeting. The movie—she forgot the title, except that it was "Dead" something or other—had come on late night TV and was actually pretty dreadful. But she'd come away from the movie thinking that the whole zombie craze was about using the zombie as a clever metaphor for some perceived social ill. There was probably also something of a more general hopelessness to it, a modern ennui with the status quo. But, ultimately, it seemed, life for the living in those movies was pretty pointless. Where was there to run when everybody, eventually, ended up as one of those decaying, venomous things? It was a good metaphor for politics and the economy, but she was baffled as to the zombie's cultural appeal. She certainly didn't get it.

But now, she found herself surrounded by real zombies, and it wasn't like anything the movie had led her to believe.

As long as you were careful, and quiet, they were easy to avoid.

So she made her way down the stairs until she got to Deck 5. There she had to stop because a group of zombies had gathered on the landing and didn't seem to be moving.

She went back up to Deck 6 and left the stairs. Six was one of the mixed-use decks, half passenger accommodations and half bars and restaurants. The Pecos House, the *Gulf Queen*'s five-star steakhouse, was here, and seeing signs for it made Rachel think of Wayne again. He'd been so looking forward to eating there.

And she'd complained about it.

What happened to them? They used to make each other so happy. But her career had exploded and his had been driven into the background. Everything he did was to support her. All the time off he'd taken. All the traveling. Everything he'd done he'd done for her, to support her. He'd been her biggest cheer-leader. He'd been the warm body under the covers when she climbed into bed at two in the morning, mentally and physically exhausted from the day. He'd been her center, her core, her foundation. He'd asked for nothing in return, and if she was honest with herself, she'd given very little more than that.

Could she really blame him for the drinking?

She hated him for it, but could she really blame him for it?

She shook her head and continued on.

She reached a foyer at another stairwell and stopped. Rachel looked around. There was nobody in the corridor, just a few bodies crumpled on the floor. She had a straight shot all the way to the stairs that she hoped would lead her to the lifeboats. And if that way was blocked, the deck was right behind her. She could simply go that way.

She listened for the sound of footfalls on the stairs and heard none.

Still, something bothered her. The hairs on the back of her neck were standing on end, and she'd survived the shark tank that was Washington long enough to trust her instincts when they told her the shit was about to hit the proverbial fan.

An instant later, her instincts proved right.

From behind her, from the corridor that led outside, she heard a roar like a packed soccer stadium.

So many voices crying out.

It's a rescue vessel, she thought, and ran for the deck railing.

She peered over the side. She saw forty, maybe more, yellow lifeboats drifting away from the ship, floating aimlessly on the current.

"No!" she said. "No, no, no!"

She looked up, toward the source of the noise.

All down the length of the ship she saw people leaning over their balconies, their faces bent and twisted in fear. They were crying out, reaching for the lifeboats as though they stood a chance of pulling one back.

About a dozen or so couples jumped.

Very few rose to the surface again.

My God, she thought. Oh, my God. We're all dead.

CHAPTER 29

Tess woke with her face pressed into the carpet and a searing pain in her chest. She tried to roll over onto her back, but it hurt too badly and the best she could manage was to explode into a fit of coughing that made her chest feel like she was being hit with a hammer over and over again.

When she tried again, she coughed again, but this time she was ready for it and she was able to control it.

A little.

Her ribs hurt like hell and her eyes were burning.

She coughed again.

It took her a moment to realize the room was full of smoke.

That sent a surge of adrenaline through her and she rolled over, her back against the bed. There was blood all over the carpet and on her clothes and she quickly patted herself down, looking for a wound.

But there wasn't one.

The blood belonged to someone else.

She glanced to her right and saw Dr. Sutton face-up at the foot of the bed, looking away from her so that she could see the clotted gunshot wound to the back of his head. So that explained the blood.

The air was thick with smoke and it made it difficult to see. She kept blinking against the tears.

But through the smoke she thought she saw movement.

"Senator Sutton?"

Then a breeze from the balcony cleared some of the smoke from the carpet and she saw the man from the hallway, the one she'd shot right before she and Senator Sutton had entered her room, crawling across the floor.

"Whoa!" Tess said, pushing her back into the side of the bed.

The man's face was barely recognizable, and most of his brains appeared to have been blasted out the rear of his skull and all over his back.

"How the hell . . . ?"

He pulled himself along the carpet an inch at a time. A noise like a tire going flat came from a hole in his throat.

Despite the pain in her chest and the smoke in her eyes Tess knew she had to stand up. Her instructors at the Secret Service Academy had never once questioned her mental toughness. Nor had Juan Perez the entire time she'd served on his team. The only person who had ever questioned her ability, her resolve, was her mother, and that had come in the form of begging her to settle down with some promising young banker, or maybe settle for a doctor if she couldn't find a banker she liked, anything but this

Secret Service nonsense. That was what spurred her on. That was what gave her the strength to stand up.

She pushed herself to her feet and onto the bed just as the man slashed at where her shoes had been a moment before. She looked down at him and the only word she could think of, the only word that made sense, was *zombie*.

The guys on her detail, when they were on the road, they played a drinking game to that TV show *The Walking Dead*.

She'd even joined them a few times.

Tess thought it was stupid, but it was a boys' club, law enforcement, and if you wanted to get ahead, sometimes you had to be one of the boys.

But now, looking down at that man she knew to be dead, she couldn't think of anything else but the word *zombie*, and what she'd thought was stupid and gratuitously violent before, now filled her mind with a horror so complete and fully realized that she wanted to curl up in a ball and cry for her mother.

And that made her mad.

She jumped off the bed, ignoring the pain and the smoke, and picked up the chair from the desk. Tess raised it her head and smashed it down on the zombie's upturned ruined face.

It barely registered the blow.

She changed her grip on the chair back so that she could wield it like a fence post digger and jammed it down on the back of the zombie's head.

A chair leg found its mark and sank deep into the softened skull.

She twisted the chair with a grunt and the zombie's arm fell to the floor.

"Mother fucker," she said, and pulled the chair

loose and jammed it back down again. "Goddamned mother fucker."

And then it was done.

She coughed and looked around, her mind starting to clear.

The senator was gone.

So too was the woman who shot her.

Juan was right, as always.

So what did she do now? That was the real question. The senator was obviously still alive. If Monica Rivas had simply wanted her dead, her body would be here in the room. There'd be no point in moving her.

But she couldn't think with all this smoke. It was making it hard to breathe, hard to see.

She went out to the balcony and breathed deeply of the sea air.

Then an explosion threw her against the railing, nearly pitching her over into the sea.

Startled and short of breath she turned and looked up the side of the ship. It was enormous, a cliff of metal and glass towering above her, and it was on fire. Smoke roiled off its superstructure, spilling across the green-black sea. She could hear people screaming. It sounded like being on the ground level at a soccer stadium, the rhythmic roar of human voices. People were jumping from the balconies into the sea, some of them holding hands. On a few, the ones close enough, she could even see the bent and broken grief on their faces.

The hopelessness of it all.

And then, an MH-47 helicopter rolled over the side, ropes hanging from its belly. The enormous twin-blade helicopter seemed suspended in midair for a terrible moment, then turned and headed out to sea.

It doubled back a moment later, but kept its distance from the enormous burning wreck that was the *Gulf Queen*.

Juan is here, she thought, her heart leaping up in her chest. He's here!

In her mind she had the whole thing figured out. Juan had somehow managed to uncover what was going on aboard the *Gulf Queen* and had called in his old Special Forces–days connections to deal with it. He was here!

All she had to do was get to him.

But it wouldn't be his style to come and save her. She wouldn't be the girl he'd hired if that was what she hoped for.

She knew that, right from the start.

She turned away from the balcony and went over to her own cabin, where her tactical gear was still spread open on the bed.

She had a Colt AR-15 with a sixteen-inch barrel there, plus a cache of fully loaded magazines.

Tess took up the weapon and examined it, checked the action on the bolt and the catch and release of its receiver. The Colt was a rock. Hardly state of the art, it nonetheless got rounds down range consistently and accurately, and it could do it in just about any weather. You could mistreat it, bang it around, fail to clean it, and still it brought the goods to the battlefield.

She loved this gun.

And it was here in her hands.

What remained was her core objective. She had to find the senator and get her to safety.

And to Juan.

But between her and that objective stood a ship full of zombies.

She slapped a magazine into her Colt and loaded the rest into the cargo pockets of her BDUs.

Juan expected her to do this.

And yes, she could do this.

CHAPTER 30

Rachel Sutton stood at the railing, watching the lifeboats drift away on the current.

What the hell was she supposed to do now?

She looked up at the cliff that was the ship's hull and superstructure. A surprisingly large number of passengers were at their balconies, pointing and yelling. Some looked as baffled as she felt. Others were angry. Some fell to the ground and wept openly. Rachel couldn't look anymore. She turned away.

Maybe the thing to do, she reasoned, was to go find an empty cabin somewhere, lock the door, and sit and wait for whatever was going to happen. It wouldn't be long before somebody came looking for a whole ship full of missing people. Surely they could find a ship this big with little effort.

At least she hoped that was the case.

She went back inside the ship, turned down a corridor at random, and walked into the first room she came to.

"Hello?" she called, and waited.

Nobody stirred. She heard nothing.

It was empty, just as she'd hoped. She went back to the door and closed it and locked it and then crawled into the still-made bed and curled into a motionless, desperate fetal ball.

It was hard for her to believe that things had gotten this bad.

And she'd never seen it coming. It totally blindsided her.

She pulled a pillow close and curled around it. Rachel pressed her nose into the fabric, breathing the clean cotton smell, and she thought of Wayne.

Rachel had no idea how long she cried, or for how long she slept after that, but she had slept, for she woke with a start and the vague impression that someone was yelling. She lay there for a long moment with her eyes open, arms clutched around the pillow, listening.

Then she heard it again, people yelling.

But different than before.

Was that elation she heard?

Curious, she rose from the bed and walked out on the balcony. She leaned over the side and stared up at the other passengers, all of whom were watching the sea and pointing.

She followed their gaze, and at first saw only a black smudge low on the horizon. Since her early forties, things viewed at a distance all looked like ink blots. But then she heard the unmistakable slap of helicopter blades against the air, and within mo-

ments, the inkblots turned into a pair of jet-black helicopters, moving low and fast over the water.

Oh, my God, she thought. They sent the SEALs
to rescue me. Yes!

Suddenly elated, she ran out of the room and
through the hallway, looking for the nearest set of
stairs.

She was going topside.

She was going to be there when they landed.

CHAPTER 31

"Make ready!" Rick Carter yelled.

Inside the helicopter, the operators around Juan started to move. The men put on their helmets and adjusted their gear, checked their weapons, but did it calmly, like the professionals they were. Fast-roping from helicopters was a basic skill set for them, one of the first things they'd mastered way back in Ranger school, long before getting selected for Delta, and none of them acted nervous or apprehensive. Certainly none of them looked as nervous as Juan felt. Most of them, in fact, had slept during the two and a half hour flight out to the *Gulf Queen*.

Juan had tried to sleep himself. After being in a constant state of motion since eight p.m. the previous day, he was exhausted, both mentally and physically. But try as he did, he just couldn't fall asleep. He was too worried. He was worried about this mission, about his own safety and the safety of these men; but even more than that, he was worried about

Tess. After fighting those dead men in the Cavazos Meatpacking facility, and watching scores of zombies staggering around the deck of the *Gulf Queen* on the drone feed, he was sick with worry over what he'd find. Tess was tough. She could take of herself. He knew that better than anyone. But she'd been alone on that boat, facing down all those zombies, for at least twenty-four hours now. Good as Tess was, could she still be alive? Would anybody still be alive?

He pushed thoughts of finding a zombie Tess out of his head and focused on the job at hand. He had fifty pounds of gear strapped on his back, and he was about to jump out of a perfectly good helicopter, something he'd hated since his days in the Ranger battalion.

He grabbed his helmet, nodding in approval at the hydraulic fluid that had beaded up on it. The stuff was on his boots and his pant legs, too. But that was okay. There wasn't an Army helicopter in service anywhere in the world that didn't spew hydraulic fluid. In fact, there was a joke in the teams that if you ever got on a helicopter that wasn't leaking the stuff, get off, because it was probably going to crash.

And then the crew chief yelled, "One minute!" and dropped the cargo door down.

The roar of the engines grew even louder. Wind whipped through the cabin. Rick Carter came over to him and held up one finger.

"It's game on," he yelled over the noise. "You ready?"

"Hell, yeah!"

"Bullshit. You hate this part of the drill."

"No," Juan said, "I've learned to love it."

Carter laughed. "Yeah, right. Hey, have you seen your ship? It's really burning."

He was right. From where he sat, Juan could see thick black smoke rising up into the sky. He pulled himself up on the overhead handrail and went closer to the open door. About three hundred feet below him, the *Gulf Queen* was dead in the water, no wake, just drifting with the current. On her deck he could see people—zombies, he reminded himself—moving around, some of them turning their attention up to the pair of helicopters moving in for the kill.

Juan glanced over at the other helicopter and was impressed by the operation they'd put together in such a short time. Both helicopters were flown by seasoned pilots from the 160th Special Operations Aviator Regiment, who were the official air delivery service for both Delta and the SEALs. His helicopter, carrying a team of ten Delta operators, was going by the designation Slasher 1. They'd go in first, secure the drop point directly above the bridge, and work crowd control while Slasher 2 brought in the rest of the operators. Once everybody was on board, each team would break into two squads. One of the squads from Slasher 2 would go forward and secure their extraction point at the ship's helipad, while the other three teams went in search of the senator.

In support of the mission, which was now officially called "Operation Iron Maiden," were a multitude of resources. The U.S. Fleet Forces Command had three Ticonderoga class cruisers headed into the area. In the air was a C130 for refueling the helicopters, an E2 Electronic Warfare Jet to manage all of the communications, the drone that was still feeding live footage to the mission commanders and, of course, the two F-15s coming from Hurlburt Field in Florida that were assigned to shut the door on Operation Iron Maiden once the senator was found.

Juan glanced up at the sky, figuring they had about an hour of workable daylight left. He hoped it would be enough. While looking over the ship's blueprints back at Corpus Christi he figured they'd need about thirty minutes to search the entire ship. Now though, seeing the thing in person and getting a feel for how huge it really was, he was starting to have doubts.

"Hold on!" the crew chief yelled into the cabin. "We're going in."

Juan grabbed the overhead handrail just as the helicopter started down. They had a primary and a backup drop site predetermined, but both were compromised. Not good, he thought. They were going to have to start shooting from the moment they hit the deck.

The pilot took them lower and Juan found himself twenty feet above the *Gulf Queen*'s Lido Deck, staring down at a rapidly growing crowd of hands and teeth.

"Ropes out," the crew chief called to his assistant, and the two men threw their heavy black ropes over the side.

"Game on," Carter said. "Let's go!"

The team started down the ropes. Juan moved forward. Carter was right in front of him, and as he grabbed the rope, he turned to Juan and said, "Reminds me of Oaxaca. I hope this senator of yours is worth it."

He slid down without another word.

Juan grabbed the rope, looked down at the deck rocking back and forth beneath him, and thought: Yeah, me, too.

And then he jumped.

CHAPTER 32

Juan dropped into a mass of hands and bloody faces. The zombies pulled and slashed at him, grabbing at his clothes and his gear, trying to pull him down. There was no way to fire his rifle without risking hitting one of the other guys on the team, so he swung it like a club, bashing a woman in the face until her hands let go of his uniform and she was pulled under by the ones charging up behind her.

Above him, Slasher 1 flared off, dropping its ropes to the sea as it cleared the airspace for Slasher 2's approach.

The downwash from the rotors blew smoke across the deck, and for a moment Juan couldn't see. But he felt the zombies reaching for him and his instincts kicked in. Juan swung his rifle again and again, crushing skulls everywhere he turned, and still they kept coming. Beside him, two men grabbed one of the team and rode him to the ground. They were smashing his face into the deck when Juan ran to help. He kicked one of the attackers in the ribs and then threw him off. When the second man turned his attention on Juan, he punched the zombie in the face until it sagged to the ground. He brought the butt of his M4 down on the man's face until it looked like meat, just one open and swollen eye staring up at him, the body not moving.

Beside him, Carter was doing the same thing. He knocked a zombie to its knees, backed up, and fired a single round into the man's face. The shot exploded out of the back of the man's head and his body fell limp.

"Secure the stairs," he ordered, and his men fanned out to do just that, firing as they went.

They'd landed on a narrow deck next to the pool. It butted up against part of the superstructure and had two sets of white metal stairs, one leading down to the casino and the other leading up to the Sun Deck. The zombies were sprinting up the stairs, so many of them that they shook the entire deck.

But the team kept their fire discipline, every shot careful and deliberate, and within seconds they had two-man teams at the head of each stairwell directing a steady stream of fire at the zombies above and below. Juan looked around the deck and saw bodies everywhere. The deck was slick with blood, and a few of the zombies were still moving. But they had knocked them all down at least and none of them were immediate threats.

"Ready, Slasher 2," Juan heard Carter say over his headset. Carter didn't sound winded or even animated. He was cool and collected, absolutely in control of the situation, just as Juan knew he would be.

He saw Carter giving the all-clear sign to Slasher 2. The helicopter was already on its approach and its crew dropping its ropes. Twenty-eight seconds later, all ten of their operators were on the deck and fanning out to their assignments.

Impressive, Juan thought. The guys were tight.

Like all Special Forces operators, the team needed very little on the ground direction, and the only radio chatter Juan heard came from the guys running the show up in the air and the helicopters circling the deck. They were calling out hotspots, giving information on numbers of zombies as best they could, but the guys around Juan barely seemed to notice. They just went about their assignments, getting the job done.

The squad assigned to secure the extraction point moved forward. Their LZ had been chosen with great care because it could be secured quickly and yet still offered direct access to the front of the ship and to several points below deck. Juan was already picturing the route he and his squad were assigned to take through the ship when he heard glass shatter behind him.

Juan turned and saw four of the guys on the extraction detail backing away from the windows to their left. The fifth member of their team was on the ground wrestling with a zombie that had just crashed through the window, scattering glass shards everywhere.

His mind was just starting to ask why they weren't helping him when all the windows along that part of the superstructure burst outward as dozens of zombies rushed them.

The men started firing, their weapons tearing into

the crowd, but they were overwhelmed and ripped to pieces in the time it took Juan to process what was going on.

He took a few steps forward, but the men were already dead.

Carter grabbed him by the handle on the back of his pack and pulled him away.

The zombies that couldn't get at the men turned toward Juan and the others and sprinted after them.

"Fall back," Carter ordered. "Leapfrog it."

It was a familiar drill, one Juan had done many times. They were standing on a narrow deck about five feet wide. To one side was the ship's superstructure and on the other, the railing that guarded against going over the side of the ship. The team split, each man taking up a position on the opposite side of the deck from the man in front of him and about twenty feet behind him. The lead man started shooting as he pulled back, pausing only long enough to slap the next man in line on the shoulder, confirming that he was now the lead. Done by seasoned professionals the method, nicknamed "leapfrogging" in the teams, could maintain a continuous field of suppressive fire down range while still allowing for a fast and orderly retreat.

The trouble was it was a method that only worked against an enemy afraid of being shot. It didn't offer much opportunity to aim, even for men with Delta's high level of marksmanship, and relied more on the shock and awe of a continuous field of fire to get the job done. It did little good against the crowd of zombies chasing them, and two more members of the team went down before they could get everybody off the LZ.

Carter put a hand on Juan's shoulder. "We're getting slaughtered up here. We need to get aft of this superstructure, and we need to do it right now."

"What about the extraction site?"

"It's compromised. We have to fall back. We'll exfil from the miniature golf course at the rear of the ship."

They were at the rear of the leapfrog line, waiting their turn as lead. The noise of the approaching crowd and the rattling guns was deafening. Carter turned to watch the team's progress when the man two positions ahead of them started firing at a group of zombies coming up the stairs next to him.

Juan tried to yell at the man to get out of the way, but he was too late. The first zombie up the stairs gathered him up in a tackle and pushed him back against the railing. As the two struggled, more zombies surged out of the opening, some of them moving forward to attack the guys still caught in retreat, while others mobbed the man who had been standing right at the top of the stairs. Juan watched in horror as the deck filled with zombies. Within seconds, they had overrun almost the entire team, and here and there through gaps in the sea of mangled faces Juan watched the men of Delta Force, one by one, get pulled down to their deaths.

Only Juan and Carter and one of the men from Slasher 2 were left. Carter and the other man ran aft, but Juan didn't run. He'd noticed something.

There was a metal door hanging open on the wall next to them. Inside was a janitor's closet. Juan wasn't interested in what was inside, though. It was the heavy metal door he wanted.

"Juan, what are you doing?" Carter said.

"Find cover," he said. "I'm going explosive."

"What? Juan, what the . . . ?"

But Juan wasn't listening. He pulled the door open so that it faced the zombie crowd. He removed all of the breaching charges he carried, peeled off the adhesive tape on the back, and stuck them to the front of the door. With luck, the door would help to shape the charge and the resulting impact would create some distance between themselves and the growing horde.

"Ready," he called out.

He got behind the door, pressing his back against it, and blew the charge.

The blast sent him flying. He knew it would. He was prepared for that, and when he hit the deck, he rolled, just like they'd taught him to do during the judo training the guys from the CIA had given him when he first joined Delta.

But he was not prepared for how much damage the blast would do to the deck they were standing on. He stopped rolling just in time to see dozens of zombies falling over the side of the ship. Many more were burning, their clothes and hair on fire as they stumbled onward.

"Christ," Carter shouted. "How much of that shit did you use?"

Juan looked over his shoulder at him. "Pretty much all of it," he said, and grinned. But the next instant the deck shifted beneath him and he dropped.

"Whoa!" he said, trying to steady himself.

He could hear the metal support struts groaning.

Something popped, and then the whole thing yawed under him and Juan slid down it and over the side.

He hit the railing and bounced, for a moment suspended in midair over the ocean a hundred ninety feet below. Juan stabbed a hand out and caught the railing. His body dangled from the twisted metal, the world rocking back and forth below him. The gear he wore on his back made it hard to keep his grip, but he knew he had to. There were no second chances at this. With a fierce yell, he heaved his weight up and managed to grab hold of the railing with both hands.

"Rick!" he called out. "Rick! A little help down here."

Carter appeared at the edge of the collapsed deck. "Goddamn, Juan. You're fucking insane, you know that?"

"You know it."

"Hang on, I'll get you out of there."

Carter got a length of black cord from his assault kit and tossed one end down to Juan. "Grab hold, man. I don't think this thing is very sturdy."

Juan stuck out his left hand and found the rope. He coiled it around his wrist and then reached over with his right to grab it. At the same time the deck shifted again, slipping a little closer to collapse.

"Better hurry," Carter said.

"I've got it," Juan said.

Carter pulled and Juan felt himself rising. At the same time there was another loud series of pops and the deck started to move. Juan put his feet up on it just as it gave way, and for a moment it was like he was Wile E. Coyote, his legs pumping a million

miles an hour even though he never moved an inch.
Then the whole thing separated from the ship and
Juan turned to watch it as it tumbled end over end,
like a broken kite, toward the ocean below.

It took a long time to hit the water.

He barely heard the splash.

Carter pulled him up the rest of the way, and
when Juan gained the deck again, the two men collapsed side by side.

There was a big gap now between them and the
zombies, many of whom stood perfectly still, watching them, waiting. Others were still burning, but
making no effort to put out the flames. In and
amongst the wrecked bodies they could see several
of their own, all dead now.

"Holy crap," Carter said.

Juan was out of breath. But he wouldn't have
been able to respond anyway. After twenty years of
fighting in some of the most god-awful places on
earth, after all the shit he'd seen, he'd never seen
anything like this.

The radio crackled in Juan's ear. It was McBride,
demanding a report.

Carter sighed before answering it. "I think they're
gonna scrub us," he said.

"What? They can't do that. I've got . . . we have
to finish the mission."

"Yeah," Carter said. "We'll see." He keyed his
radio. "Echo 2, we've taken heavy casualties. No joy
on the target."

"Extent of your casualties," McBride said. By ne-
cessity, all radio communications were clipped and
terse. This was already a longer radio conversation
than Juan had ever had on an operation.

Carter took a deep breath. "We've got me, Garrity, and Sierra 1. Everyone else is dead."

A long silence followed, and Juan figured McBride was consulting with his bosses, trying to reassess the situation. He'd never been on a mission that had gone this wrong before. But there had been others in the past. There had been precedents. Mogadishu, in 1993, the famed Black Hawk Down fiasco, came to mind. That one had been a bigger operation than this one by far and resulted in eighteen American fatalities, a small percentage of the total operational elements on the ground, and still the powers that be had pulled the guys out and regrouped for a rescue operation for the personnel wounded and captured during the initial assault. But in Mogadishu, they had gone back in. They didn't leave anybody behind. And that made Juan think of Tess, somewhere down in the belly of the ship. He was so mad he wanted to scream. He knew the way these things worked. The brass up in the air would make a cost-benefit analysis, and in the end, they'd scrub the mission, extract the assets they still had, and call in the F-15s to clean up the mess.

"Okay," McBride said when he got back on the radio, "proceed to the secondary exfil position. Prepare for extraction."

"Understood," Carter said. He turned to Juan and said, "You ready?"

"I can't leave her."

"Who, Senator Sutton? Dude, fuck her. I already told you, a politician's not worth all this."

"I mean Tess," he said. There were so many feelings churning inside him he hardly knew how to express them. In the end, he said the only thing that really mattered. "She's mine."

But it wasn't enough for Carter, for his expression, normally so neutral, so unemotional, suddenly turned to disdain. "Seriously?" he said. "Juan, look over there. Look!" He pointed across the gap left from Juan's breaching charges. "I just lost seventeen of mine. Seventeen!"

"I know," Juan said. "I know that. It's just, I . . . Rick, I can't leave her. I can't."

"No," Carter answered. He was speaking slowly, deliberately. There was menace in his voice. "You can, and you will. Unless, of course, you want to get your ass shot out of the water by a pair of F-15s."

Carter got up and motioned for Garrity to take the lead. "We're headed aft," he said over his shoulder, "to the miniature golf course. Lead us out."

Garrity nodded and headed that way.

Carter stood over Juan, hands on his hips. "You need to make up your mind, and you need to do it pretty damn quick."

Juan didn't move.

"Hey, Garrity," Carter said. "Hold up a sec."

Garrity stopped and waited.

"What's with this?" Carter said. "You got a thing for this woman, is that it? You want to go risking your life and the life of my men because you're afraid you'll lose your favorite piece of ass. Is that it?"

Juan stood up.

"Oh, I get it," Carter said, without looking away. "You love her. That's it, isn't it? You did all this because you're in fucking love with her."

"I did it because it's my fucking job!" Juan said.

"Uh-huh," Carter said. "You know what? You never could lie for shit."

He turned away and motioned for Garrity to lead on. Garrity started up the stairs that would lead them around the pool deck, his weapon at the ready. Carter got as far as the second step before he stopped and turned back to Juan.

"According to the game grid, you've got thirty-two minutes. If you're gonna do this, that'll have to be enough."

Juan nodded. "Thanks, Rick."

"Just make sure I don't regret it, okay?"

Garrity led them up the stairs and they crossed another observation deck. Below them, the pool deck was a mass of broken bodies and spent shell casings glittering in the setting sun. A crowd of zombies was keeping up with them on the opposite side of the pool, but couldn't figure out how to get to them.

"You're gonna have to get by them if you want to get below," Carter said.

"Yeah."

"How you gonna do it?"

Juan scanned the three levels of deck space he could see, trying to figure his way through them.

No matter where he turned, it looked like he was in for a fight.

And then, without warning, a zombie ran up the stairs in front of Garrity and lunged for the young soldier. Garrity's response was automatic. He raised his rifle and fired a three-round burst into the zombie's chest.

It had no effect.

The zombie launched itself at him, wrapping him up and sending him into Carter's legs.

Carter staggered back, but managed to keep his feet.

"Get off him, you fuck!" he said as he kicked the zombie in the side of his head. The zombie's head snapped back, but he didn't let go.

Garrity got his hand under the zombie's chin and pushed it up and away from him.

"That's it," Carter said. "Hold him there."

He stuck the muzzle of his rifle into the zombie's ear, his finger on the trigger, when more zombies lumbered out of the stairway. There was little room to maneuver. Carter leveled his rifle at the approaching crowd and started to fire, but the weight of the group surged forward, overrunning Garrity and the man with whom he was fighting. They ran into Carter and knocked him down, too.

Juan grabbed Carter by his pack and tried to pull him away from the crowd, but there were too many hands on him. Juan pulled and they pulled back, and somewhere in that mass of bodies, a few began to tear into Carter's legs with his their teeth, ripping through his uniform.

Juan fell back . . . and into the arms of more zombies.

He lurched to the side, crashing into the railing. They surrounded him, pressed in upon him, pulled his goggles from his face and tore at his body armor.

In desperation, he rolled over the railing and let himself fall to the deck below.

He landed on his back, the impact knocking the wind from his lungs.

Juan stared up at the railing from which he'd just fallen, gasping for breath, and saw the crowd staring down at him, frantic for the kill that had literally slipped through their fingers.

In between gasps, he told himself he had to get up. Just get up.

CHAPTER 33

The fires were getting worse. All the smoke was making it hard to breathe, and even harder to see. Pilar struggled through the worst of it with her shirt pulled up over her mouth and nose, slowly but surely working her way up to the Lido Deck. She'd been hearing gunfire, a lot of it, and explosions, too, and she was afraid she knew what that meant.

She'd run out of time.

Still, she had no idea if the senator was dead or not, and she had to have that confirmation. Get it or don't bother coming home.

But the smoke was making it hard to find her way and she didn't even see the zombie until she ran into him. It was a man of about twenty, tall and skinny with a full sleeve of tattoos on his right arm, most of which was caked with dried blood. Part of his foot was mangled; otherwise, he might have been faster. As it was, Pilar had time to get behind him and shove him hard into the wall. His face hit the metal and he bounced off, tumbling to the floor.

She'd used up all her ammunition up on the bridge, and without a weapon couldn't afford to stay and fight with this zombie, especially as there were likely to more of them. With all the noise up on deck, they'd almost certainly be flocking her way.

Pilar left the man flailing on the ground, still trying to get at her, even though hitting the wall had shattered his teeth, and ran for a nearby flight of stairs.

They led up to the pool area, where the gunfire was starting to slack off.

She crawled behind a line of chaise longues to a small bar, careful to keep her head down. What she saw both surprised and thrilled her. A pair of black helicopters were circling overhead as though searching for somebody. There were bodies everywhere. Hundreds of zombies lay chewed to rags by automatic gunfire, and here and there amid the bloody piles of mangled bodies lay soldiers in black Nomex flight suits. There were no insignia on any of the uniforms, but Pilar didn't need to see any to know with whom she was dealing. These men were either SEALs or Green Berets, possibly Delta Force. She'd seen their kind, always equipped with the most amazing weapons, working clandestine raids in Ciudad Juarez. They hit hard and fast and were always deadly.

Except that today didn't seem to be their day.

There were three still alive that she could see. They were moving along the deck above her, covering each other as they fell back one at a time toward the front of the ship. There was a helicopter landing pad just in front of and below the bridge. Perhaps they were headed there for extraction.

They didn't make it far though. As she watched, a wave of zombies poured out of a doorway directly in front of the soldiers. Even with their automatic weapons, they never stood a chance. Two of the men were knocked down and swarmed, while the third fell over the railing and landed on the deck next to the pool directly across from her.

She saw him roll over onto his back, staring up at the balcony where his fellow soldiers were dying, and it was then she recognized him. It was the Secret Service agent from the Washington Hilton, the one who'd stopped the assassination. He was tenacious, that one.

But the zombies weren't done with him. Several of them jumped over the railing, and the agent was forced to scramble out of the way as they fell all around him.

He got up and ran.

They charged after him, and the next instant he disappeared into a darkened corridor, twenty of them right on his heels.

And then there were none, she thought. Very nice.

She scanned the carnage left over from the botched raid, her gaze finally settling on one of the soldiers. He was facedown in a pool of blood, the back of his uniform torn open and his body shredded. But his weapon was intact, and so too were the extra magazines he carried.

One of the helicopters was still circling, and she

waited for it to pass overhead and orbit away from her. When it did, she ran over to the body and took his rifle, an imposing-looking M4 carbine with a collapsible stock. The best money could buy, she noticed. These guys had to be Delta Force.

"Too bad it didn't do you any good," she said.

She went through the man's magazine pouches, pulling out as many as she could carry. She was stuffing them in her pockets when she heard a woman yelling at the helicopter from across the pool.

Pilar's mouth fell open. It was Senator Sutton. Right there in front of her.

"Hey!" Sutton yelled, waving her arms at the helicopters. "Hey, down here!"

Pilar glanced up at the circling helicopters. They were starting to come back around. She had no idea if the gun crews had seen the senator yet, but it didn't really matter. Pilar only had a few seconds to move. All the noise Sutton was making was drawing a crowd, and zombies were already running toward her from the deck above them.

Pilar raised the rifle, stepped over the dead soldier, and started firing.

Sutton must have seen the movement out of the corner of her eye, for she gasped at the sight of Pilar and ran inside a video arcade just as the bullets started flying.

"Damn it!" Pilar said.

She started after Sutton, who was headed for the stairs at the back of the arcade. If she managed to get down those steps she would find herself in a junction from which she could take any number of paths through the ship. That couldn't happen.

Pilar sprinted after her, gaining on the older woman almost immediately.

Just outside the doors of the arcade Pilar slowed, raised her rifle, and sighted in on the senator's back. It was a clear shot, a kill shot, but before she could pull the trigger, the senator turned and fired a spray of bullets from a pistol. Several of her shots hit the video game next to Pilar and exploded sparks all over her.

Pilar ducked behind the doorframe.

Holy crap, she thought. Where'd she get a pistol?

Pilar turned, pointed the rifle toward the stairs, and backed away from the doorframe so she could put some rounds down range as soon as she got a glimpse of the senator. But what she saw was the senator's shadow sinking down the stairs. She didn't have a shot.

And she was running out of time. The zombies that had attacked the soldiers above her were coming off the stairs now, and they were running right for her.

More were coming out of the café next to the video arcade.

For a moment, Pilar thought of charging down the stairs after the senator, but she knew she'd never reach them in time. She looked behind her and saw a gap in the zombies that would take her around the far side of the pool.

There were stairs there.

She'd have to go that way. It was her only chance of cornering the senator, even if she had to do it down there in all that smoke.

And what other choice did she have, really? She

had been put on a set of rails by decisions—her own and those of others—long ago, and those rails led inexorably to this end. Kill Senator Rachel Sutton or die herself. There was no other option.

Not for her anyway.

And so she ran.

CHAPTER 34

Rachel Sutton got to the foot of the stairs and had to stop. So out of breath. So scared. Where in the hell was she going to go? That crazy cartel woman was everywhere.

Before her was an enormous open area three stories high and ringed by colonnades that offered a view of the main floor, where half a dozen zombies were picking their way across the mosaicked floor. She was on the third floor, at eye level with a blue, white, and red chandelier so huge and bright it reminded her of the belly of the alien spacecraft from *Close Encounters of the Third Kind*. On the far side of the main floor was a curling staircase, carpeted in blue that led to the second floor. The ship's casino was there.

Where to go, where to go?

She needed to find a place fast. That cartel woman was right behind her, and while she'd managed to surprise her with a few shots from her pistol, she knew she wouldn't get that lucky again.

Her best bet was to hide and wait. Hopefully those SEALs would come soon.

But everything was so open. Where could she go?

She was still trying to make up her mind when the cartel woman emerged from the stairs to her left.

The assassin saw her and immediately broke into a sprint, charging her.

Sutton ran without any idea of where she was going. She was too scared for that. She just ran as fast as she could go, arms and legs pumping, her breath leaving her in short, panting bursts. But Rachel couldn't run as fast as the younger woman, and almost immediately she began catching up. With a desperate burst of speed, Rachel sprinted on, the only sound the roaring of her blood in her ears. A moment later, Rachel glanced back over her shoulder, her mouth dry from panic and exertion, and in her confusion nearly slowed to a stop.

The other woman wasn't chasing her anymore. She had stopped running. Now she was leaning against a metal column, her rifle aimed at an open spot in the railing just ahead of Rachel.

When Rachel realized what was happening, she did stop. Her heart was pounding out of control, but she was alert, hypersensitive like an animal in a hunt, and she saw the sniper's trap the woman was setting for her. Had she gone another ten steps, she'd have crossed that open area where the scrollwork on the railing ran out. She'd have been an easy target.

Wasn't going to happen, she told herself. Not today. She had no intention of going down that easily.

There was another stairwell just ahead of her, to the right, and she flew down it, legs pumping as fast as she could go, arms out to catch herself in case she fell.

She came out on the second level and doubled back the direction she'd been running. With luck, the assassin would try to follow her down the stairs. Or maybe she would stay in place, hoping to catch a clear shot of her again. Either way, it didn't matter. The stairs leading down to the casino were just ahead. All she had to do was get there.

But then, from somewhere above and behind her she heard the clang of metal on metal and she made the mistake of looking back.

The younger woman hadn't taken the bait after all.

She had her rifle slung over the railing again, trying to sight her in.

Rachel veered hard toward the wall as bullets chewed up the floor beside her. She screamed and tripped, catching herself against the wall. Pure fear was driving her now. She struggled to her feet and ran on. She reached the stairs a moment later, took them two at a time, and didn't stop running until she was inside the casino. To her right, she saw a number of blackjack and craps tables; to her left, row upon row of slot machines.

She went left.

Rachel meant to head for the back, but as she rounded a bank of slot machines, a hand stabbed out of the shadows and caught her by the shoulder.

Gasping, she twisted away from it and fell over, landing on her hip. The zombie holding her shoulder didn't let go, though, and it came down on top of her. Rachel twisted again, and succeeded in pushing the man off her. She rolled over onto her hands and knees and with a breathless grunt pushed herself upright.

The man was dressed in a bloody waiter's uniform. The nametag still hanging from his chest read MARIO. He shoved his bent and bleeding hands into her face and she somehow managed to swat them away.

Then she turned and ran, only to find herself walled in by slot machines.

She spun around, unable to believe she was trapped. But she was. The only way out was through that zombie.

"Stay back," she said. She pulled the pistol from the waistband at the small of her back. "I mean it, stay back!"

The waiter lumbered toward her, oblivious to the gun.

It felt enormous in Rachel's hands, like some kind of cannon. She tried to aim it, tried to hold it steady, but she was shaking too badly to hold the sights on the man's forehead.

And then he was too close. She had to fire. She winced as she squeezed the trigger, and when the thing went off, it jumped in her hands. She let out a startled gasp. The noise was deafening, especially in here, but when she looked, the man was facedown on the floor, moving, but only a little.

At the same instant, the cartel woman ran into the casino.

Rachel saw her coming and hit the ground. She crawled past a dozen slots before she found a small alcove that housed an ATM machine. There was a gap of maybe six inches to one side of it, just wide enough that she could crawl through, if she squeezed hard.

She had to turn her head to do so, and it still put a big scratch down her jawline, but she got in there and wedged herself behind the ATM.

Now, all she had to do was be quiet.

If that was even possible. Her heart was thundering in her chest. Every wheezing breath she took sounded so loud there was no way that woman could miss it.

But she couldn't do anything about that. She hunkered down, shivering, and waited.

Rachel couldn't see anything wedged back in that little space, but she could hear the cartel woman's footsteps passing by the front of the ATM machine.

Back and forth the woman passed.

Wayne had taken her hunting whitetail deer a few times over the long years of their marriage, and she knew the drill of following a wounded deer to the place it finally dropped.

Just follow the trail.

Move silently. Look methodically.

Sooner or later, you'd hear it wheezing, bleeding out. It was only a matter of time.

And if the cartel woman was doing that, it meant she knew Rachel was somewhere close. It would have been easy to figure out. Rachel had been forced to shoot that zombie, and the cartel woman had probably already found the body. There weren't many places to run from there. That woman was probably already picturing the kill in her mind.

She had to run for it. That was her only chance. Moving slowly, wincing at the pain in her legs,

Rachel stood up. She peered out from behind the ATM machine and saw the cartel woman walking away from her, two rows over, machine gun pointed toward the gaps between the slot machines.

Her back was turned, and she probably had another ten steps before she rounded the corner and started searching the row one over from Rachel's hiding spot.

If she was going to go, it had to be now.

Rachel pushed herself through the narrow gap through which she'd just passed. It was easy this time because she was slick with sweat.

She got through it, the only noise coming from her cracking knees and the soft wheeze that escaped her nostrils. She crept quietly down the aisle to the middle of the casino floor and there stepped right into a woman's arms.

Rachel let out a startled gasp.

"Shh," the woman said, and only then did Rachel realize it was Tess. She looked awful. Her face was smudged with dirt and spattered with blood. The hair on the side of her face was caked and matted with dried blood from her wounded ear. She looked every bit as bad as the zombies Rachel had seen wandering the ship.

Except for the look in her eyes.

There was still life in those eyes.

"How?" Rachel asked. "I saw you die."

Tess tapped the shock plate on her bulletproof vest. She looked like she was about to say something else, but then her gaze shifted over Rachel's shoulder and her eyes went wide. "Oh, no," she said. "Get down!"

Tess pulled her toward a blackjack table, practically throwing her behind the heavy wooden bar and into the dealer's pit. Rachel landed hard, her hip smacking against the opposite side of the bar. She looked up just in time to see Tess firing in the direction of the slot machines.

The next instant, bullets smacked into the table, exploding splinters of wood and bits of green felt into the air.

"Damn it!" Tess said, landing on the ground next to Rachel. "She's got us pinned down."

Rachel could see the cartel woman's reflection in the windows at the front of the casino. She was moving like a soldier from one row to the next, always crouched behind the slot machines, firing every few seconds to keep them from moving.

With every step, she was drawing closer.

"What are we going to do?" Rachel asked.

"Just stay down."

Tess fired back, and an instant later, her shots were joined by another burst of automatic rifle fire. At first, Tess seemed to think it was coming from the cartel woman, except that bullets had stopped hitting the blackjack table. "Oh, my God, yes!" she said, dropping down next to Rachel.

"What is it?"

"It's Juan."

Rachel looked up at her, at the shocked half-smile on her face, and peered around the side of the table for a better look.

It was Agent Juan Perez, and he was firing on the cartel woman.

He had *her* pinned down now. Every time she tried to move, he fired again. The slot machines exploded all around her. Rachel could see her with her back to one of the slots, her hands thrown over her black hair against the flying glass and plastic.

"Get down!" Juan yelled at them.

Tess's eyes went wide. "Oh, no, grenade! Down!" she said, throwing herself over Rachel.

The explosion shook the entire room and left a ringing in Rachel's ears. A fine wave of dust and aerosolized ash drifted over the room, covering her. She couldn't see the assassin. That entire half of the casino was awash in floating dust and smoke, and there was debris everywhere.

Juan motioned for them to get down again, and Rachel had just enough time to see him throw another grenade before Tess pushed her face into the carpet.

The second explosion shattered every window in the place, and when Rachel finally pulled herself out from under Tess, she saw the ceiling was on fire. Tess wouldn't let her up, though. She kept a hand on her shoulder, her pressure gentle, but firm, and gave her a warning look to stay down.

Then Tess leaned her rifle against the blackjack table and started making hand signals to Juan. Rachel didn't speak sign language, but she could tell from Tess's body language that she was arguing with Juan.

"What is it?" Rachel asked.

"He wants us to go to the lifeboats."

"But they're all gone. I watched them go."

"That's what I told him. He said there's a few still onboard though, starboard aft."

"But . . . ?"

"Don't argue. If he says they're there, they're there. Just get ready to move."

Tess's pressure let up just a bit, and Rachel was

able to push herself up onto her hands and knees. She scanned the rubble where the slot machines had just been, the dust settling down over the wreckage.

She was about to ask Tess what they were waiting for when a sudden blur of movement caught her eye.

It was the cartel woman.

She jumped up from behind a toppled slot and ran for the busted-out windows near the front of the casino. She was through the window and running around the corner before either Juan or Tess could open fire.

"Go!" Juan yelled at them. He motioned at Tess to go the other way. "Get her to the lifeboats. I'll meet you there."

"Where are you going?"

"After her. I can't let her get to the senator."

"Come with us. I don't want to get separated."

He used sign language again, and when he was done, Tess didn't bother to respond. She simply reached a hand down to Rachel and said: "Get up. We need to go right now."

"Why? What did he say?"

"We have eight minutes to get you on a lifeboat and away from here."

"But why?"

"Because there are a pair of F-15s on the way to blow this ship out of the water."

CHAPTER 35

The second grenade was the worst. The slot machine she was using for cover took the full brunt of the blast. She was lucky her back was to it because the blast launched the slot machine into the air, throwing her into the wall and nearly crushing her. Had she been turned the other way it might very well have caved her head in.

But she wasn't much better for all that.

She was hurt badly. Her side was bleeding again, as was her mouth and nose. Her left shoulder was screaming at her, and there was a fierce and painful ringing in her ears.

She tried to get to her feet but she was so dizzy and disoriented that she gave it up and collapsed into the ash that coated everything. She rolled over onto her back and coughed. The air was swirling with dust and smoke, and the ceiling was burning. She needed to move or she'd die here. Pilar knew that instinctively.

Yet she couldn't move.

But then she saw a fish-eye security mirror near the front of the casino, and in it, the man who had nearly killed her.

The lady agent's boss.

Pilar coughed again.

He was doing something. It took her a moment to realize exactly what, but when she saw him using sign language she perked up.

Years before she'd tried to convince Ramon's men to learn it, but they were all stupid and shortsighted. None of them saw the tactical value in a silent language, and so they'd just laughed at her.

But she had seen the value in it, and she had learned it well.

And what she read in the signs this agent was sending both alarmed her and gave her hope.

She hadn't gotten rid of the lifeboats after all.

Most of them, but not all.

And now she knew where the senator was going.

She was still in the game. She still had a chance.

Mustering all the strength she had left, she climbed to her feet. Blood dripped from her mouth, pattering into the dust at her feet. Her vision was doubling and tripling everything around her. But she was determined, and she finally managed to stand.

She drew a deep breath, ignoring the sudden pain in her ribs, and ran.

CHAPTER 36

Juan jumped through the busted windows of the casino and chased after Pilar. She'd rounded a corner near the back, headed, it seemed, for the main hallway that ran the length of the ship, but when he got there, he saw no sign of her.

He stopped and listened, hoping to hear her footsteps.

Nothing.

"Where did you go?" he said.

There were three ways to choose from. The main hallway he could see already was a nonstarter. From the mouth of the hallway he could see quite a ways. There was a lot of smoke, and it got pretty dark farther in, but he felt certain she hadn't gone that way. That would be too easy.

There was a shorter hallway to the right that looked like it led outside, but he could tell she hadn't gone that way either. A zombie was at the far end of it, making its way toward the casino explosion. Juan figured there would probably be others attracted by all the noise, but they wouldn't still be headed his way if they had seen Pilar. They would have tried to go after her.

And that left the passageway to his left. There was a bad fire somewhere down there, because the smoke was pretty thick. He remembered the helicopter ride in, how heavily burned that side of the ship had been. Down there was the source of it. But it also made for the best hiding spot. If he were in her shoes, on the run and outgunned, that'd be the option he'd take. Level the playing field a little.

He took a few steps in that direction and almost immediately realized that he'd guessed right. The ash from the casino explosion had gotten all over her, and she was leaving traces of it on the maroon carpet.

Like footprints in wet sand, he thought.

He heard Tess's voice behind him and he turned. She was standing with Sutton, watching him, and in that moment he surprised himself with the depth of his feelings for her. They welled up in him all at once, unbidden, yet real and immediate. He wanted to pull her close and kiss the bruises from her face. He wanted to make all this go away.

Tess signed to him. *Should I follow you?*

He shook his head and motioned for her to go down the main hallway to the back of the ship.

She signed again. *You'll be careful?*

Yes.

She paused, and then signed: *I love you.*

That stopped him cold. He stared at her. The warmth seemed to leave his face. Her expression didn't change at all, but she started to turn away.

He gestured for her to look at him, and when she did, he signed back: *I'm in love with you. Get off this ship alive and I will, too.*

Her only reply was a thin, wistful smile, but it lit her bruised and bloody face.

Then she grabbed Sutton by the arm and pulled her along.

CHAPTER 37

Juan knew he was going to need help. With all the smoke, he could walk right by her if he wasn't careful. He dropped his pack and fished out his night vision goggles. They hadn't worn them going in because they'd had an hour of daylight left and no one thought it would take them even half that time to finish the mission. But they'd packed them anyway, and Juan was thankful for that now.

All at once the interior of the ship dropped into a greenish haze. He could see through the smoke without any difficulty now, and he advanced down the hallway. This one wasn't a straight line like the main corridor on the other side of the ship. It twisted constantly, opening up on shops and observation decks and even onto an ice skating rink. It made for slow going. Corners were a constant threat. He'd have to stop and check to see if it was clear before continuing, and he was never certain if she'd be waiting with her rifle at the ready, or if he'd turn a corner and step into the waiting arms of another zombie. So he went as fast as he could, studying the carpet for more telltale signs of ash.

He found it on one of the corners, a patch of it on the wall.

She must be getting tired, he thought, for it looked to him as though she'd leaned against the wall before continuing on. There was blood there, too. That was good news.

Then he heard a cough, very faint, muffled, but distinct. And it sounded like it was coming from right around the corner. He raised his rifle and stepped back so he could pie the corner.

As he swung around, slowly revealing the passageway beyond, he heard the sounds of a struggle. He went a little farther and saw a zombie struggling near the next corner. But his attention went immediately to Pilar, who was standing behind the zombie, holding it by the back of its shirt like a shield. And she had her rifle over the thing's shoulder, ready to shoot.

Juan dove for cover just as Pilar shoved the zombie in his direction and started firing. Bullets chewed up the wall right beside him and he felt a sharp, hot pain in his neck from the flying splinters.

He stuck his rifle around the corner and fired blind, swinging the rifle back and forth to hose down the whole corridor. His weapon was suppressed and he thought he heard the sound of bullets thudding into flesh, but he wasn't going to be taking any more chances like that. He swapped out the magazine for a fresh one and fired blind again, emptying the second magazine.

He swapped out magazines again and pied the corner.

Pilar was gone.

The zombie was on its knees in the middle of the corridor, bullet wounds all over its thighs and chest, trying to get back onto its feet.

Juan stepped around it and resumed the hunt.

CHAPTER 38

There was a knock on the metal cabinet door and Paul flinched. The little boy huddled next to him cried out. A moment of awful, complete silence followed. Paul had been folded up inside the cabinet for what felt like hours now and everything hurt, but he didn't move.

The boy began to whimper.

The knock came again. "Paul?" It was Kelly. "Are you guys okay in there?"

Paul tried to move but couldn't. "I can't get the door," he said.

There was click and the cabinet door opened, light spilling across his face and stinging his eyes. He hadn't noticed it inside that cramped space, but he was soaked through with sweat.

Kelly helped the little boy out and then reached a hand in for Paul. He took it, and let her pull him out of the cabinet.

He rolled onto the floor, the muscles in his back screaming at him.

"Are you okay?"

He groaned, then slowly pulled himself up to a seated position. He looked up at her and nodded. "I think so. My back hurts."

"We ought to go," she said. "I think there's a fire onboard."

"A fire? Where?"

"I don't know. Can't you smell that, the smoke?"

He sniffed the air, but all he could smell was his own body, the funk of all that tequila working itself out through his sweat.

"I don't smell anything," he said.

"Paul, I really think we need to go. I've been hearing things, too. Like gunshots."

Paul listened. He looked around and saw the kids were all listening, too, their faces and clothes wet with sweat. He turned back to Kelly.

He shrugged. "I'm sorry, I don't . . ."

"There were a lot of them just a few minutes ago. Do you think it's a rescue team?"

Paul studied her. If she didn't sound so rational, so calm, he'd think she was hallucinating. He didn't smell anything. He didn't hear anything. He shook his head, his expression apologetic.

"The Secret Service agent you guys had with you, did she have a submachine gun?"

"Uh, yeah, I think so. She said she had a lot of weapons."

"Maybe it's her."

"Maybe," he said doubtfully. "Here, help me up." She offered him a hand and he stood. His back was killing him, but so were his legs and neck. "Oh, God," he said, stretching his neck.

"Are you sure you're okay?"

He managed to chuckle. "Yeah, just getting old. How about the kids? Are they okay?"

"We need to get some water in them. It was hot in there."

"Yeah, you're not kidding. I don't think the air conditioning's working."

As soon as he said it he thought he smelled smoke. Very faint, but still there.

There was a sink along the back wall. Kelly went over to the coffee cups and handed each of the kids a cup and told them to drink as much water as they could. Several of them complained of being hungry, but there was nothing they could do for that. Not right now anyway.

"You should drink some, too," she told Paul. "You look like you're sweating pretty bad."

Paul mopped a hand across his face and it came away soaking wet. She wasn't kidding. He felt light-headed and a little dizzy. His stomach felt queasy, too. He leaned against one of the metal prep tables and tried to catch his breath.

"You don't look so good," she said.

"Yeah? I feel even worse."

"You're dehydrated," she said.

"Yeah, maybe." He wasn't sure if it was that or his hangover coming back. Could be either at this point, he thought. His head hurt so bad.

And then: *Gunfire!*

It was high above them, but the metallic clatter of small arms fire was unmistakable.

"Was that . . . ?"

"Yeah," he said. "Yeah, I think it was."

"What do we do?"

Paul thought for a moment. He had absolutely no idea what they were supposed to do, or even what they could do. A fire onboard was bad enough, but with gunfire, it was even worse. It probably was a rescue team up there. But if they were still firing, and the fire was still raging, they probably weren't doing much good in taking back the ship. Things would still be nuts out there.

"Should we go up top to see what's going on?"

"No," he said quickly. "God, no. Not all of us. I'll go. You and the kids can stay here."

"Like hell," she exclaimed. "You're crazy if you think we're staying here."

"There's water here. And you've got shelter here, too. It's a whole lot safer than trying to get twenty-three kids through a ship full of zombies. Especially if the ship is on fire. We won't make it three decks."

"But it's our chance for rescue. Paul, what do you think is going to happen if we get separated? Even if you do make it topside, how long do you think it'll take to get a rescue party down here? Paul, we can't stay here much longer."

"All right. All right, well, maybe there's another way."

"Like what?"

"Those lifeboats, they've got signal flares, right?"

"Yeah?"

"Well, maybe all that gunfire will attract the zombies up top. You know, they key on sound, I guess. We've seen that already, back at the pub."

"Okay. Yeah, that makes sense."

"So, if they're all moving topside, maybe it's not such a good idea to go that way after all. Maybe now's our chance to make a break for the lifeboats. Once we get there, we could use the signal flares to let them know where we are."

He had no idea if any of that was true, but it sounded good.

"And if they don't see the flare?"

"Well, then we get in the lifeboat and drop overboard. They'll have to see a big yellow lifeboat drifting away from the ship. Either way, we get rescued."

"Off this ship anyway."

"Yeah," he agreed.

She hugged herself as she stared off at nothing, not blinking, barely breathing. Her lips were trembling at the corners slightly, but her eyes were steady, and he sensed her strength in them. She was tough, this one. Had to be, not to abandon all these kids.

"Okay," he said. He nodded towards the kids, most of whom were still in line for more water. "Do you think they're ready to go?"

"I think so," she said. "I know I am."

A few minutes later, they were walking through one of the interior corridors toward the stairs at the rear of the ship. They had tried to walk along the exterior deck, but the smoke was bad out there. It'd only taken a few moments outside for Paul to admit that the ship was really burning. And if he needed any more proof, once they got to the railing and looked aft, they could see the enormous tail of black smoke trailing out behind the ship. It was hugging the water like fog.

And there were more zombies out on the deck. Not so many that they couldn't avoid them, but enough to make getting caught a matter of when and not if. There were fewer inside, and most of the ones they saw were so badly torn up that they could do little more than moan and raise a feeble hand in their direction.

The smoke was bad, too, but Paul and Kelly had the children pull their shirts up over their mouths and they trudged onto the aft stairwell that would take them up to the lifeboat deck. The kids kept to their line, just as Kelly said they'd do, and as they started up the stairs Paul began to feel a little better about their chances.

They made it several flights before they ran into any real trouble.

As they approached each landing, Paul would turn and motion for the kids to duck down and stay quiet. He would inch his way down the stairs, staying low so that he could see the landing they were about to take without being seen in turn by zombies who might be wandering by.

But as he was checking the landing on Deck 6 he realized they were going to have to come up with a different plan. There were two zombies there, a woman and a teenage girl, both of them feeding on what looked like the body of a waiter from the main dining room.

The stairwell ended there on the landing. To go farther, they'd have to cross the landing behind the two zombies to reach a separate flight of stairs that curved down and out sight behind them. They had maybe fifteen feet of clearance between the path they'd have to take and the zombies. The younger one was facing their direction, but still had her mouth buried in the waiter's open chest and hadn't noticed them yet.

There was no way they were going to make this happen, he thought.

Paul looked back at Kelly at the end of the line.

When he did she screamed.

"No," he whispered. "Oh, God, no!"

He saw some kind of commotion among the kids in the back of the line, and then grunts and more screaming and the sound of Kelly swinging her baseball bat against somebody's head. The next instant she and the rest of the kids were running down the stairs. There was blood all over her shirt.

"Go!" she yelled at him. "They're coming!"

"Can't go this way either," he said.

She ignored him and continued charging down the stairs. "Hurry!" she said, pushing some of the smaller kids in front of her.

"Wait!" he said.

But the next instant he saw that wasn't going to happen. There were ten, maybe fifteen zombies coming down the stairs, and more behind them. He had no choice. He ran to the foyer where the two females were rising from their kill, eyes locked on him. Three more zombies were coming up the stairs behind them.

"Crap."

Paul turned and gestured the kids toward the exterior door. They were going to have to chance running down the deck again. "Get them out there," he said to Kelly, and before she had time to acknowledge him, he turned and charged the two female zombies.

The older of the two lunged at him, fingers swiping at his face. Paul ducked under her arms, jamming the baseball bat under her breasts and shoving her back. She tumbled over the dead waiter and into the younger zombie. The younger one was fast though, and she sidestepped the woman completely.

Paul raised the bat to swing at her head, but the girl slipped in the waiter's blood and went facedown on the tile.

Paul was running for the deck before she could even look up to find him again.

When he rounded the corner, smoke was drifting down the deck. Up ahead he saw Kelly and the kids, their legs pumping as they sprinted away from him. He looked behind him and saw half a dozen zombies clamoring toward him. He ran after Kelly and the kids, his legs driving him over a chaise longue and onto the wooden deck beyond. His heart was thudding in his chest. *They're right on me,* he thought! *Christ, right on me.* The thought wouldn't go away. He'd managed to quiet his fear for several hours, but now it was back with a sudden vengeance.

The kids couldn't run nearly as fast as he could. He was on the slowest of them almost immediately. One of the little girls looked over her shoulder at him, smoke curling off his face, and her eyes went wide.

"I got you," he said, and scooped her up into his arms.

One of the kids ahead of him tripped and crashed to his hands and knees.

"Get up!" Paul shouted. "Let's go, move!"

With a whimper, the boy scrambled to his feet and continued running, Paul right behind him.

"Keep going," he said. "I won't let them get you."

For an awful moment there was no sound but the thudding of his sandals on the deck. The little girl was getting heavy in his arms, and he felt like his muscles were about to give out. He slowed long enough to put the little girl down and look over his shoulder.

There had to be twenty of those things coming up behind them, coming up fast.

He reached for the nearest chaise longue and threw it into their path. There was a whole row of the things and he began throwing them at random across the deck. The first zombies to reach them tried to jump but misjudged the distance and tumbled over them to the deck in a tangle of arms and legs. Working quickly, he went down the row, throwing chaise longues into their path, and when he ran out of those, he started to run again.

He gained on the little girl again and heard the tortured rattle in her chest. The girl was frightened beyond her understanding, but there was no time to sooth her. Paul scooped her up again and started to run as fast as the added weight allowed.

They reached a small, white metal stairwell. Kelly was at the top, gesturing them forward.

"Hurry!" she yelled to Paul. "It's clear all the way to the lifeboats."

Paul didn't chance another look back. He didn't need to. He could hear the snarls and panting of the dead as they ran after him, closing the gap. He hit the stairs at a run and slogged his way up.

Kelly was right. The way was clear right up to the lifeboats.

But something was wrong. He saw that right away, and slowed to a walk.

He could see the davits where most of the lifeboats had been, but weren't now. They were empty. He saw a lifeboat that was hanging from one of its davits, and another that had partially dropped but was still caught up in the side of the ship, but most of the others seemed to be missing.

There was only one still attached to both its davits and ready for boarding.

"What happened?" he asked Kelly.

She got to the lifeboat first and popped the doorway in the hard shell roof. "Hurry, kids, everybody inside!"

"What happened to the other boats?" he asked her.

When she met his gaze her eyes were wild with fear, and the thought struck him then that maybe they were among the last of the living to leave the boat.

"Do you think—"

Gunfire cut him off mid-sentence.

He spun around and saw Monica Rivas with a submachine gun. She was advancing on the stairs, firing down at the zombies trying to make their way up. He lost track of the number of rounds she fired. They came so fast, so constantly. But then she stopped firing, ejected her magazine, and slapped in a new one from her belt.

When she turned to him the look on her face was so horrifying he flinched. She was covered in sweat and grime and smoke seemed to cling to her black hair. Her eyes were on fire. Her black shirt was soaked with blood.

"Where is she?" she growled.

Paul couldn't speak. He set the little girl down and she backed away. Kelly grabbed her and helped her down into the lifeboat.

Paul said, "Monica, I—"

"Quiet!" She raised the muzzle of the submachine gun and he could swear he saw smoke leaking out of the barrel. "Get your hands where I can see them."

"Monica, please—"

"Shut up! Hands behind your head!"

He did as she ordered.

"Get down on your knees. Move. Faster. Face the water." She spun him around, and then jammed the gun into the back of his neck. "Get down on your knees."

"Okay, okay." He knelt down. He could barely breathe.

She moved in close and pressed the muzzle against his cheek.

It burned his skin.

"Where is she? I swear I'll blow your brains all over this deck if you don't tell me."

"Senator Sutton? I don't know."

"Bullshit."

She pressed the muzzle down into his cheek so hard it hurt his teeth. He tried to pull his head away, but she kept the pressure up, pressing his face against the railing to stop him from moving any farther.

"I'm not playing with you. I want to know where she's at right now. Tell me!"

"I don't know," he said. Tears were running down his face. "I swear, I don't know. I haven't seen her since last night."

She pressed the rifle deeper into his cheek, and he could feel the inside of his mouth tearing against his teeth. But she didn't say anything, and for a long, terrible moment there was no sound but the wind whistling through the deck struts and the pennants slapping in the breeze.

Then she pulled the rifle away. He could see her walk over to the lifeboat and look inside. When she turned away, the look on her face was different. She looked softer, hurt somehow, more like the girl he thought he'd come to know that night at the Washington Hilton.

But the look was gone in the next instant.

She turned on Kelly and motioned her toward the lifeboat with the barrel of her gun. "Get on board," she said. "Move."

Kelly obeyed without another word.

Then she turned her full attention on Paul. She put the gun in his face and her expression grew hard, unrecognizable.

"Tell me where she's at and I'll let you live."

"I don't know," he said again. "God, I swear. I don't know. Please don't."

She slapped him.

Startled, he stared at her. No one had ever slapped him before.

"Where is she?"

He was breathing hard, but he was in control of himself now. He looked her right in the eye, his gaze going right past the rifle, and said, "I told you I don't know."

She nodded. She had been right in front of him, but she took a step back now and pointed the rifle at his chest.

"Go ahead," he said, his hands still locked behind his head. "Go ahead, Monica. Shoot me. Do it. But please," he said, and nodded over his shoulder toward the lifeboat, "let them go first. They're just kids. They didn't do anything to anybody."

"Everybody dies," she said.

"Yeah, but not kids. Kids shouldn't have to die."

She moved so suddenly he barely had time to register the change. One moment he was trying to bargain with her, the next her rifle was pressed between his eyes and she was so close he could smell the sweat on her skin.

"Kids die," she said. "Kids die every fucking day. You Americans, you don't get it, but kids die every fucking day where I come from."

He swallowed. For a long moment he was too scared to respond, but then his courage found him.

"But not these kids. Not today. Monica, please. Not today, not these kids. If you need someone dead I'm right here, but not them. Please."

He could feel her breath on his skin, hot and angry.

Paul wanted to look away, but knew he couldn't. Too much was at stake.

She said, "Where is Senator Sutton? Tell me and I will let you live. I'll let you all live."

"I don't know," he said. "I swear it, I don't know."

She stared at him. Paul could only look at the front sights on the gun, the hole in the muzzle looking like a mouth that might swallow him in a sea of blackness. He was shaking, though he barely noticed.

"Stand up," she said.

He forced himself to look past the gun and into her eyes. He didn't recognize the person he saw there.

"Move!"

He climbed to his feet, his hands still raised over his head.

"Get on board," she said, and flicked the end of the rifle toward the opening in the lifeboat, where Kelly stood holding the hatch. "Hurry."

He moved in a daze.

He turned in the opening and studied her, the woman he thought he knew.

"Why are you doing this?" he asked. She said nothing, just stood there with her gun aimed at his chest. "Monica, tell me please."

She reached up to the lever that controlled the davits. She pulled it down and the lifeboat lurched like a carnival ride, then swung out over the ocean. They were going down to the waterline.

"Monica, why are you doing this?"

"You don't know me," she said as the boat lowered down. "And my name is not Monica."

CHAPTER 39

Tess watched in disbelief as the woman she knew as Monica Rivas lowered Paul's lifeboat over the side. She thought she was about to watch him die. Instead, she sensed she'd just witnessed some kind of act of contrition.

She sank back down behind the ice machine she and Senator Sutton were using for cover and tried to sort it all out.

"Did you see that?" Sutton said, too loudly.

"Shh," Tess whispered. "Keep your voice down."

"I don't understand," Sutton went on. "Why did she do that? I thought she was going to kill him."

"Keep your voice down," Tess said through gritted teeth. "You're gonna get *us* killed."

Sutton looked like she'd been slapped. She started to object, then seemed to come to her senses. She sank down to the deck next to Tess and whispered: "Sorry."

"Just . . . no more noise," Tess said.

She fingered the trigger on her Colt, trying to figure out how they were going to get out of this. They had come down the aft stairs, threading their way through one crowd of zombies after another, before finally ending up in the right place. They were stepping out onto the deck when they heard gunfire, and ducking down behind this ice machine, they had witnessed the cartel's assassin with a military-issue machine gun at Paul Godwin's face.

For a moment there, it really did look like she was about to kill him.

And then she'd just let him go.

He'd collected the last of the kids he had with him, and that older girl, and together they'd gotten in the lifeboat and she'd actually pulled the lever to lower them down.

What was said, she hadn't heard.

What that woman had seen that made her change her course, Tess could only guess. But to her, watching from sixty feet away, it looked like someone trying to apologize to ghosts that could never be appeased.

She'd come within a breath of firing on her then. The woman was standing in the middle of the deck with absolutely nothing for cover, her rifle slung over her shoulder. She was a sitting duck. Hell, at that range, Tess could have put a bullet right through her ear. And she was about to do just that when the first zombie staggered out onto the deck, attracted by all the shooting.

Tess eased off the trigger. Where there was one of those things there were always more, and she couldn't take the chance with a standup fight.

A moment later, her caution proved her right.

Four more zombies staggered out of the same doorway.

The cartel assassin turned at that moment, her gaze going from the zombies on the deck to Tess, with her rifle aimed straight at her.

Beyond the reticle of Tess's sights, the cartel assassin smiled.

And then she dove for cover around a corner and disappeared.

Tess had sunk down behind the ice machine at that point and barked at Sutton to keep quiet. But it was too late for that, because already more zombies were piling out of doorways behind them. It took only a few seconds, but they were surrounded.

"Agent Compton," Sutton said. She pushed herself up until she was standing, her back to where the assassin had just been.

Tess fought the urge to pull her down. Perhaps she was right. Perhaps this was the time to move. Perhaps it was their only option.

"Come on," Tess said.

"Where are we going?"

"There," Tess said, and pointed a lifeboat hanging from one of its davits.

"What? No. I . . . I can't do . . ."

Tess pushed her to the door on the side of the lifeboat. "You can and you will." Tess threw the door open, grabbed Sutton by the collar of her blouse, and pulled her toward the door. It was swinging in and away from the hull, a good four feet down from the opening in the railing.

"Get in," Tess said, and shoved her forward.

Sutton screamed and tumbled into the open door. Tess heard her knocking about in the fiberglass tub of a hull and knew she was safe. At least she'd made it into the lifeboat, which was one step closer to safety.

"Just keep your head down," she said.

"What about you?" Sutton's voice echoed up from the lifeboat.

"I'll jump. Just hang on."

As the zombies closed in on her, Tess hit the lever that released the lifeboat from its one remaining davit. She figured it must have malfunctioned when the cartel assassin released the other lifeboats and she hoped the manual control would be enough to reengage it.

The lifeboat lurched and creaked, and then dropped free of the restraints holding it to the *Gulf Queen*.

"Yes," Tess said. "That's it. Keep going."

The pulley snapped and creaked against the cables, but the lifeboat was going down.

"Oh, thank God," Tess said.

A noise behind her made her spin around. The zombies were closing in. There were at least twenty of them now. Certainly more than she could shoot. She glanced over the railing and saw Sutton's lifeboat dropping rapidly down the side of the *Gulf Queen*. Below the lifeboat, the Gulf of Mexico, a deep black now with the setting sun, was shifting and indistinct. But it was a long way down, she knew that.

If she was going to do this, she needed to do it now.

Swallowing hard, she swung her legs over the railing and held her breath. "Oh, shit, oh, shit, oh, shit," she said, trying to muster up the courage to jump.

The lifeboat was rocking so much, swinging back and forth. It looked like a postage stamp there against the ever-expanding distance down to the sea.

"Go!" the voice in her head roared.

She couldn't, wouldn't, go.

The zombies closed in. They clutched at her hair, at her clothes.

And then the voice in her head turned to that of Juan Perez's. She could see him standing in the air in front of her, beckoning to her.

"You have to jump," he said. "Do it now!"

Without a moment's hesitation, she jumped, and for a terrible moment, she doubted everything.

Right until her feet hit the lifeboat's roof.

CHAPTER 40

He picked up her trail again near the back of the ship. She had gotten here ahead of him, and maybe even gotten to Tess and Sutton. He prayed that he wasn't too late.

Her footsteps indicated she'd suddenly veered to her right, down a passageway that looked like it might go all the way through to the other side of the ship. That was where the few remaining lifeboats were, which wasn't a good sign. Not at all. But he was surprised to see that she hadn't followed that passageway. She'd gone past a gift shop, where nearly every window and breakable object seemed to have been destroyed, and then turned down a flight of stairs. It was dark down there, but with his NVGs he could see down to the next landing and it looked clear.

But why had she come this way? It made no sense.

Her tracks were there, so she must have seen

something down there. She must have had her reasons.

He went after her, quietly working his way down the stairs. Juan made it halfway down the first flight when he stepped on broken glass. The popping sound echoed down the stairs, and he froze. He looked down at his feet. There, carefully arranged so as to cover the entire step, was a layer of shattered wine glasses.

"Holy crap," he said. She'd tricked him. "You clever fucking bitch."

But there was no time to beat himself up for being careless. From below he could hear the pounding of running feet, and he knew what that meant.

As if in answer to him, a man appeared on the next landing down. He was infected. His glowing eyes told Juan that.

He'd spotted Juan, too.

More just like him were climbing the stairs right behind him, and they all sprinted toward Juan.

"Time to go," he said, and ran up the stairs and around the corner. His arms and legs pumping with all he had, he ran for the lifeboats.

It looked like they'd all deployed.

He ran to the railing and looked down. Sure enough, two lifeboats were drifting away from the side of the ship, one much farther out than the other.

A huge explosion rocked the ship and Juan had to catch himself against the rails to keep from going over the side. He looked down the length of the ship and saw a slowly dissipating fireball clinging to the side of the *Gulf Queen*. The water below was choked with trash and debris . . . and bodies.

"Oh, no," he said.

He took off his NVGs and looked at the dark water around the closer of the two lifeboats. Sure enough, the water was clogged with dead bodies, many of them beating against the water without really managing to get anywhere.

But there was someone else down there. A swimmer.

It was Pilar, and she was swimming toward the lifeboat.

Juan looked over the side.

It had to be an eighty-foot drop, maybe more.

Darkness had fallen while they were making their way to the lifeboats and now the sea below looked as black as ink. He could see zombies writhing in the water but couldn't make out any details. All he could discern was movement.

Which made Pilar easier to spot. He raised his rifle and sighted in on her back and squeezed the trigger. But instead of hitting Pilar, the bullets slammed into a zombie. Whether out of luck or skill it didn't matter. At the last possible moment, Pilar had grabbed a zombie in the water next to her and rolled under it. Juan saw its body jerk with the gunshots, and knew right away he'd lost the element of surprise. She would stay under as long as she could now, and every time she surfaced, it would be somewhere else. He couldn't anticipate where. Not with any accuracy anyway. He was going to have to go in there and get her.

Juan looked back over his shoulder and saw a crowd of zombies coming for him. He didn't have the time to stay up here and play sharpshooter anyway.

He had to go.

Juan dropped his rifle to the deck and pulled his pistol. He stared down at the water, breathing fast.

"Go," he ordered himself, thinking of the aircrew boss that had yelled in his ear right before his first parachute jump. "Go, go, go!"

He jumped.

For one long moment, one terrible moment, he was weightless, suspended over blackness that wanted so very desperately to consume him. Free fall seemed to go on and on, and yet he couldn't form a single coherent thought. He couldn't even breathe.

It took hitting the water to do that.

He hit hard, and he was pretty sure he hit a glancing blow on one of the zombies, too. He went under, went deep, but now he was in a known element. Water survival had always been one of his strengths. He tucked and rolled, flattening his body out to stop his descent. Then, when he'd gone as deep as he was going to go, he relaxed and let his body drift upwards so that he knew which way was up.

He kicked for the surface.

Juan was almost there when he ran into a mass of legs. He didn't panic though. He stayed under, dolphin kicking away from the mass of zombies.

When he tried to surface again, he was more careful. He felt above him, waving his arms in a circle to make sure he was coming up in a clear spot. He broke the surface a moment later. Treading water, he turned around to see where he was, and found himself staring a zombie right in the face.

The man started clawing at him, slapping at the water, but he was clumsy. He was staying afloat from the decomposition gases in his belly, and he couldn't control himself. He was like a balloon with arms. Juan spun him around easily and kicked away from him. Pilar was still far out in front of him. He had to reach her though. He ducked his head and swam.

It didn't take him long to catch up with her. Pilar was clearly a pro, an expert in survival, evasion, resistance, and escape, as good, maybe, as any operator he'd ever known, but she wasn't a particularly good swimmer. He closed the gap easily, and when she realized that, she started shooting.

He ducked behind a badly burned mattress, lowered himself into the water and tilted his head back so that only his face remained above water.

But he had seen enough. He had a plan.

He took a deep breath and slid under the water. To control her rifle she needed both hands, and that meant she was kicking frantically to stay afloat. He had little trouble following the sounds of her distress.

Except that it wasn't her he was after.

At least, not directly.

There was a female zombie a few feet to her right, and Juan swam for her. She was much like the man he'd dealt with before, bloated and out of control, and it was easy to turn her in whatever direction he wanted her to go. He pulled the zombie down and spun her around so he could grab the back of her shirt. She tried to put her hands on him, but he was able to keep her at arm's length without much effort. Only then did he chance opening his eyes. The ocean was nearly black, and the salt water stung his eyes terribly, but a few feet away he saw the bubbles rising from Pilar's kicking, and he pushed the zombie in that direction.

When he surfaced, he shoved as hard as he could, praying at the same time that he'd guessed right about Pilar's location.

Turned out he had.

The zombie, in its own dim way, realized it had prey right in front of it and went into kill mode. Pilar was caught off guard. She swung her rifle at the zombie's head, and over the splashing Juan heard her scream, *"Suéltame!" Get off.*

He saw his chance and he took it.

He gulped a deep breath and went under. He found Pilar's legs and wrapped her up in his arms. She couldn't fight the zombie and his pressure pulling her down, and as soon as he felt her start to buck and twist, he grabbed her belt with one hand and her ponytail with the other and swam straight down. He swam until he felt the pressure build against his eardrums, which he knew from many hours in the pool was about fifteen feet. There he stopped, and there he held Pilar at arm's length. She thrashed, she kicked, she tried to throw her hands over his arms and fight, but he wouldn't let her go. He held her there until her thrashing turned to spasms, and until even those stopped.

Just like he'd been trained, he kept the time in his head. He counted two minutes, and then he let them both rise to the surface.

She wasn't dead, though. Not yet. It takes five to ten minutes for the human body to fully die by drowning, and he wasn't going to take any chances with her. Besides, he didn't have that kind of time.

In fact, by his watch, he was out of time already. He kept her motionless body at arm's length though, refusing to give her an opening in case she was faking it, which he wouldn't put past her. He swam with her to the nearest zombie he could find and shoved her motionless body into the zombie's arms.

It tore into her with a ferocity that made him retreat in horror. How in the hell such things existed he couldn't begin to describe, but at least this was the end of her.

He watched until her blood hit the water, and then he swam for the lifeboat. Out of the corner of his eye he saw a flash of light. He glanced at his watch. His time was up. The missiles were on their way.

Desperate now, he swam for the lifeboat and circled around it.

He could hear the high-pitched Doppler shriek of the missiles' approach, and he knew this was it. He reached the lifeboat and swung around the far side of it, putting it between himself and the *Gulf Queen*. There was a life preserver hanging off the side and he grabbed it, pulled it close.

Overhead, the missiles shrieked.

He braced himself against the lifeboat, his mouth open, muscles tensed against the impending shock wave. The missiles hit a moment later, and every cloud overhead, every burning ember sent aloft on the blast wave, every shred of sky filled with light, and though he held on to the life preserver for dear life, he was thrown clear, far away from the lifeboat.

His vision blurred and dimmed.

He felt his weight sinking beneath the waves. He gulped for air and took in water. He panicked. His mind knew what to do, how to save himself, but his arms and legs wouldn't work, and the water pulled him down. He was drowning, and he was powerless to stop it.

Juan sank beneath the waves.

He felt hands on him, pulling him up. He fought against them. In his delirium he thought for sure it was Pilar coming for him, joining the fight one last time.

But then he saw Tess's face, felt her arms around him, her hands on his back, but it didn't register. In that moment, he didn't know her.

"Easy," Tess said. "Juan, I've got you."

Juan thrashed against her hold, but he couldn't break free. She had him wrapped up tight. She wasn't about to let him go. Not until she put her hands on his face and made him look at her.

"Juan, it's me. It's Tess. I've got you."

He stopped fighting. He stared about, stunned by an ocean on fire, and by the burning *Gulf Queen* sinking below the waves. He turned to her, and though he couldn't hear for the ringing in his ears, he could kiss her. He pulled her to him, and this time, he was the one who wouldn't let her go.

CHAPTER 41

By morning's light Juan and Tess stood side by side on the rear deck of the Coast Guard Legend Class Cutter *William Allen*. They were still about two hours out from Galveston, but already the media frenzy had begun. Helicopters circled overhead, and a whole lot of smaller boats had gathered in the area. The Navy and the Coast Guard were keeping the curious at bay, but they were letting the media come aboard the *William Allen* for a press conference that was supposed to start any minute now. They already had fifteen reporters standing by, and smaller boats were still shuttling more over. Juan heard somebody say that the blast had been visible as far away as Sarasota, Florida.

He had spent much of the night on the phone with Mr. Crouch. The White House, Crouch said, was furious for how wrong the operation had gone. So many mistakes, so many missed opportunities, so very many lives lost. But, maybe now the American people would finally wake up to the threat Mexico's cartels really were, Crouch said. Maybe. They were going to lean heavily on Juan's report, though. Crouch said that was the silver lining to this whole mess. They were calling it a terrorist attack, and according to Crouch it would most likely lead to a full-scale U.S. military involvement in Mexico as the battle against the cartels came out of the shadows of black ops and into something much more like a war. There were troubling times ahead.

Juan didn't doubt a word of it.

But the phone calls were done for now, and he and Tess and everybody else were waiting for Senator Sutton to come up from the *William Allen*'s infirmary. The ship's doctor had done a pretty good job fixing up Juan and Tess, but they both still looked like they'd been run over by a truck. Juan certainly felt that way.

It was getting better, though. The breeze was cool, and the smell of the sea was back. No more smoke and burning oil fumes.

And he had Tess at his side.

That was the biggest surprise of all. After all this time of working with her, side by side, day after day, he should have realized she was what he needed. He'd been stupid. He let so much time go by. For so long he'd thought of himself as nothing but a soldier cast adrift. He was good for fighting and killing and not much else. Maybe it was the ghost of his first marriage that had done it to him. When he looked back over his life outside of the military and the service, all he saw was the wreckage of that marriage. When Madison left him, he'd put up a wall, and for more than a decade he'd been dead inside. But that was done now. He wasn't going to live his life in the rearview mirror anymore. That stopped today.

He reached over and took Tess's hand. She laced her fingers together with his. Her face was bruised and the corner of her mouth swollen, and her smile sad and damaged. She was a deep one, that woman. Juan sensed that he had only begun to explore her depths.

Together they watched the sun coming up over the water. Tess raised her chin to the breeze and closed her eyes. He watched for a moment, then let his gaze wander back over the sea. The crowds and the noise swirled all around them, but to Juan it all felt a million miles away.

"Are you okay?" she asked him.

He turned to her and nodded.

"I don't recognize that look."

He shrugged. "That's because I'm thinking."

She chuckled, but that didn't last long. The smile shrank away and she sighed. "It's not quite the happy ending I would have liked. But I suppose it couldn't have ended any other way. Not from where we started."

He squeezed her hand. "I don't want to think about endings anymore. I'm tired of things being over."

She squeezed his hand. "Me, too."

There was a commotion behind them and they turned to see Senator Sutton hobble onto the deck, flanked by a pair of Coast Guard sailors. Her right arm was bandaged and she had a lot of little cuts on her face like red thread. She looked across the deck to where the media was chomping at the bit to talk to her and for just a moment Juan thought he saw a note of apprehension in her eyes.

"That is a woman with a lot on her mind," Tess said.

"Yeah. A lot of ghosts."

He watched her tug her shirttails down, composing herself, and then head into the mass of journalists. Cameras went off all around her.

"Rick Carter," he said, "one of the Delta guys I was with, asked me if I thought she was worth it."

"Worth what? Of rescuing, you mean?"

"Yeah."

"Of course," she said without a moment's hesitation. He glanced at her. She was of course thinking of the service's philosophy that an attack on a U.S. politician is not an attack solely on a person, but on the institution of American government. To attack a senator, or the president, or some federal judge in Wyoming was to attack the American way of life, and when you thought like that, yes, she was worth it. No question about it.

"He meant as a person, I think. Will she be a leader, or just another politician?"

"What do you think?" Tess asked him.

The reporters closed their ranks around Sutton, and she started the most important speech of her life.

"I don't know if anybody can truly say. Not yet."

"I hope she leads," Tess said. "I want to believe in her."

"Yeah, me, too."

But it was like Mr. Crouch told him on the phone. There were troubling times ahead.

GREAT BOOKS,
GREAT SAVINGS!

When You Visit Our Website:
www.kensingtonbooks.com

You Can Save Money Off The Retail Price
Of Any Book You Purchase!

- **All Your Favorite Kensington Authors**
- **New Releases & Timeless Classics**
- **Overnight Shipping Available**
- **eBooks Available For Many Titles**
- **All Major Credit Cards Accepted**

Visit Us Today To Start Saving!
www.kensingtonbooks.com

All Orders Are Subject To Availability.
Shipping and Handling Charges Apply.
Offers and Prices Subject To Change Without Notice.